NEIL'S
WAS IN SEMIDARKNESS

The lights from the pool outside and the movement of the water cast wavering shadows of blue and green on the walls and ceiling, giving the room an ethereal atmosphere that was enhanced by the scent of Neil's after-shave.

Dinah could feel him tremble as he placed his hands on her shoulders.

"If I kiss you, Dinah, I won't be able to stop."

She looked up at him, realizing that she'd been waiting for this moment, been denying her attraction to him, denying her need . . . and her desire. And suddenly, the things they'd argued about seemed insignificant.

"Kiss me," she whispered.

A low moan escaped him, but still he held back. "Are you sure? We won't be able to go back. . . ."

Smiling, she drew his head down to hers.

ABOUT THE AUTHOR

Beyond Compare marks the Superromance debut of
Risa Kirk. A former medical technologist, this
author of a dozen novels cheerfully admits to being
obsessed with writing. She shares her California
ranch with her husband, Ray, four horses and
various cats and dogs.

Risa Kirk

BEYOND COMPARE

Harlequin Books

TORONTO • NEW YORK • LONDON
AMSTERDAM • PARIS • SYDNEY • HAMBURG
STOCKHOLM • ATHENS • TOKYO • MILAN

Published February 1986

First printing December 1985

ISBN 0-373-70200-0

CHAPTER ONE

BY THE TIME Dinah arrived at the network awards dinner in New York, the room where the ceremony was to take place was packed. Round linen-covered tables for six dotted the vast hall, tiny islands of white surfacing only briefly among the undulating waves of the milling, glittering crowd, and Dinah paused a moment in the doorway to get her bearings. Her flight from San Francisco had been late and after the hectic rush to her hotel to get ready, and then another dash here, she felt breathless and out of sorts. The fact that she didn't look it was evident in the stage-whispered comments she overheard as she stood, deep green eyes scanning the crowd to find anyone she knew.

"Isn't that Dinah Blake?"

"She's even more beautiful in person than she is on TV!"

"She's the one with that San Francisco talk show I told you about—you know, *Personalities*. I never miss it when I'm there!"

Flattered despite herself that she'd not only been recognized but apparently admired, Dinah's mouth curved into a smile. A few seconds later, the smile became a little wry.

"Do you think her hair's *really* that shade of red?"

"You know—I think she's had a nose job."

"I read somewhere that she writes all her own material. I don't believe it, do you?"

Dinah's expression had become a little rueful by the time a page approached to escort her to her table, and as she followed the young man through the crowded, noisy room, she was aware that more eyes and whispers accompanied her. When she found herself wondering if her long teal-colored skirt and matching beaded jacket had passed muster, she thought amusedly that it might be safer to ignore the rustlings in her wake. Fixing her gaze on the page's back, she lifted her head and summoned the professional smile she'd cultivated for the show. But her eyes sparkled with private humor as she wondered whether she should have worn a sign to satisfy all this curiosity. Mentally, she ran over the list.

Yes, I am the hostess of Personalities. *That's why I'm here tonight. To my own great surprise, I've even been nominated for an award.*

No, I don't dye my hair. And if you think it's red now, you should have seen it when I was younger.

No, I've never had a nose job. It's as straight as it ever was, even if it is a little too long for my taste.

And finally, yes, as difficult as it is to believe, I really do write my own material for the show.

That last thought caused her smile to fade a little as she remembered what a battle it had been to gain even that concession from her boss, Roger Dayton. She sighed inwardly, wondering when he was going to allow her the chance to prove herself on more significant issues. They had been sparring about that for months now, but no compromise was in sight. She'd tried to tell him that she wanted to do more with the show than interview celebrities or talk to the newest author pushing his or her latest diet book, but so far Roger had been unmovable. One didn't tamper with success, he pontificated, and even she had to agree that *Personalities* was that. No one had been more surprised than she when the show zoomed to the top of the ratings chart for morning television, and sometimes she wondered why she couldn't rest on the laurels she'd already gathered.

"Your table, Miss Blake," the page said, interrupting her thoughts.

She was just turning to thank him for pulling out the single unoccupied chair for her when the man seated across the table from her rose. She was dimly aware that the rest of the men followed suit. *Good Lord,* she thought, awed in spite of herself, *that can't be Daniel Rawlings!*

But it was. She recognized him instantly—who wouldn't? Everyone at the network and all its affiliates, from the highest-paid star to the lowest production assistant knew who Daniel Rawlings was. A word from his New York penthouse office could extinguish or skyrocket a career, a nod or shake of his head could keep a program on the air or bury it forever in the archives. Daniel Rawlings was head of programming and probably wielded more power than anyone in the room.

"Miss Blake," Rawlings said smoothly, extending his hand. "How nice that you could join us."

"Thank you," Dinah responded, summoning all her poise. Why hadn't Roger warned her that she'd be sitting with one of the most powerful men in television?

Daniel Rawlings seemed unaware of her inner confusion as he turned to introduce her to the rest of the

table. Still stunned, Dinah turned bemusedly to acknowledge the introductions and found herself staring into a face she'd seen only on the screen. Panic
overtook her: the man was none other than Neil Kerrigan, host of the acerbic Sunday-night news program, *The Kerrigan Report*, which had broadcast
several months earlier a blistering segment on talk
shows—like hers. Cursing Roger again for not warning her about this, Dinah fought the impulse to recoil
and instead calmly extended her hand.

"Miss Blake," Neil Kerrigan said in that deep voice
that had enthralled millions of viewers, including
her—until that one program, "may I present my son,
Andrew."

Annoyed by Neil's confident assurance, Dinah
glanced coolly away from the startling blue eyes to
look at the young man who stood beside his father. He
wasn't quite as tall, but the family resemblance was so
strong that without the age difference they could have
been twins. Father and son had the same jet-black
hair, the same intense blue eyes. Neil's jaw was
stronger, the planes of his face more mature, but
seeing them together almost gave her a sense of déjà
vu. In Andrew, she could see a young Neil; in Neil, the
man his son would become.

She smiled, acknowledging the introduction, and to
her astonishment, he actually bowed slightly over her
extended hand. "Call me Andy, Miss Blake," he said
with a grin that banished the illusion that he was just
a slightly younger version of his father. Dinah realized then that he wasn't much older than sixteen, despite his height.

Dinah smiled again. "Then you must call me
Dinah."

Andy's smile was suddenly shy, and Dinah realized she had made a conquest. She glanced involuntarily at the conquest's father to see if he had noticed and then was annoyed with herself again. Who cared if he had noticed? Reminding herself that behind that strikingly handsome face was a mind known for clever, sarcastic repartee, Dinah knew she had to keep her wits about her. She had no intention of being subjected to what had become known as "The Kerrigan Interrogation."

She'd heard it said, and she believed it after seeing some of Kerrigan's broadcasts, that even though appearing on his program was more an ordeal than a pleasure, very few guests refused an invitation. It was more dangerous not to appear than to be present; those who declined were likely to find themselves the subject of one of Neil's "Special Reports," a fate worse than death. Neil was known for digging up certain facts and figures that had been intended to remain buried forever.

Dinah suspected that was another reason why his program was so popular: no subject was sacred to him, and no person—whether highly placed government official or member of the private sector—was too intimidating not to feel the sting of public exposure by Neil Kerrigan.

But he displayed none of that during dinner. In fact, by the time coffee was served, Dinah was beginning to tire of the superficial conversation. Then he turned to her with a sardonic expression, and Dinah suddenly knew how the butterfly felt when it was about to be impaled by a pin. She hadn't misjudged him after all.

"Dan seems pleased with the success you've had in San Francisco," he began. "Your program is

called—" he frowned slightly, as if trying to recall
"—*Personalities*, isn't it?"

Dan? Dinah was distracted for a moment, astonished. She'd heard it said that even Rawlings's closest
friends referred to him as Daniel, and after meeting
him tonight, she could see why. He didn't seem to be
a man who would approve of nicknames. In fact, she
couldn't imagine calling him anything but Mr. Rawlings, unless it was "sir." Either Neil Kerrigan knew
the network's top executive very well, or he was so
confident of his own sphere of power that he could
afford to be irreverent. She suspected that it was a little of both. Irritated at the thought, she answered
coolly.

"Yes, it is," she replied, and thought that he knew
very well what her program was called, since he'd gone
to such lengths to crucify her before a nationwide audience. It hadn't been a pleasant experience listening
to him snidely labeling her kind of programming as
pabulum for the mind; he'd even singled out *Personalities* as an example. She hadn't forgotten the humiliation she'd felt the night she watched it; the fact that
she agreed with him to a certain extent had only contributed to her emotional turmoil. She'd been so irate
that she'd marched into Roger's office the next morning prepared to do battle. She'd told him that if they
couldn't demand a retraction, at least they could air a
rebuttal. Roger had stated they'd do no such thing.
Kerrigan's program might stimulate viewers to tune in
to hers to see what the fuss was about, and that was
worth at least a tenth of a rating point, maybe more.

"But I doubt you've seen much of it," she added,
looking pointedly at Neil.

"On the contrary," he disagreed. "I watched several clips before I did the piece on *Report*."

Clips? *Clips?* For a moment, Dinah was speechless. He'd criticized her, made fun of her, ridiculed her before an entire viewing nation, on the basis of a few clips? She was so infuriated that it was a struggle to control herself. "Oh yes," she made herself say indifferently, determined not to let him see how angry she was. "I saw that program."

"What did you think?"

Was there no end to his arrogance? For an instant she was tempted to tell him exactly what she did think. But then she realized that they'd managed to catch the attention of Daniel Rawlings, who had abandoned his own conversation to listen to theirs. She could hardly respond in the way she wanted with Rawlings listening, but she couldn't help a cool, "I didn't think it was particularly well done."

She'd struck a nerve there; she could tell by the tightening of his expression. Dinah held back a toss of her head. So she had made him angry—it served him right.

"How so?" he asked finally, obviously trying to control his irritation.

She deliberately raised an eyebrow, as if surprised at the question. "Well, it wasn't quite up to your usual standards, do you think? Usually your information seems so well researched."

"There was nothing wrong with my information," he replied stiffly. "I've got the best research staff in the business."

"Oh, no doubt you do," she agreed pleasantly. "But I'm afraid they were off the mark that time."

She saw his fingers tighten around the stem of his wineglass and had to look down before he saw her pleased smile. *How does it feel, Mr. Kerrigan,* she wondered, *when* you're *the one on the defensive?*

"In what way were they off the mark?" he asked, recovering. "Give me an example . . . if you can."

She hadn't missed the heavy sarcasm, and she smiled sweetly. "I didn't mean to upset you, Mr. Kerrigan. Perhaps we should talk about something else."

"I'd rather talk about this," he said harshly. Several heads turned in their direction at that, but he seemed unaware of the interest. Dinah saw Andy look from his father to her and grin; when he gave her a thumbs-up gesture, she almost laughed.

"Well, if you insist . . ."

"I do."

"All right, then," she said, abandoning her meek role. "Correct me if I'm wrong, but I believe you stated in that program that the talk-show format is . . . what did you call it? Oh, yes—an intellectual wasteland."

If he was startled by her sudden change of manner, he didn't show it. Leaning back, he nodded arrogantly. "I did say that, yes. And furthermore, I believe that any person of even moderate intelligence would have to agree with me."

Dinah's green eyes flashed at that, but she was determined not to lose her temper. She was aware that Daniel Rawlings was still following the conversation with interest, and it suddenly occurred to her that this might be her chance to prove that she could do more with her show than just trade diet and exercise secrets with the newest self-proclaimed expert.

"Moderate intelligence, Mr. Kerrigan? Those talk-show programs you belittled that night are watched by millions of people every day. Are you trying to say that the vast majority of those viewers are incapable of judging good programming from bad?"

Neil wasn't deflected by that salvo at all. "I wouldn't have put it quite that way, but yes. Just because those millions of viewers tune in doesn't mean that the programs they're watching have any value in themselves. Popularity is not a measure of content, as I'm sure you will agree."

Dinah was on dangerous ground here, and she knew it. Despite her impassioned defense, she wholeheart-edly agreed with Neil. That's why she'd been so angry that night he'd aired his own broadcast about the subject: she hadn't been smarting so much from his attack as she had been from the uncomfortable knowledge that he'd been right. But she could hardly admit that when she'd been nominated for an award for the very type of programming she privately de-spised, so she said, "I think the ratings prove you wrong, Mr. Kerrigan. Talk shows—"

"Ratings are hardly a measure of the quality of a program, Miss Blake," he interrupted. "At best, our revered Nielsens only indicate how popular a certain program is. It's not the same thing at all, at least in my book."

Her reply was just as sharp. "Then perhaps you're reading the wrong book, Mr. Kerrigan!"

"Am I?" he asked sarcastically. "I don't believe that listening to a celebrity babble about his or her latest role on some insipid sitcom requires any partic-ular mental prowess. Nor have I been intrigued by in-terviews with all these self-indulgent authors who believe they're writers because they've managed to get a book published.''

Despite her poised facade, Dinah was beginning to wish she'd never pursued the topic. It was ironic that she'd put herself in the role of defending a position she didn't believe in herself. She'd said so many of these same things to Roger Dayton that it was almost like hearing an echo of one of those fruitless arguments, Neil playing her role, she parroting the station manager's.

Dinah had begged Roger to let her start inviting guests who really had something to say, people who had made a real contribution. She wanted to give these men and women a chance to share their accomplishments. She was content to leave the hard-news analysis to reporters like Neil Kerrigan, because she knew that people needed to be informed about the graft and corruption that sometimes seemed to permeate every aspect of government and politics. But she also knew that there was a real need for people to know, and to hear, that there were positive things going on out there, too.

Roger had called her a romanticist, a bleeding heart. He'd reminded her that her audience tuned in to watch a beautiful woman interview people they'd like to be themselves. They expected that, and that's what they'd get. Period.

But she wasn't through yet with Roger Dayton, and she certainly wasn't going to go down in defeat before Neil Kerrigan, not with Daniel Rawlings listening so intently.

''I concede your point—to a certain extent,'' she added when Neil smiled in that superior way she already detested. ''But there's more to the format than interviewing celebrities and writers. Millions of people have been helped by discussions about the newest research, for example—''

"I agree," he said smoothly. "But not on talk shows."

He didn't say "like yours," but the inference was there, and Dinah bristled. "And not on programs like *The Kerrigan Report*, either," she retorted sharply. "From what I've seen of your show, you're more interested in tearing people apart than—''

He raised an eyebrow. "Do I detect the cry of a bleeding heart?"

Dinah's eyes flashed again, and she could feel her color heighten. "I detest that term," she said flatly.

"So do I," he said, surprising her. "But then I detest labels in general." He bowed his head slightly. "I apologize."

Dinah was so taken aback that she didn't know what to say. Wondering if he was mocking her in some subtle way, she looked at him suspiciously. He returned her glance blandly, but for a moment as she gazed at that handsome face, her heart began to pound. In an effort to cover her sudden confusion, she glanced quickly away, reminding herself that she didn't like this man. He was so self-confident that he was impervious to criticism, and it was obvious after their discussion—if she could call it that, she thought blackly—that he valued no opinion but his own, and yet . . .

There was something about him that made her forget all that. She'd sensed the electricity the instant she'd met him: she had felt it in his handshake and in the casual brushing of his arm against hers during dinner. She felt it now, in the warmth of her face and in the inexplicable heat flushing her entire body.

But she had fallen for another set of blue eyes and another handsome face once, and she wasn't interested in going through all that again. Her divorce last year from Ted had been a painful time for her. The only thing that had kept her from falling apart completely had been the show. As irritating as Roger Dayton could be, she was still grateful to him for insisting that she had to go on.

Roger hadn't been entirely selfless in his motives. She knew he would have done anything to avoid replacing her in midseason, but she'd been thankful anyway. If she hadn't been forced to keep up her grueling schedule—the five-in-the-morning risings, the makeup and wardrobe calls, and all those hours of preparation involved in putting together a show like hers—she would have had too much time to think about why her marriage had failed. As it was, she thought about it too much anyway. She'd almost driven herself crazy wondering if she'd been totally to blame. It had taken a lot of soul-searching to accept that she hadn't been entirely at fault.

The plain truth, she'd realized so many agonizing months later, was that Ted couldn't handle her success. It had been his ego problem, not hers, and even though that didn't make it any easier to accept now, at least she understood it better. She ought to, she thought sadly: she'd spent endless nights in their empty, echoing house after Ted left, trying to figure it out.

The irony of the whole thing was that she'd never believed she was a success—not in the true sense of the word. What she'd achieved was fame, a kind of notoriety, the dubious distinction of becoming a Public Figure.

She still felt that way. Even the fact that she'd been nominated for Best Morning Talk Show hadn't changed her passionate belief that the show could be better if Roger would only let her prove it. She'd even drawn up a detailed prospectus of her ideas months ago to present to him. She'd worked for weeks on it until it was as polished and professional as she could make it, and she was sure he would give it the consideration it deserved. To her fury, he'd refused to read beyond the first page.

"Ladies and gentlemen, may I have your attention please!"

Dinah started. She'd been so preoccupied that she hadn't realized someone had gone to the dais to begin the ceremony.

"Saved by the bell," Neil murmured. "You were a million miles away just now, you know. Were you gathering your forces...or retreating in defeat?"

He was definitely mocking her now. Lifting her chin before she turned away to gaze pointedly at the master of ceremonies, she said haughtily, "I never concede defeat. And certainly not when I'm right."

To her annoyance, he wasn't abashed by that at all. She actually heard him laugh softly before he said, "We'll see who's right and who isn't."

Really, the man was incredible! She looked at him again for an instant, and then wished she hadn't. A spotlight was now on the dais and the rest of the room was dim, and Neil's face looked almost chiseled, like a sculpture she had seen once of a Roman warrior, proud and defiant, exulting in the heat of battle. His eyes were in shadow, but she didn't have to see his expression to know that he could have been the model for that Roman warrior. For a moment she felt as she had felt then: in awe of such strength and proud endurance, almost aroused by the sight of the conquering male. Annoyed and disturbed by the comparison, she glanced quickly away again.

"I hope you're as confident after the ceremony as you are now," she said as cuttingly as she could. "Or don't you believe in awards, either?"

He laughed again. "Only when I win one."

But by the time the lights came up again and the presentations were over, it was Dinah who sat triumphantly with an award for Best Morning Talk Show, while Neil watched empty-handed.

"Well done," he said when the applause faded away and she returned to her seat, flushed and pleased, and unable to prevent a triumphant glance in his direction because she had won—and he hadn't.

"Thank you," she responded coolly.

Andy, who had been following their earlier conversation with as much interest as had Daniel Rawlings, leaned across his father. "Congratulations, Miss Blake . . . Dinah," he said, grinning as he looked from her to Neil and back again.

Dinah's response was infinitely warmer toward the son than the father. "Thank you," she said with the dazzling smile that had contributed so much to her success.

Andy blushed, started to say something, floundered in the middle of it and finally burst out with, "You know, I think it would be great if you and Dad did a show together."

There was a silence. It couldn't have lasted more than a few seconds, but it seemed like an eternity to

Dinah, who was so stunned by the suggestion that she couldn't think of anything to say. It didn't help to hear Neil snicker, but before she could gather her wits long enough to tell Andy his idea was out of the question, the boy had turned eagerly to the head of programming. In horror, Dinah heard him say, "Don't you think that's a good idea, Mr. Rawlings?"

"What was that?"

Dinah knew she had to regain her composure, and quickly. Aware of Neil beside her, shaking now with laughter, she barely repressed an urge to jab him sharply in the ribs. What was he laughing about? He couldn't possibly think this was funny! "Andy was just making a joke," she said hastily. "Weren't you, Andy?"

Andy didn't hear the warning in her tone; he was too carried away by his own enthusiasm. "No, it wasn't a joke, Dinah," he said earnestly. "It came to me when I was listening to you and Dad argue. I think you two would be great together."

Dinah couldn't believe that Neil was allowing his son to go on with this. "Say something," she hissed.

He gave her an amused look. "I take it you have some objection to my son's idea."

Dinah tensed even more. She didn't dare look toward Daniel Rawlings; she just hoped that he was regarding Andy's suggestion with amused tolerance, as she might have done in any other circumstances. Right now, she didn't find any humor in the situation. The thought of the two of them on the same program filled her with dismay; she had no intention of engaging in a verbal brawl on the air with Neil Kerrigan. After the discussion they'd had tonight, she knew with devastating certainty that that would happen. She had seen it before: his delight in baiting an opponent, his habit of saying the most outrageous things just to provoke a thoughtless reaction or remark. He wasn't going to have the opportunity to do that to her; she absolutely would not put herself in a position where he could make a fool of her.

"What do you think, Dad?"

Before Neil could answer, Daniel Rawlings leaned forward. "I think your boy has something there, Neil."

Dinah and Neil looked at each other again. When she saw the sudden speculation in his eyes, she knew it was hopeless to appeal to him. He was actually enjoying this, she thought furiously, and still unable to believe that the head of programming might actually be considering Andy's suggestion, she tried to protest again.

"Mr. Rawlings—"

Rawlings raised an imperative hand, stopping her in midsentence. He smiled suddenly, and his expression chilled her. She knew what he was going to say, and it was all she could do to prevent herself from leaping up and dashing from the room. She sat there instead, her thoughts churning as she tried to think of a way to get out of this gracefully. She couldn't think of a thing.

"Neil," she whispered desperately. "Do something."

"What do you want me to do?" he asked, amused again.

"Something! Anything!"

Rawlings spoke again, the great pronouncement from on high. Dinah cringed. To her, it was louder than the crack of doom.

"Hmm. Yes, the idea definitely does have merit."

Neil finally bestirred himself at that. Sure that he finally believed this had gone far enough and he wasn't going to play along anymore with the joke, Dinah was just letting out a breath of relief when she heard him say, "Are you really serious about this, Dan?"

"I was eavesdropping on your conversation, too," Rawlings answered unperturbably. "And I have to agree with Andy that you two are certainly, er, dynamic together. However, I think it might be a good idea to do a trial run before we commit to a special."

A special! Dinah couldn't believe her ears. She realized at once what that would do for her career, and for a tempting moment she pictured the enhanced image it would give her...the prestige...the power. She saw herself walking into Roger's office and demanding—demanding—a change in format for her show; she imagined the satisfaction she'd feel when Roger was forced to concede. She was so carried away by the fantasy that it took her a few seconds to understand fully just what Rawlings had said. The tantalizing images vanished abruptly in the light of this new catastrophe.

"A trial run?" she asked, hoping she didn't sound as fainthearted as she felt. "What do you mean?"

Rawlings smiled again. She was learning to hate that smile; every time she saw it, her situation became worse. "Well, Neil can hardly have you as a guest on his program. The format isn't quite...right for that. But you could certainly have him on your show, and we could test audience reaction to the two of you then. What do you think?"

What did she think? She thought it the most hideous idea she'd ever heard. Neil Kerrigan had spent the entire evening telling her exactly what he thought of programs like *Personalities*, and she had no doubt that if he appeared on her set, he'd waste no time telling the whole world the same thing. It didn't take much imagination to picture what a complete disaster that would be. She was a good interviewer and she knew it, but she was no match for Neil Kerrigan. He had sparred with the best of them—and won. No, she wasn't going to put herself in that position. She'd worked too hard to lose it all now simply because Neil had a personal vendetta against entertainment programming.

But she could hardly tell Daniel Rawlings that, and he was waiting for her answer. She had to say something, so, summoning her considerable poise and her most charming smile and trying not to choke on the words, she said, "I would be honored to have Mr. Kerrigan appear on my show, Mr. Rawlings, but I'm sure he has too many commitments of his own to take the time now." She turned to Neil, willing him to take up the cue. "Don't you, Mr. Kerrigan?"

His glance held hers for a long moment before a slow smile curved his mouth. Dinah held her breath. Why wasn't he saying anything? Rawlings's idea must be as repugnant to him as it was to her; she couldn't imagine that he'd consider for a second appearing on her show. *But why was he smiling like that?*

It seemed an eternity before Neil's eyes left hers. When he finally looked away, she felt limp, as if that contact had entirely drained her of energy. Now, surely, he would think of something to get them out of this appalling situation his son had so innocently thrust upon them. All he had to say was—

"I'd be delighted to appear on Miss Blake's program, Dan. I'll have my secretary call and set up a time."

Dinah bolted upright, exhaustion forgotten. As she stared in furious consternation at Neil, he looked at her again. And winked.

NEIL'S SON WAS SILENT on the taxi ride back to the hotel. When Neil emerged from his own reverie to ask why, Andy put his head back against the seat and sighed. "She sure was beautiful, wasn't she, Dad?"

Neil didn't have to ask who Andy meant; he'd been preoccupied with thoughts of Dinah, too. Recalling those flashing green eyes, he was chagrined to realize how mistaken he'd been about her. He'd expected a vapid woman who traded on her beauty, but she'd been so much more that he'd been taken aback. His attraction had been so instantaneous and so powerful that he'd deliberately provoked an argument just to maintain some emotional distance. Some inexplicable impulse had made him agree to appear on her show, but he didn't regret it. Just the thought of seeing her again made his blood race, and when he turned to stare out the window without answering, Andy looked across at his father, and grinned.

CHAPTER TWO

DINAH FUMED ALL THE WAY across the continent from New York to California. She had intended to spend the night in the city, but she'd been so furious after the awards ceremony that she'd changed her plane reservations and took the first flight back to San Francisco. She hadn't cared that it left in the middle of the night; she knew she'd never be able to sleep anyway after what had happened. So while her fellow passengers slumbered uncomfortably even in first class, Dinah sat seething under the tiny cone of light that illuminated her seat. Flight attendants came and went, asking if she'd like champagne or something to eat, and at first Dinah was tempted to demand all the champagne they would give her. She settled for innumerable cups of coffee instead, which of course only had the effect of jangling her nerves even more.

She should have known Neil Kerrigan would come up with something like that, she thought irately. He had actually enjoyed putting her in an untenable position, and she'd been so furious when she saw that wink that it had taken all her control to act self-possessed and poised when she'd been practically speechless with fury. She hadn't trusted herself to stay a second longer than absolutely necessary; if she had, she would have erupted like a volcano.

"'I'll have my secretary call and set up a time,'" she mimicked savagely. "'I'd be delighted to appear on Miss Blake's show....'"

Well, *she* wasn't delighted at all, and the first thing she was going to do when she got back was to instruct her secretary to inform Neil Kerrigan's office that she was booked solid for the next eighteen years. *That* would give him something to think about!

But as tempting as the thought was, she knew she couldn't do it. Roger would have a fit if he found out, and while she knew she could handle her immediate boss, she shuddered at the thought of what she would say to Daniel Rawlings if he discovered she'd ignored what amounted to a direct order. Even someone in Neil's position couldn't do that.

And that was another thing. She knew Neil had only accepted Rawling's suggestion because he'd thought it would be amusing to see how she would handle it. Oh, she had no doubts about his motives whatsoever; they had been written all over his smug face. He had taken revenge on her because she'd dared to argue with him—dared, in fact, to disagree. He had deliberately backed her into a corner from which she couldn't escape, and if by some superhuman feat she managed to get out of this unscathed, she'd let him know exactly what she thought of him.

She was still plotting what she'd say when the plane finally landed at San Francisco International. When she saw Leigh's flaxen head bobbing among the few hardy souls awaiting the flight's early-morning arrival, she let out a breath or relief and waved. She'd called from New York and asked if Leigh could meet the plane, but her friend had been so groggy from being awakened in the middle of the night that Dinah hadn't been sure she'd even remember the conversation.

"Thanks," she said gratefully as Leigh came up to her. "I really needed to talk to someone."

"Wouldn't a cab driver have done?" Leigh asked with a yawn as they made their way to her car. "Whatever possessed you to come back at such an indecent hour? I thought you were going to stay overnight."

"I was," Dinah answered briefly. "It's a long story."

Leigh started the car and they headed out onto the deserted freeway. It was the beginning of February and exceptionally cool this morning, so Leigh turned up the heater. "Want to tell me about it?"

"Yes...no.... Oh, I don't know." She had wanted to discuss what had happened when she called Leigh, but now there didn't seem much point. She was tired of thinking about it anyway, so she added, "Let's just say it wasn't one of my better nights."

Leigh glanced across at her. "What's the matter? Didn't you win?"

Dinah laughed shortly. She'd been so upset about what happened afterward that she'd completely forgotten her triumph during the ceremony. "Yes, I won."

"You did? But that's wonderful! Congratulations!"

"Thanks," Dinah said, and frowned as she rested her head against the back of the seat. Somehow it didn't seem so important—now that Neil had emerged the victor in their encounter instead of her.

Leigh looked at her again. "You don't sound very happy about it," she said with the ease of long friendship. "What's wrong?"

Dinah and Leigh had been friends since high school, when they had both suddenly sprouted to their adult heights of five foot eight. Towering over the rest of the class hadn't seemed quite so grotesque when there was someone else to share the misery, and in the years since their friendship had deepened. Leigh was the sister she'd never had, and she knew Leigh felt the same way about her. She'd helped Leigh open her first exclusive little boutique when she got her break at the station, and earlier this year, Leigh had been able to open another after Dinah had been given approval to credit Leightique for her on-camera wardrobe. Leigh had appeared on *Personalities* several times to give fashion shows, and her friend was one guest Dinah always enjoyed.

That last thought reminded Dinah of another guest she knew she wouldn't enjoy at all, and she grimaced. "Oh, I'm happy about the award. It's just that there was a . . . problem afterward."

"A problem?"

"Yes. I met Neil Kerrigan."

"You met Neil Kerrigan?" Leigh echoed with a shriek. She almost drove off the road as she turned in her seat to stare at Dinah. "*The* Neil Kerrigan?"

Dinah clutched the armrest. "Leigh, watch where you're driving!"

Leigh glanced around quickly, swerving back into her own lane with a jerk. But her mind was still obviously not on her driving as she exclaimed, "Wow...! Neil Kerrigan. I can't believe it!"

Dinah was exasperated with herself. How could she have forgotten that Neil was one of Leigh's idols? Her friend watched *The Kerrigan Report* religiously every Sunday night; she absolutely refused to make any plans that might prevent her from getting home in time for that precious hour. Leigh even took her phone off the hook so that she wouldn't be interrupted. Wishing that she'd never mentioned the subject, Dinah said flatly, "There's nothing to get excited about. He's certainly not what you think."

"How could he not be?" Leigh demanded excitedly. "Oh, Dinah, you must tell me everything that happened! What he said, what he did...how he looked! Especially how he looked! Is he really as handsome as he is on TV?"

Dinah thought of that chiseled face with its straight nose and strong chin, the well-shaped sensual mouth, the dimple that had flashed once or twice in his left cheek. Annoyed that her heart gave a little leap at the picture, she said curtly, "No. He isn't. Not unless you like predators."

Leigh threw her an amused look. "That handsome, huh? It sounds like he really got to you."

"Oh, he got to me all right," Dinah muttered, slouching back in the seat again now that Leigh didn't seem in danger of driving them into a freeway divider.

"Was that the problem?"

"No." Dinah didn't want to talk about this anymore. She wanted to get home and soak in a long, hot bath and forget the whole thing. She was exhausted and disheveled from all this rushing around, and maybe after a few hours' sleep, she'd be able to grapple more successfully with the problem of Neil Kerrigan. Right now, she couldn't seem to think coherently about anything.

"So why didn't you stay in New York?"

Dinah sighed. Leigh was like a terrier sometimes; she just wouldn't let go until she found out every little detail. "Because I was too upset to stay," she answered, and then was annoyed with herself again. Knowing Leigh would never let her leave it at that, she took a deep breath and told her the whole story.

"He's going to be a guest on your show!" Leigh cried as Dinah concluded the humiliating tale. "Oh, how are you ever going to *stand* it? I'd be so thrilled I know I'd make a complete fool of myself!"

And that's exactly what would probably happen to her, Dinah thought depressingly as Leigh rhapsodized on. Staring out the car window at the houses starting to take shape in the growing light, she just hoped that by the time Neil got back to his home base in Los Angeles, he'd be bored enough with the joke not to follow through.

Her spirits rose at the thought, and the more she considered it, the more hopeful she became. By the time Leigh dropped her off at the house and she fell into bed, she had convinced herself that the whole thing would blow over and she wouldn't have to deal with it after all.

"HE DID WHAT?" Dinah cried later that afternoon in Roger Dayton's office.

"I knew you'd be thrilled."

"Thrilled!"

Roger grinned, the cat who'd just been presented with the cream. He'd been so excited about the Los Angeles call that he'd practically been pacing as he waited on tenderhooks for Dinah to come in. Neil

Kerrigan's office had called a few minutes after Dinah had phoned in herself to tell Roger she was back and on her way.

"I don't know how you did it, Dinah," he said as she stared at him in utter dismay, "but you deserve a bonus. It's not every day we book a guest of Neil Kerrigan's caliber, and the only thing I can think of is that he must have been impressed by that award you won." Pausing, he added almost as an afterthought, "Oh yes, congratulations on that, too, by the way. Good job!"

"Thanks," Dinah said. She'd always felt a vague distaste for Roger Dayton, but it had blossomed into real dislike now. His throwaway remark about her winning the award irritated her, and she glanced away from him. "Unfortunately, I don't think that Neil Kerrigan is impressed with anything but himself. In fact—"

Roger leaned forward at that, placing his doughy hands flat on the desk in front of him. "That's not a very civil attitude, Dinah. You won't get very far with him if you act like that."

"I won't get anywhere with him at all," Dinah retorted.

Roger's eyes narrowed. "What is that supposed to mean?"

Dinah stood. She was too agitated to sit still, and she began to pace. "It means that Neil Kerrigan is the most egotistical, self-involved, arrogant man I've ever met," she stated. "And if we have him on the show, it's going to be a disaster."

"What do you mean, 'if'? Of course we're going to have him on the show. He's scheduled to appear at the end of this week."

Dinah stopped abruptly. "This week!"

Roger's gaze was flat. "Do you have some kind of problem with that?"

She thought of several things to say in response, but when she saw his challenging expression, she knew she'd die first before admitting how unnerved she was at the thought of doing a show with Neil. Reminding herself firmly that she'd dealt with difficult guests before—although none as difficult as she knew Neil Kerrigan was going to be—she lifted her chin. "No," she said coolly. "I don't have a problem with that at all."

"Good," Roger said, smiling that unctuous smile that so annoyed her. "I'll have research get right on it. You'll have every detail we can get our hands on about Kerrigan's life by Thursday night. I want you to know him so well by Friday that—"

"Don't worry, Roger," she interrupted curtly. Did he really think he had to explain her job to her? "I'll be prepared. I always am."

"You'd better be," he said as a parting shot. "This is going to be an important segment for the show. A lot is riding on this, Dinah. We can't blow it."

But during the next few days, whenever she thought about it, she knew she was going to do just that. She was so distracted that she practically sleepwalked through the other segments they taped, and by the time she and Leigh met for dinner two nights before D day, she was so tense she couldn't even eat.

"What's the matter with you?" Leigh asked finally in exasperation. "You haven't heard a word I've said all night."

Dinah pushed away her untouched plate. Grabbing her wineglass instead, she wondered why she had given up smoking three years ago. She could use a cigarette now—a whole pack of them. Taking a sip of the wine, she said, "I'm sorry. I've just got a lot of things on my mind, that's all."

"I can see that," Leigh said dryly. "Come on, what gives?"

Dinah hesitated, wondering if she could explain. She felt such conflicting emotions about the situation that she wasn't sure she knew how she felt about it herself. But then she remembered how Leigh had helped her through her divorce, and through so many other crises before, and she knew she ought to give it a try. "It's this thing with Neil Kerrigan," she admitted finally.

"What thing?" Leigh demanded, leaning forward excitedly. "Don't tell me you've been going out with him!"

Dinah drew back. "Of course not!"

"What then?"

"He's going to be on the show Friday—"

"This Friday? Why didn't you tell me?"

"Because I didn't want my best friend to see me make a fool of myself, that's why."

"You've never made a fool of yourself in your entire life."

"Haven't I? Well, in that case, you're about to see a first."

Leigh started to smile at that, but when she realized that Dinah wasn't joking, she sobered again. "It can't be as bad as that, can it?"

Dinah forced a smile. "It's ridiculous, I know, getting so shook up simply because Neil Kerrigan's going to be on the show. You'd think I was going to interview the president or something."

Leigh wasn't fooled. "You really are worried about it, aren't you?"

Dinah glanced away. "Yes, and I don't know why. It's not as if I haven't had difficult guests before...."

"What makes you think he's going to be difficult?"

"You haven't met him. I have."

"But he must have wanted to be on the show," Leigh persisted, "or he wouldn't have agreed to come."

"It's his reason for coming that bothers me."

"What reason is that?"

Dinah sighed. "We had a terrible argument at the awards dinner—"

"You didn't tell me that!"

"Some things are better left unsaid."

Leigh was fascinated. "What was it about?"

"Do you remember that segment he did about entertainment programming?"

Leigh winced. "How could I forget? He came down a little hard on you that night."

"A little?"

"All right, a lot," Leigh amended. "Was that what the argument was about?"

"Sort of. At least, that's how it started. We never got a chance to finish it."

"And that's why you think he agreed to come, so that you could finish it on the air?"

"I'm afraid so," Dinah said with a grimace. "But what's even worse is that I have to take part of the blame. I guess I started it."

"You!"

"Well, I was so angry at what he'd done, and there he sat, so satisfied with himself, so...so damned arrogant about it, that I—"

"Oh boy," Leigh muttered. "No wonder you're worried."

They were silent for a few moments, both lost in thought. Then Leigh said hopefully, "Maybe he's forgotten all about it by now."

Dinah looked at her again. "Oh sure."

"Well, maybe it won't be as bad as you think."

"Right," Dinah said dryly, and knew that it was going to be a hundred times worse than either of them had imagined.

DINAH RECEIVED the research material on Neil Kerrigan Thursday night just as she was leaving the office. All the way home, she kept glancing at the folder on the seat beside her, wondering what it contained, perversely delaying the moment when she had to open it.

But the innocent-looking file seemed to mock her, and finally she couldn't stand the suspense any longer. Ripping open the envelope when she stopped for a light, she stared with dismay at the two sheets of paper inside. She realized immediately that there wasn't enough information here to keep the conversation going two minutes, much less a half hour, and for an instant she was overcome with fury at the research department. Was this all they could find? She'd heard that Neil was a fanatic about his private life, but this was ridiculous. What were they going to talk about?

Agitated, she stuffed the pages back inside the envelope and drove the rest of the way home, telling herself firmly she wasn't going to think about it until she'd had dinner and a bath and a glass of wine. Naturally, she sat down to read the meager report the instant she walked in the door.

"Neil Andrew Kerrigan," she read aloud. "Age thirty-eight...."

Born: Great Falls, Montana, November 13, 1947.

Parents: John Nelson Kerrigan, father; Eileen Galworth Kerrigan, mother.

Siblings: One. Andrew Riley Kerrigan, brother, died 1966, Vietnam.

Education: Yale University, 1964-1967. Graduated magna cum laude, Bachelor of Arts, Journalism.

Service Record: Volunteered U.S. Army, 1967. Two Purple Hearts, one Medal of Valor. Service: Korea, Germany, Vietnam. Discharged as Captain, 1969; two months' convalescence, V.A. Hospital, Long Beach, California.

Marital Status: Married Elise Marie Grayson, 1969; divorced, 1982.

Children: One son, Andrew Nelson Kerrigan, born 1969.

Previous Employment: See attached.

Current Employment: Host of *The Kerrigan Report* (see attached), Los Angeles, California.

Hobbies: ?

Special Interests: ?

Dinah stopped reading. Grabbing the envelope, she looked inside. There had to be more, she thought, trying to quell her panic at the idea of going on the air with this smattering of information.

But the envelope was empty, and as she sat staring at the two pages in her hand, the question marks after Hobbies and Special Interests caught her eye and she became furious with Research all over again. Did this mean that Neil didn't have any hobbies, or that they couldn't find out what they were? A man like Neil Kerrigan, graduated with honors from Yale, decorated for bravery during the Vietnam War, had to have some outside interests. He didn't just go home to luxurious Pacific Palasades every night and lock himself in, did he?

Dinah threw down the envelope and flung the type-written pages on top of it. Groaning, she put her head in her hands, wondering what she was going to do now. She couldn't grab facts and figures out of thin air tomorrow, but it seemed that that was exactly what Research expected her to do.

The only personal thing she had of any interest were the medals he'd won during the war, and she could just imagine Neil's reaction if she pressed him about that: he'd probably tell her flatly that he didn't want to discuss the war, and then where would she be? She'd have to ask him about *The Kerrigan Report* then, and she quailed at the thought of introducing that subject at the outset, before she knew how things were going to go.

But she already knew how things were going to go, didn't she? The whole show was going to be a disaster from start to finish, so it didn't really matter what they talked about first. She knew he planned to make her look ridiculous tomorrow, and after reading the information she had on him tonight, she suspected that was exactly what would happen. Feeling helpless and angry at the same time, Dinah went to bed.

SHE WAS AT THE OFFICE early the next day after spending one of the worst nights of her life. When she had finally dropped off to sleep sometime in the wee hours of the morning, she'd been chased by nightmares of Neil laughing triumphantly while she stood amid the ruins of her career. By the time five o'clock came and the alarm went off, she was already in the kitchen, drinking her second cup of coffee and cursing the circles under her eyes.

She had wanted to look absolutely radiant this morning, filled with confidence and so outwardly poised that Neil would think twice about being anything other than a gentleman—if he knew how to be one, that was, she thought irritably. Forcing herself, she went into the bedroom to dress, wondering what Roger would say if she just called in sick today. The idea was tempting.

It was also out of the question. As she looked at herself in the mirror, she knew that the last thing she was going to do was give Neil Kerrigan the satisfaction of not showing up. No, she'd be there even if she had to spend the next two hours repairing the damage her sleepless night had caused. If she had to surrender, at least she could look her best in defeat.

Twenty minutes later, Dinah gave herself a final inspection in the mirror. A satisfied smile curved her lips, and suddenly she felt more like herself. The blue silk dress with dolman sleeves that Leigh had brought over the other night complimented her eyes and her shoulder-length hair, which mercifully had decided to behave itself this morning. No one had to know that she didn't feel as confident and assured on the inside as she looked on the outside. The important thing was the effect, she thought, and determinedly ignored the butterflies gathering in her stomach as she went briskly out to her car and drove to the station.

When she arrived, the receptionist was aflutter and the two secretaries were agog. "He's here!" one of them whispered as Dinah passed. "He's really here!"

Dinah's mouth was suddenly dry. "Where is he?" she asked, and hoped that her voice didn't sound as tremulous to them as it did to her.

"He's in Mr. Dayton's office," the receptionist breathed. "I just took him a cup of coffee."

If she hadn't been so unnerved at the thought that Neil really had come, Dinah would have been amused at the adoring expression on the girl's face. It irritated her instead, and she asked more sharply than she intended, "When did he get here? Has he been to Makeup yet?"

The receptionist looked surprised and hurt at her tone. "He got here just a few minutes ago, Miss Blake. I...I don't think he's had a chance to get to Makeup." Her eyes lit up again. "Do you want me to find out?"

"No, I'll do it myself," Dinah said, and strode off down the hall.

She heard one of the girls sniff, "What's the matter with *her*?" and another reply, "Maybe she's just nervous."

Nervous? Dinah felt like laughing shrilly at the idea. What could possibly make them think she was nervous? Wasn't it every day that her career crashed down around her ears?

Roger's office door was closed, and as she approached, she heard voices inside. She couldn't hear what they were saying, but Neil's deep baritone was unmistakable and her heart gave a painful lurch. As much as she dreaded the thought of going in there, she knew she couldn't just stand out in the hallway like a schoolchild waiting for the principal, so she raised her hand to knock on the door before she lost courage.

The door opened at that precise moment, and suddenly she was face-to-face with the man who had preoccupied her every waking thought for days. She was so startled that she stood frozen for a long moment, her hand foolishly raised in the air.

Neil seemed just as surprised as she when he saw her standing there. He stopped so abruptly that Roger, coming up behind him, jostled him forward, and before either of them could move aside, Neil had bumped into her. His hands involuntarily clasped her waist, and at the contact, they both jumped back as if stung.

"Sorry, Miss Blake," Neil said, recovering more quickly than she.

"Think nothing of it, Mr. Kerrigan," Dinah replied stiffly, despising him all the more because he was so obviously composed and she wasn't. She knew by his smile that he wasn't sorry at all, and she was amazed that she sounded so cool and self-possessed when inside she was a quivering bundle of nerves. Now that they were face-to-face and she felt the impact of the man, what little confidence she'd gathered seemed to evaporate. The supremely self-assured look in his eyes made her feel panicked again and she knew she couldn't go through with this. Not today, not ever.

But just then someone called down the hall, "Ten minutes, Miss Blake," and Dinah knew there was no time to think of an excuse to delay the show. She'd have to go through with it after all.

NEIL WATCHED DINAH from the wings, unable to take his eyes off her as she waved to the waiting audience before turning to confer with the director. Unconsciously he flexed his fingers, still able to feel her slender waist in his hands. Resisting the impulse to run his hands through his hair, he tried to compose himself. In a few minutes he was expected to go out there and deliver the Neil Kerrigan everyone knew. It seemed a difficult task: he'd forgotten the power of those green eyes of hers, and for a moment back there, he'd been so shaken that he could hardly remember his own name. Suddenly annoyed that she looked so poised when he felt so out of control, he made himself recall her impassioned defense of her program and felt more calm. He'd play the game her way, he decided. He'd be the perfect guest, exactly the kind she said she wanted, the kind her audience expected.

Smiling to himself, he relaxed and waited for his cue.

CHAPTER THREE

"FOUR . . . THREE . . . TWO . . . ONE . . . ."

The camera swung her way, the voice-over introduced her, and suddenly Dinah was on the air.

"Good morning, ladies and gentlemen," she said, flashing that brilliant smile that always roused the audience even before the applause cue lit up over their heads. "Welcome to *Personalities*."

The applause exploded, and although Dinah couldn't see the audience beyond the blinding glare of the hot klieg lights, she breathed a sigh of relief when she sensed that she had a good group today. These first few seconds were always tense: the audience could set the tone of the show, and if they happened to be uncooperative, the program could turn into a disaster. It had only happened once or twice to Dinah, but she remembered all too well that sinking feeling as she played to a silent, watchful and completely unresponsive crowd. That was the last thing she needed today. She was already so nervous that her palms were damp, and she was sure that the mike was picking up the loud thudding of her heart.

"Keep it light," Roger had muttered in her ear at the last minute.

She had looked up at him from a final perusal of her notes, impatiently waving away the ministrations of the makeup girl who was fussing with her hair. One of the production assistants was fluttering around, tripping over herself and everything else as she checked to make sure the set was ready, but she wasn't the only one who was affected by Neil's presence. Everyone seemed awed and distracted today, and as Dinah watched them all rushing around, she barely restrained herself from screaming at them to stand still.

Realizing Roger was still hovering, waiting for her reply, she wondered how she was going to "keep it light" with a guest like Neil Kerrigan. She just knew he planned to open the show with some acid comment specifically designed to put her on the defensive, but she muttered, "I'll try."

"You'll have to do better than that," Roger snapped, unnerved himself. "You don't know how important this is!"

Irritated at his tone, Dinah said evenly, "Why don't you tell me?"

But just then the director, a normally unflappable veteran of nearly twenty years behind the camera, called out from the control booth in a voice an octave higher than usual, "Thirty seconds!" and Roger didn't have a chance to tell her what he meant. He disappeared at a run toward the booth, and Dinah had no choice but to take her place on the set.

"Oh no, the coffee!" the assistant exclaimed, and dashed off to fetch the carafe and two cups as the director, his voice vibrating, called out, "Places, everybody!"

Dinah herself had experienced a moment of complete panic as the camera's red eye impaled her and she knew she had to begin the intro; for a few horrifying seconds she couldn't even remember the name of the show. Mercifully, instinct had taken over, and she was amazed to see after a quick glance at the monitor that she looked like she always did—poised, cool and in total command of the situation. She felt like an absolute wreck.

"This morning we're pleased to present a very special guest," she said, "a man I'm sure you all know from his own popular news program, the Los Angeles-based *Kerrigan Report*. He's graciously consented to take time from his demanding schedule to share with us a behind-the-scenes glimpse at one of the most renowned and successful personalities in television today, so please . . . give a warm welcome to the handsome and dynamic . . . Mr. Neil Kerrigan!"

And suddenly there he was, striding across the stage from the wings, his black hair with its boyish wave gleaming under the lights, his lean face wreathed in a smile. The applause became deafening as the audience rose to their feet, and he stopped to face them—tall and self-assured, casually elegant in a tailored blue sport coat, tan slacks, crisp white shirt and striped tie. He was so handsome that Dinah's heart gave a leap, and she reminded herself firmly that she couldn't afford to be distracted even for an instant by those outrageously good looks. But an image of that moment in the corridor flashed into her mind, and she could feel his hands on her waist. To her horror, she felt her color heighten.

Furious with herself, she didn't dare look at the monitor again. She was sure her flushed face would be painfully evident, and if it was, she didn't want to see it. She hadn't been this unstrung since the first time she'd appeared on camera, and suddenly she was annoyed that Neil Kerrigan had the power to do this to her. *Get a grip on,* she thought to herself, and held her smile while she waited for the applause to die down.

The crowd finally subsided, and in the rustle of people seating themselves again, Neil turned and bounded up the two steps to the dais. Dinah was sure that her cheeks were still flushed and she just hoped he would think it had something to do with the lights. But then their eyes met, and when she saw the expression in that deep blue glance, she felt her color rise again. Utterly composed, he knew how nervous she was and she saw at once that he was actually enjoying her discomfort. Cursing the fair complexion that had betrayed her at such a critical moment, she gestured quickly for him to be seated opposite her. But as she sat down gracefully herself, the perfect hostess on the outside, she wondered how she was going to get through the next half hour. Feeling as though she'd been sentenced to thirty minutes of pure torture, she turned to him and began.

"As you can hear from the response, we're all delighted to have you here, Mr. Kerrigan—"

Neil smiled. "Call me Neil, please . . . Dinah."

Dinah didn't trust that smile at all. She knew he had something up his sleeve; she had seen it in his eyes. But she nodded in gracious acknowledgment, braced herself and plunged in.

"Before we talk about your news show," she said, willing her voice under control, "perhaps you could tell us when you first became interested in journalism as a career. Was it the pursuit of a youthful dream? Did you always know that someday you'd be where you are now?"

Neil hesitated so long that Dinah was sure he was going to make some devastating comment that would make her look like a total fool right at the outset. It seemed an eternity before he grinned wickedly and replied, "Well, it was really an accident—"

"An accident?" She wasn't sure if he was putting her on or not.

There was a distinct gleam in his eyes that made her distrust him even more. "I didn't know I'd major in journalism until I was a freshman in college," he began.

"So it wasn't a childhood dream."

"Oh, no." He grinned again. "Do you remember the first day on campus, when all the freshmen have to declare a major course of study?"

"Yes," Dinah replied warily. She definitely didn't trust that evil glint in his eyes.

"Well, when I got there I saw this beautiful girl heading into the journalism department..."

"And...?" Dinah prodded even more cautiously. It was like waiting for the other shoe to drop.

"I followed her."

There was a delighted burst of laughter at that in which Dinah felt compelled to join. But her response was forced, and the quick look she directed at him told him she didn't care for this boyish act he'd adopted, even if it did endear him to the crowd. As the laughter died down, she decided to fight fire with fire.

"But you did graduate from Yale with a bachelor of arts in journalism, didn't you?" she asked sweetly. "As I recall, you were magna cum laude."

Neil winked broadly at the audience. "That gorgeous girl was also smart," he said. "We, er, did a lot of studying together."

The resulting laugh was louder this time—the crowd already loved him. Dinah should have been relieved that it was going so easily, but alarm bells were beginning to sound in her mind. What was he trying to pull here? She didn't believe for an instant that he'd gone through Yale University on the skirt tails of some adoring girl; she wasn't even sure if Yale had been admitting women at that time. But there was no way to check that right now, so she plodded doggedly on.

"I've read that right after graduation you volunteered for the army. That seems—"

A shadow passed briefly over his face, but it was gone so quickly that Dinah wasn't sure she'd even seen it. "Oh, let's not bore the audience with that," he interrupted, and turned away before she could object. "I'm sure some of those wonderful people out there have a few questions they'd like to ask. How about it?"

There was a renewed swell of applause, and Dinah knew instantly that she was defeated. Neil had deftly taken control out of her hands; if she tried to get it back, she'd lose the crowd. There was nothing to do but smile in agreement and gesture for the houselights, but as she did, she couldn't wait for a commercial break so that she could ask him just what he thought he was doing. Seething, she looked out over the sea of raised hands and wondered what he had up his sleeve now. Nodding toward the first hand she saw, she waited for the ax to fall.

"Mr. Kerrigan, are you married?"

"I was," Neil responded genially while Dinah held her breath. "But she decided on our thirteenth year that I was bad luck."

There was a tittering of laughter, and Dinah glanced at him quickly before she selected another hand.

"Then you're divorced, Mr. Kerrigan?" the second questioner asked unnecessarily.

Neil didn't flicker an eyelash. "At the present time," he answered courteously.

"Does that mean you plan to get married again?"

"I don't think so. Isn't one wife enough for any man?"

The laughter was loud this time and Dinah nodded abruptly in the direction of a third waving hand. She didn't like the way this was going at all. Why was he being so flippant about everything? She wanted to steer the questions to some of the important issues he had covered on his show, to treat the crowd to the kind of incisive analysis for which he was famous. But she knew she couldn't change course now; the audience was too enthralled with his clever replies, and if she tried to bring the discussion back to a more serious level, she knew the mood could turn sullen. Feeling a little sullen herself, she sat back and waited for her chance to gain control again.

"Do you have any children, Mr. Kerrigan?"

"Yes, a son. His name is Andrew—Andy. He's sixteen now, and already thinking about all those good-looking girls at Yale."

More laughter as another hand shot up. "Does Andy live with you?"

"No, I sent him off to boarding school because he's going to be taller than I am, and I don't want any competition."

"What kind of car do you drive, Mr. Kerrigan?"

"What kind of car do you think?"

The speaker, a middle-aged man with thinning hair and a paunch, replied shyly and wistfully, "A Rolls?"

Neil grinned. "I'm not old enough for that yet. How about a Ferrari?"

"Even better," the balding man breathed reverently, and sat down with a thump, reddening at the renewed laughter around him.

The questions continued all through the commercial break. Dinah tried several times to interject something, but Neil waved a hand in her direction as if he was enjoying himself too much to be interrupted. In the control booth above them, Roger was ecstatic. Every time Dinah glanced up there, he made a signal with his thumb and forefinger, smiling broadly to let her know how pleased he was. Dinah wasn't pleased at all; she wanted to grab Neil by the lapels and shake him. Gritting her teeth behind a professional smile that was getting more and more difficult to hold, she promised herself that she'd get back on track in the second half if it killed her. This time, she'd be prepared for him.

When the break ended the camera opened with a tight shot on her face. Dinah summoned all the considerable poise. "Welcome to the second half of *Personalities*," she said smoothly. "We're pleased to have with us today Mr. Neil Kerrigan, host of the Sunday-night show, *The Kerrigan Report*."

Then, as the camera pulled back to a shot of them both, she turned to Neil. Before he had a chance to continue his ridiculous charade, she said, "We haven't had much opportunity to discuss that popular program of yours, but I'm sure our audience would like to know, as I would, how you put together a show as successful as *The Kerrigan Report*. Perhaps you could share with us now a behind-the-scenes look at one of the most fascinating programs on television today.''

After such a gracious intro, Neil could hardly refuse to answer. His face in profile to the audience, he mockingly saluted her with a look, and it was all Dinah could do to keep her expression neutral when she felt like grinning with satisfaction.

But Neil wasn't about to admit defeat as easily as that. He might have conceded her a point just now, but she saw from the look in his eyes that she was still going to have to fight for anything she got. ''What would you like to know?'' he asked so agreeably that Dinah heard those alarm bells again.

She was determined to remain unruffled. ''*The Kerrigan Report* speaks to central issues that affect all of us,'' she said evenly. ''Perhaps you can enlighten us on how you select your material when there are so many problems to address.''

Neil smiled. Evilly. ''It's very simple, really. I just have everybody in the office write down a grievance on a piece of paper, we put them all into a hat and then I pick one.''

There was a smattering of laughter at that, but Dinah decided that if he wanted to play rough, she could, too. ''I see,'' she said, and added sweetly, ''and then do they all write your copy for you, too?''

Above them in the control booth, Roger groaned and made a slashing motion with his hand. Dinah ignored him, smiling composedly at Neil as she waited for him to answer. She should have known that he would be equal to the occasion.

''Oh, I generally write that myself.'' He paused a beat, and then asked innocently, ''Why, don't you?''

Dinah barely prevented herself from giving a sharp retort. "Of course," she said courteously, although it cost her an effort. "But we were talking about you. How do you select your guests for the show?" She couldn't resist adding, "Or are those names put into a hat, too?"

Roger was gripping his hair with both hands now, shouting something at her from behind the glass. Glad the booth was soundproof, Dinah ignored him again. She knew she was going to pay for this, but at the moment, she didn't care. This contest between her and Neil was exhilarating; she saw by the look in his eyes that he felt it, too. So did the audience. Everyone was waiting in breathless silence to see who would emerge the victor in this unexpected skirmish.

"No," Neil drawled finally in answer to her question. "We put those names in a coffee can instead."

The moment of tension passed. The audience let out its collective breath in a rush, bursting into delighted laughter at Neil's sally. Roger, who had thrown himself across the transom in despair, looked up hopefully as the waves of laughter reached the booth. When he realized that he wasn't utterly ruined after all, a relieved smile split his fleshy face, and by the time Dinah was signaled to wrap up, he was actually beaming. Wondering who had really won this verbal battle of wits, Dinah turned to face the camera. She wasn't through yet.

"And there you have it, ladies and gentlemen," she said. "The humorous side of the man who brings us the more sobering issues in *The Kerrigan Report* every week." Reaching out to offer her hand to Neil, she added graciously, "Thank you, Mr. Kerrigan, for being here. It's been a pleasure and an honor to have you on the show.''

Neil took her hand, but he didn't release it as they both stood to acknowledge the thunderous applause. When Neil knew their mikes were off, he murmured under the whistles and shouting and loud clapping, ''A pleasure and an honor? Don't you think that was overdoing it a little?''

''Why no, Mr. Kerrigan,'' Dinah murmured, trying to extract her hand. ''You were all I thought you'd be...and more.''

He raised an eyebrow. ''I'm not sure how I should take that.''

''Take it any way you like, Mr. Kerrigan,'' she said sweetly, acutely aware of the warmth and pressure of his fingers holding hers. ''Let's just say it was an... interesting experience.''

He laughed at that, but still wouldn't relinquish her hand. ''Interesting enough to have dinner with me?''

''Dinner?'' she repeated, startled.

''Eight o'clock?''

''No, I'm sorry,'' she said hastily, recovering from her surprise. ''But I—''

''How can you refuse?'' he asked. ''After all, I was such a perfect guest.''

Dinah lifted her chin. ''I would hardly call you the perfect guest!'' she retorted, remembering all those anxious moments during the show.

''But I answered every question, didn't I?'' he persisted. ''And you have to admit, the audience loved me.''

Squirming inwardly, Dinah had to admit that was true. But she had no intention of acknowledging that to him, so she said, ''That doesn't mean I do.''

"But surely I should have a reward for giving such a sterling performance!"

"I'm sure there are hundreds of women who would be delighted to oblige," Dinah answered haughtily. "Unfortunately, I'm not one of them."

Her sharp retort seemed to amuse him even more. "Don't tell me you're afraid to go out with me."

"Afraid!" she repeated, stung. "That's absurd!"

"Is it?"

"Of course it is!" she insisted, moving back a step. The power of his gaze was too compelling; she knew she had to excuse herself before she found herself blurting out that she'd have dinner with him after all. "I'm sorry, but—"

Just then Roger came rushing up, interrupting them in a flurry of congratulations. Pumping Neil's hand and squeezing a frowning Dinah's arm at the same time, he exclaimed, "Wonderful show! Just wonderful! The audience loved you, Mr. Kerrigan. You had them in the palm of your hand!"

Neil shot Dinah an amused I-told-you-so look, and she glared back at him as Roger went on rapturously, "I really think it's the best show we've ever done, don't you, Dinah?"

"Well, I—"

"We're so glad you agreed to come, Mr. Kerrigan!" Roger swept on, interrupting her. "Is there anything I can do to show my appreciation? If you're free, I'd like to invite you to dinner, at least."

"Thank you," Neil said suavely. "But Miss Blake has already been kind enough to extend an invitation."

Dinah's chin jerked up. "That's not exactly..." she began, but the damage had already been done. Roger was beaming at her now, and she knew that a refusal from her would wipe that fatuous smile from his face in an instant. He had forgiven her for the moment because the show had turned out successfully, but she knew from experience how quickly his mood could change, and she wasn't going to have a scene with him in front of Neil.

Then she saw Neil grinning openly, aware of the position she was in and enjoying himself immensely, and she tossed her head. She might have to go out with him, but she'd do it on her own terms. "I was just going to tell Mr. Kerrigan that I'd meet him at Ernie's," she said, naming one of the most exclusive restaurants in the city. "Eight o'clock, wasn't it, Mr. Kerrigan?"

"Eight o'clock is fine," Neil replied, not batting an eyelash. "But I'll pick you up, of course."

"Oh, I wouldn't dream of putting you to all that trouble," she answered, and walked away before he could object.

DINAH DIDN'T HAVE TIME to think about the show until she was getting ready for her dinner date that evening. As she wearily drove home at five, she reflected that it was fortunate she hadn't had another taping scheduled for that day. Even if she hadn't been so exhausted from the show with Neil, she wouldn't have had time to think about another guest. She'd been inundated with well-wishers from the moment she entered her office after leaving Neil in Roger's clutching hands. Everyone in the station, it seemed, had called or stopped by to congratulate her and tell her what a wonderful show it had been. Even Leigh had phoned, and her friend had been so ecstatic that

Dinah hadn't had the heart to tell her what an ordeal it had been—or that she was having dinner with Neil that night. She knew she couldn't have listened to Leigh rhapsodizing about how fortunate she was, not when she was dreading the evening. Leigh wouldn't have understood at all.

She didn't understand it herself, Dinah admitted when she finally arrived home. Any woman in her right mind would have been thrilled to have been asked out by a man like Neil Kerrigan; why wasn't she? It wasn't as if she hadn't dated since her divorce; she'd gone out several times.

But those dates had been pleasant, uncomplicated, enjoyable because she'd made it clear she had no intention of getting involved. She knew that someday she would be ready for another relationship, but she wasn't now, and she had decided after her divorce that she would concentrate on her career for a while. There were plans to be made and goals to accomplish, and she couldn't do that and be romantically involved, too. Ted had taught her that.

Dinah was annoyed that the thought of becoming involved with Neil had even crossed her mind. There certainly wasn't any danger of that, was there? She didn't even know the man; she wasn't sure she even liked him. So she was working herself into a state over nothing.

Determined not to think about it anymore, she took the tape of the show she'd brought home from the station and inserted it into her VCR so she could listen to it while she fixed her face and dressed. With the dialogue droning in the background, she went to the closet and selected an elegant gold watered-silk pants outfit. It had almost a military look: pointed collar and cuffed sleeves, the pants falling in a straight line to her high-heeled sandals. But the contrast between the delicate material and the tailored construction created just the right hint of femininity, and after studying herself in the mirror, Dinah was satisfied with the effect.

She was just finishing her makeup and hair when she realized that the tape of the show was almost over. She'd been listening absently to it while getting ready, but something had been nagging at the back of her mind, and she turned now to stare at the screen, struck by a sudden horrible thought. Rushing over to the recorder, she rewound the tape and then stood there, jabbing the Fast Forward button, stopping every time Neil was on the screen to listen to what he'd said. By the time the tape was finished again, she realized what he had done, and she was almost speechless with anger.

"The perfect guest," he'd said, and she'd been so relieved that the ordeal was over that she hadn't caught the implication of his words.

She did now, and suddenly she knew why everyone had been so pleased with his performance. He'd given them exactly what they wanted, exactly what he'd said at the awards dinner that her viewers expected. Rewinding the tape again, she played it once more, listening to his glib answers, his oh-so-clever replies. Appalled that she hadn't caught on sooner, she listened again and again, forced finally to accept the galling knowledge that he'd made a fool of her just as she had suspected he'd do.

"An intellectual wasteland," he'd said of shows like hers. "Pabulum for the mind."

He'd been intentionally flippant and facile today, just to show her that her audience would love him even if he didn't say a single thing of any substance. And as he had predicted, the crowd had responded delightedly. No one had asked him about the program he'd done on arms control; no one had asked him about world hunger or inflation or government deficits or energy. Knowing he had covered all these subjects in depth on his show, not one person in that audience today had questioned him about anything more important than what kind of car he drove! Dinah was so furious at what he'd done that she jerked the tape out of the recorder and slammed it down on the table.

That's why he'd taken control of the show away from her, she thought, pacing angrily back and forth. He'd wanted a chance to prove his point. And he had. He had!

The realization made her stop abruptly in the middle of the room. Gritting her teeth, she told herself that she never wanted to see him again. If she did, she'd strangle him with her bare hands. How could he have done this to her? How could she have let him?

The clock struck the half hour just then, reminding her that it was time to leave. She glanced irately at it, telling herself that she wasn't going to go. She wouldn't meet him tonight and admit that he'd made her look ridiculous; she'd die first!

About to change into a robe, she was struck by a sudden disagreeable thought. If she didn't go, he'd have the satisfaction of knowing that she was too humiliated to face him, and that was even worse than admitting that she knew what he'd done. Angry all over again at the impasse, she stood debating her alternatives.

Abruptly she made her decision. Grabbing her cape, she left the house in a cold rage that became even more icy as she approached the restaurant. By the time the valet took her car and she went inside, she knew exactly what she was going to say. His commentaries might have struck fear into the hearts of government officials, but she had a few comments to make of her own right now. By the time she finished with him, he'd know exactly how it felt to be on the receiving end of the same kind of blistering commentary he was so accustomed to meting out.

CHAPTER FOUR

DINAH SAW NEIL the instant she entered the restaurant. It was impossible not to: his was the only table surrounded by a cluster of adoring women. Pausing in the entry to watch a sultry-looking brunet lean suggestively over his shoulder, Dinah gritted her teeth. She should have known this would happen; even if Neil hadn't been the most handsome man in the room, he was certainly the most recognizable, and it had been too much to expect that they would be left alone. Now her opening salvo would just have to wait. She could hardly march up and throw down the gauntlet with his fan club hanging all over him. So irritated that she didn't even notice the admiring glances thrown her way by the men in the room, she tried to think of how she was going to handle this.

"Miss Blake!" The maître d' appeared magically at her elbow, a smile of genuine delight on his face. "So nice to see you again! Mr. Kerrigan is already, er, waiting for you."

Dinah looked at the table where Neil was obviously enjoying all the attention. "So I see," she said dryly.

"Allow me..."

Dinah was stopped several times herself as she followed the man through the restaurant, and as she signed someone's menu and acknowledged a profusion of compliments about *Personalities*, she couldn't prevent a private smile of satisfaction. Neil might be popular, but she wasn't exactly unknown in this city, and although she deliberately avoided looking at him again, she hoped he noticed the attention being paid to her. It was obvious that others liked her program even if he didn't, she thought smugly, and her confidence soared as she slowly made her way to the table.

Aware that he was watching her as she approached, Dinah covertly glanced at him and couldn't miss the admiration in his eyes. Determined to stay angry with him, she told herself she wasn't flattered, but of course she was, and as their eyes met, the strangest thing happened. She was distantly aware of the maître d' hovering by her elbow, and of Neil's fans sensing an intruder, but she couldn't look away from his face. There was something so compelling about his expression that for a moment she couldn't remember why she was angry with him.

This is absurd, she told herself, and as Neil rose to his feet, she tried to recapture her earlier feelings of outrage and indignation. The cluster around him turned to look at her, and in the delighted squeals from several of the women as they recognized her, that inexplicably powerful eye contact with him was broken. Relieved, Dinah turned almost eagerly to acknowledge the attention, and the excited babble of questions thrown at her gave her time to gather her composure.

Or so she thought. Finally seated, she looked at Neil again, and she knew she wasn't composed at all.

"That was quite a reception," Neil commented dryly as he sat down again, too.

"You attracted a little attention yourself, I see," she replied, and wondered why she felt so distracted. Even though he hadn't touched her, she felt his impact almost physically, and she knew her color was rising. Relieved when the wine steward appeared with champagne, she willed herself under control as Neil and the man went through the ceremony of taste and approval.

By the time the steward had poured two glasses and vanished, Dinah had remembered that this was the man who had tried to make a fool of her this morning. Angry again, she was about to demand an immediate explanation when she realized there was a much better approach. Recalling that Neil enjoyed lulling his opponent into a false sense of security before he attacked, she decided to treat him to his own tactics. Suddenly she began to enjoy herself, and when he raised his glass, she lifted hers, as well.

"What are we celebrating?" she asked sweetly.

"The show today. I thought it went rather well, didn't you?"

"Everyone certainly seemed to think so."

He frowned slightly. "You don't seem to agree."

"Oh, but of course I do," she said. "As you pointed out earlier, you were the perfect guest."

His frown deepened. "Well, that might have been a slight exaggeration."

"An exaggeration? You're too modest. You were witty, clever, amusing. What more could anyone ask for?"

He sat back, regarding her with a mixture of puzzlement and irritation. "So you're pleased with the show?" he asked, as though he couldn't believe it.

"Why shouldn't I be?" she responded, affecting surprise. "It's not everyone who's allowed to draw out the hidden side of Neil Kerrigan. In fact, I'd like to propose a toast: to the man who after this morning is certain to be nominated for the Mr. Congeniality award.''

Neil had begun to raise his own glass. He set it down abruptly and stared at her. "What is that supposed to mean?"

Dinah pretended astonishment. "Why, just what I said. I didn't realize until I ran through the tape of the show tonight that Roger was right. You had the audience eating out of your hand today—they absolutely loved you. And who could blame them? You were the most entertaining guest we've had in a long time.''

"Entertaining?" He almost choked on the word.

"And you said you detested entertainment programming!" Dinah admonished him, hiding her smile. "I should have known you were only joking with me that night."

Now his voice had an edge. "What makes you think I was joking?''

Dinah heard his irritation and almost laughed. "But of course you were," she said archly. "If you hadn't been, why else would you have said all those things today? You put on quite a performance, you know. I really think you missed your calling. You should have been an actor.''

Neil looked even more affronted at that, and Dinah was elated. It was so refreshing to see him off balance for a change that she couldn't resist another thrust. "I hope Andy saw the show," she said, her voice honeyed. "I know he would have been just as amused as everyone else to hear that he'd been shipped off to school so that he wouldn't be able to compete with you."

Neil actually flushed. "I didn't—"

"Or that you went through Yale on the skirt tails of some adoring girl," she went on blithely. "I thought that was particularly clever myself—almost as witty as your remark about the kind of car you drove."

"That was—"

"And it was so amusing when you said you select the issues for your show by pulling them out of a hat— or was it a coffee can? I was laughing so hard by then that I can't remember."

"That's enough, Dinah," he said harshly. "I didn't ask you to dinner so that you could—"

"Could what, Mr. Kerrigan?" she interrupted, her own voice suddenly frosty as she abandoned the game. "Make a fool of you, as you tried to do to me this morning?"

There was a sudden silence. Finally Neil said, "I don't know what you're talking about."

Dinah leaned forward. "You know very well what I'm talking about," she said fiercely. "Did you enjoy turning my show into a circus? Did you derive some perverse pleasure out of making me look ridiculous?"

"That wasn't what I intended at all!"

"Well, what did you intend, Mr. Kerrigan? I doubt it was winning Entertainer of the Year!"

"Are you finished now?" he demanded. "Because if you are, I'd like a chance to explain."

Her voice was steely. "Go ahead and try."

"All right. I admit I was superficial—"

"Ha!"

"But only because I thought that's what you wanted."

She looked at him contemptuously. "And just what made you think that?"

"Your defense of your show and others like it the night of the awards dinner," he snapped. "Or don't you remember waxing eloquent on that very subject?"

"I remember," she said evenly.

"All right, then, I just thought I'd oblige by being the kind of guest your audience expected. Was it my fault that they were only interested in what kind of car I drove or how long I've been divorced?"

She wasn't going to let him get away with that. "You deliberately encouraged those kinds of questions," she said flatly.

"That's not true. I gave them every opportunity—"

"By starting out with the fact that you chose a career in journalism because of some adolescent fantasy about a girl?"

She'd hit home with that one. He flushed again and looked away. "All right, I admit that was overdoing it."

"Overdoing it!"

She couldn't suppress her anger any longer. Did he really think she'd accept a specious excuse like that? How dare he patronize her! "No, Mr. Kerrigan," she said. "What you wanted was to prove your point about talk shows pandering to idle curiosity. Well, you did. And in the process you made a fool out of me. I hope you're satisfied!"

She started to rise. Anger and humiliation nearly choked her, and she knew if she stayed, she'd lose her temper completely.

"Wait!" Neil exclaimed, getting up himself.

"Why?" she demanded bitterly. "So that you can destroy what's left of my career?"

He took her arm, forcing her back momentarily into her chair. "If you felt like this, why did you defend your format in the first place?" he demanded.

Dinah almost hated him at that moment. She despised his smug, superior attitude; even more, she envied the power he wore so casually, as if it were his right.

Oh, it was all so simple for men like Neil; they had only to say a word and the thing was done. His reputation was such that he was secure in his position, absolutely assured of his power.

But it wasn't the same for her. She was supposed to be grateful for the crumbs offered her; she wasn't supposed to make waves. She knew, given the chance, she could really make something of her show. But she'd never get the chance, not while unimaginative men liked Roger Dayton held sway, and that was the most galling thing of all.

"Answer me, Dinah."

Dinah looked at Neil with loathing. "You wouldn't understand," she said coldly, and stood again. Grabbing her cape, she whirled around and swept out the door.

It was too much to expect that he wouldn't follow. He caught up to her as she reached the sidewalk and took her arm again, forcing her to stop and face him.

"What's the matter with you?" he demanded harshly. "You can't just leave like this!"

"I certainly can. Please let go of my arm."

"Not until you explain."

"There's no point!" she said, furious that he was preventing her from leaving. She could feel tears of humiliation gathering, and she willed herself not to cry; her pride had been battered enough today.

"I want to know why you said those things that night if you didn't believe them yourself," he said stubbornly.

"Because I had no other choice!" she cried, and finally pulled away from him.

The valet mercifully appeared with her car just then, a late-model sporty Mercedes in forest green. It was her one extravagance, and normally she was proud of it. Tonight she didn't care if he had brought her a battered old Jeep; all she wanted to do was escape.

Neil took her arm again. "I don't think you should drive, not until you calm down."

"I am calm!" she shrilled, and then realized that despite his averted eyes, the valet was all ears. With an effort she lowered her voice. "I am perfectly calm," she said between her teeth, "so if there are no more objections, I would just like to leave."

"Fine," Neil said brusquely. "In that case, I'm going to drive you home."

"You are not!"

His expression became even more grim. "Then I'll follow you to make sure you get there safely."

Dinah was furious. "This is absurd!"

"I agree. But if you won't listen to reason..."

Keenly aware that the valet was now agog, Dinah hissed, "You're the one who's being unreasonable."

"Why, because I want to talk about this?"

"We have nothing to talk about!"

"I think we do," Neil said, his voice hard. He glanced at the valet. "Put the car away. Miss Blake isn't leaving yet."

Dinah was outraged. Whirling around, she commanded, "Leave that car exactly where it is!"

The young man hesitated, half in, half out of the car. The look Neil gave him propelled him inside, and with a squeal of tires, he put the car in reverse and backed hastily away, leaving Dinah almost speechless with rage.

"Now," Neil said, "are we going to talk or not?"

"We are not! You have no right to—"

"Look," he interrupted harshly. "You objected to the way I handled the show today, and yet I behaved exactly the way all your other guests do. Maybe it's time you decided what it is you really want. You're capable of doing better, Dinah, and we both know it."

"You don't know anything about me!"

His glance held hers. "I know that you're too intelligent to be interviewing vapid celebrities who haven't an original thought in their heads. If you were really serious about your career, you'd—" A newspaper stand caught his eye just then, and he nearly dragged her over to it. An article on the front page headlined the problems of teenage alcoholism and drug abuse, and he pointed to it as he continued, "You'd be exploring topics like that on your show. Isn't that a little more important than talking to the latest guru about the benefits of mud baths?"

"Of course it is!" Dinah cried. "Don't you think I know that? Don't you think I haven't tried to—"

She stopped, shocked at what she'd revealed. She hadn't meant to tell him that. How could a man like Neil, so powerful himself, understand her own powerlessness and frustration? She couldn't admit that to him; she wouldn't! Whirling around, she met the valet just as he was returning from parking her car. He took one look at her face and instantly reversed direction, practically running back to where he'd left the Mercedes. Dinah followed close on his heels. Neil wasn't going to stop her this time.

But Neil didn't follow her. When Dinah roared out of the parking lot a few seconds later, he was still standing where she'd left him, staring after her with a bemused expression on his face. Dinah averted her eyes as she passed him. She didn't see him shake his head wonderingly, nor glimpse the beginnings of an admiring smile on his handsome face as he waited for the valet to bring his own car.

DINAH WAS STILL FURIOUS when she arrived home. Flinging her cape and sequined evening bag on the couch, she marched into the kitchen and poured a glass of wine. Taking the glass with her, she went back to the living room and threw herself on the couch.

"I'm not going to think about it," she muttered, and knew the instant she said it that of course she was. The evening had been such a complete disaster that she couldn't think of anything else.

Frowning, she slumped against the pillows and wondered what had happened to her tonight. She'd trained herself long ago to control her quick temper, but it seemed this evening that all she'd done was lose it. Despising herself, she realized that the only thing she'd accomplished was to make a bigger fool of herself than Neil had done of her this morning. The thought aggravated her and she took another swallow of wine.

What was it about him that made her lose control like that?

Restless, she flung herself off the couch and began to pace. A picture of her and Ted was propped on one of the bookcases and it caught her eye. It was one of

the few she had kept after the divorce because it reminded her of happier times: before Ted had changed
so much, before she'd gotten her big break . . . before
her marriage had started falling apart. Shaking her
head sadly, she wondered if she would have been so
thrilled at the chance of hosting her own show if she'd
known the strain it would put on her marriage.
Knowing what she knew now, would she have made a
different choice?

She had met Ted in college when he was prelaw and
she was majoring in communications. She hadn't
dreamed then that she would one day have her own
show—her ambition at that time had been to become
a producer. Secure in his choice of career, Ted had
encouraged her. He'd been supportive after they married, pleased when she'd gotten a job at the station as
a production assistant and then when she moved to set
design. They'd been married six years when she was
promoted to guest-relations director, and by then Ted
had been accepted in a major San Francisco law firm.
They'd both known it wouldn't be long before he was
invited to be a partner; he was already well on his way
to establishing a reputation as a fine criminal lawyer.

And then Allen Fogerty had visited the station. The
ratings on their morning talk show had slipped, and
there was talk of replacing Melanie Grainger, the star
of the show. As director of guest relations, Dinah had
met Allen at the airport; by the time he left that day,
he had spoken to Roger about hiring Dinah as Melanie's replacement. Dinah had been thrilled at this unexpected bonus and had immediately accepted the
position as hostess of *Personalities*.

Of course, it hadn't been called that at the time. A
directive had come down from the network detailing

a change in format, and she had been so ecstatic at the career opportunity that she hadn't questioned it—then.

Ted had been thrilled, too, Dinah remembered wistfully. She hadn't dreamed there would be a conflict. After all, he was established in his own career and they were involved in two completely different professions. But then the show started taking so much of her time and energy, and she began to be recognized in public. Ted hated being referred to as "the husband of," and he became angry at being ignored or pushed aside when Dinah was approached by fans. She was hurt but not surprised when he moved out; almost resigned when he filed for divorce. They were quarreling so much by then that it was nearly a relief.

Sighing, Dinah replaced the photograph on the shelf and wandered back to the couch. But the wine she'd left on the coffee table tasted sour to her now, and with a grimace of distaste, she took it back to the kitchen and poured it down the sink. Glancing at the phone, she debated about calling Leigh, but then shook her head. Leigh would be full of questions about Neil, and that was one subject she still didn't want to think about.

It was impossible not to think about it. She kept seeing Neil's face in her mind, she kept hearing echoes of the things he'd said tonight. But most of all she remembered that disturbing moment when she realized he was watching her. Something deep within her had responded to that look in his eyes—something she had thought she'd never experience again.

Dinah angrily snapped out the kitchen light and went into the bedroom to get ready for bed. She had an early taping tomorrow, and after all the confusion today, she hadn't had time to go over her notes.

In bed with the file propped on her knees, Dinah tried to concentrate on the pages. She realized eventually that she had read the same sentence over and over again without having the faintest idea what it said, and in disgust threw the papers aside.

"I am *not* attracted to him," she muttered. "He's the most egotistical, self-centered, pompous man I've ever met, and I'm glad I'll never see him again. If he were the last man on earth, I wouldn't give him a second look."

But if that were true, why was she so preoccupied?

Because this entire day had been a catastrophe from beginning to end, and he'd been the cause of it, that's why. Oh, it had been so easy for him to give advice!

"'It's time to decide what you really want,'" she mimicked savagely. "'You're capable of doing better. If you were really serious about your career, you wouldn't be interviewing vapid celebrities...'"

Didn't he think she knew that? Didn't he think she was serious about her career? The nerve of the man! What gave him the right to dispense recommendations from on high? He hadn't the faintest idea what he was talking about.

Didn't he?

Annoyed with the superior little voice inside her head that overrode all her rationalizations, Dinah reached up and switched off the light.

But that night the mattress had never seemed so uncomfortable or the pillow so hard, and by the time the alarm shrilled the next morning, she was so exhausted she had to drag herself out of bed. She arrived at the station in a black mood and went immediately to her office, annoyed to find Roger Dayton there waiting for her.

"Well, good morning," he said happily, rising from her chair behind the desk.

Dinah wasn't in the mood for Roger right now. She still had the file to go over and a list of calls to return, and the last thing she wanted was to listen to him rave about what a wonderful guest Neil Kerrigan had been.

"What is it, Roger?" she asked curtly. "I've got a lot of work to catch up on before we tape today."

"Oh, yes, of course. This will just take a minute of your time."

Dinah paused in the act of hanging up her coat. It wasn't like Roger to be so congenial, and she was suddenly suspicious. "All right," she said flatly. "What's going on?"

Instead of answering directly, Roger stepped aside and gestured toward the chair. "I think you'd better be sitting down when you hear this," he said with a grin.

Dinah ignored the chair. "Hear what?"

He actually rubbed his hands together in glee. "Do you know how many calls we got about the show yesterday?"

She wasn't in the mood to play games, either. "No," she said, and just barely prevented herself from adding that she didn't care.

"Take a guess."

Dinah didn't want to guess; she didn't even want to know. "Roger..." she said impatiently.

"All right, I'll tell you," he said, too pleased with himself to take offense at her tone. "Fifteen hundred."

She stared at him. "Are you serious?"

"Never more. Of course we'll have to wait for the ratings, but if Daniel Rawlings is satisified, I guess we can be, too."

He dropped the name so casually that it took her a few seconds to absorb it. "Daniel . . . Rawlings?" she stammered. "You've been in touch with him?"

Roger laughed, so delighted that he actually threw an arm around her shoulders. "He called this morning to congratulate you—us. He was pleased, Dinah, most pleased. So pleased in fact that he's decided to—" he paused dramatically "—to go ahead with the special."

Dinah had been trying to extricate herself from his clutching embrace. She froze now, completely forgetting in her shock that Roger still had his arm around her. "A special!" she choked.

Roger didn't hear the dismay in her voice. He was too thrilled at the idea himself. "Didn't I tell you this show would be important?" he asked, releasing her at last.

Dinah was still in shock. "Yes, but—"

Her tone finally penetrated Roger's euphoria. He looked at her sharply. "You don't sound very pleased."

"Pleased!" She had recovered now. "You can't possibly expect me to be *pleased* after what happened here yesterday!"

"What are you talking about? I just told you that show received the highest number of calls of any we've ever done! Do you have any idea what this is going to mean?"

She knew exactly what it meant. If this opportunity had been with anyone other than Neil Kerrigan, she would have been jumping with joy. But when she thought of the things he'd said last night and they way they'd parted, she cringed. She couldn't do a special or anything else with him—it was out of the question. She'd never be able to face him with any equanimity, and she refused to allow him the chance to humiliate her again.

"I can't do it, Roger," she said. "I can't."

"What do you mean you can't? Of course you can—you will!"

"No. No, I won't. I mean it, Roger. I'm not going to do it. I'll... I'll quit first!"

"Quit!" Roger was shouting now, his face crimson. "Are you out of your mind?"

She had to be, she thought, to throw away a golden opportunity like this. It didn't make any sense; she wasn't making any sense. But she couldn't help it. The idea of working with Neil filled her with such dread that she shook her head helplessly. "I'm sorry, Roger...."

"Sorry!" His face had purpled now, veins leaping out on his temples. "You listen to me, Dinah! When Daniel Rawlings calls and says he wants you to do a special with Neil Kerrigan, you're damn well going to do it! You don't have any choice—it's already been scheduled!"

"Well, unschedule it then!" Dinah cried.

"*You* unschedule it!" Roger shouted, and reached for the door. Jerking it open so violently that it almost flew out of his hand, he stood on the threshold, actually panting with outrage. "Go ahead, Dinah. Call Mr. Rawlings. You tell him you won't do it, if you dare! But I warn you, if you do, you'll never work in television again. If he won't see to it, I certainly will!"

The door slammed behind him with such force that one of the pictures fell off the wall. Dinah didn't notice. Flinging herself into the chair, she closed her eyes.

She had to do it. Roger was right: this was the chance of a lifetime, and she couldn't throw it away. She'd be a fool if she did.

Abruptly she lifted her head, the light of battle once more in her green eyes.

This was her chance to demonstrate to Neil that she was just as serious about her career as he was about his. He'd challenged her integrity and her ability last night, sure that she wasn't capable of rising to the occasion. Well, she was about to prove him wrong. She'd seize this opportunity and make the best of it, and if he thought she was going to take second place to him, he was sadly mistaken. She'd agree to the special, all right, but on her own terms. He'd accept her as an equal, or not at all.

CHAPTER FIVE

DINAH ARRIVED IN LOS ANGELES two days later, piqued that the production meeting had been scheduled on Neil's home ground instead of hers. She knew it was a logical choice—the network's affiliate offices were here, and Neil did have more seniority than she—but it was still galling to have to come to him when she would have preferred it the other way around. Only slightly mollified when she was met by a chauffeured limousine, she settled into the plush interior vowing that no matter what happened, today she would not lose her temper. She was determined to show Neil that she was every inch the professional he claimed to be.

The only problem was that she didn't feel like a professional. As the car whisked her along the freeways, she looked out the tinted windows and tried to tell herself she wasn't nervous. She hadn't spoken to Neil since the scene at the restaurant, and she didn't know what his reaction would be now that the project was about to become a reality instead of a joke.

She wasn't sure how she felt about it herself. It could be a tremendous opportunity for her, something that would enhance her career and lead to better things—or it could be an unmitigated disaster, if Neil decided to be arrogant and abrasive. He could pull rank on her, refusing to work with her at all unless she deferred completely to him, and in a way, she couldn't blame him if he did just that. She might feel resentful if she was in his place, compelled to share the limelight with a relative newcomer who had so much less experience.

Maybe that was why she felt so intimidated. Neil's reputation as a tough, incisive journalist was nearly unsurpassed in the industry, and while she knew her own capabilities, it was obvious that he regarded her as a lightweight. Sighing heavily, she thought she couldn't blame him for that, either. How was he to know she'd been agitating for months with Roger for the chance to prove she was capable of doing more? She'd been too proud to tell him the other night because for some reason he'd become a symbol to her of success and power and authority—all the things she wanted for herself and hadn't yet attained.

But was that what she really wanted? Sometimes this quest for power seemed so cold and calculating to her. She'd sacrificed a lot to get where she was today; would she sacrifice even more to rise further? She knew she had a streak of ambition; she just hadn't realized how wide it was until she'd had to choose between Ted and her career. She could have saved her marriage if she'd resigned from the show.

But at what cost to her, Dinah wondered as the limousine purred along the Los Angeles freeway system. As Ted had proved, some men couldn't handle a woman's success even if they were successful themselves. Women were expected to respect that, even to defer to it, as though it was a virtue instead of a fault. But Dinah resented the fact that Ted had demanded she deny her abilities and aspirations. Frowning, she wondered if Neil felt the same way, and suspected he did. Was that why his own marriage had failed?

Dinah shook her head impatiently. Instead of speculating about Neil, she should be preparing herself for this production meeting. She had to marshal her arguments, steel herself for the battle that would undoubtedly take place when she stated her demands. She had planned exactly what she was going to say and how she would conduct herself. She had even dressed carefully for the occasion in an understated suit of raw silk that Leigh had assured her made her look confident and assured. Now she had to act as though she was.

But she still wasn't ready when she arrived at the imposing steel-and-glass building that housed the network's offices. Gazing up at the glittering expanse of mirrored windows as she got out of the car, she nearly asked the driver to take her straight back to the airport. The impulse passed and she squared her shoulders. This was her opportunity, and she was going to make the most of it.

The five men seated around the vast conference table were laughing uproariously as a receptionist ushered Dinah inside. The laughter was choked off the instant she appeared, and as they all stood, a few faces reddened.

Dinah halted on the threshold, instantly suspicious that the joke had been at her expense. Then she told herself firmly that she was being ridiculous. She had absolutely no reason to think they'd been laughing at her, and even if they had been, she was certainly capable of rising above such childish behavior. She lifted her head and summoned a professional smile, fixing her gaze on one of the two men in the room she knew. Approaching him, she held out her hand. "How nice to see you again, Allen."

Allen Fogerty was one of Daniel Rawlings's legion of vice-presidents. He'd been the one who recommended her for *Personalities*, and they had worked together on implementing the show's new format. Dinah had quickly realized after spending that time with him that he was attracted to her, but although she was fond of him, she just couldn't return his interest. From the expression on his face now, he obviously was still interested in her, and she hated herself for feeling relieved. But she knew she was going to need all the help she could get, and his admiring glance immediately restored her flagging confidence.

Allen greeted her with genuine pleasure, holding her hand a moment longer than necessary before he turned to introduce her to the others: the station manager, Brad Gentry, and Chuck Seaborn and Larry Holt, who had been assigned to help tape the program.

Dinah acknowledged the introductions graciously, inwardly bracing herself as she looked at last toward the other man in the room. When she finally faced Neil, her expression was suddenly as guarded as her tone.

"Mr. Kerrigan," she murmured, and didn't offer her hand to him as she had to the others.

Neil's expression was just as wary as he responded. "Miss Blake...."

"Oh, let's not stand on formality," Allen exclaimed with forced heartiness. He had sensed the sudden tension between his two principals and was clearly anxious to defuse it. "Since we're all going to be working so closely, we might as well be on a first-name basis, don't you think?"

He glanced nervously from one to the other, and at the curt nods of assent they gave him, went on hastily. "Good. Now why don't we get down to business? Dinah, would you like some coffee first?"

Dinah would have liked something stronger than that. She'd believed she had prepared herself for seeing Neil again, but it had taken only a brief glimpse for her to realize how wrong she'd been. He dominated the room without saying a word, and she was annoyed to find her eyes drawn to him again and again as a secretary entered with coffee for all. As she accepted her cup with a murmured thanks, she noticed that the woman's glance lingered on Neil, too, and that annoyed her even more.

Neil seemed oblivious of the attention. He was conversing in low tones with the station manager as everyone settled around the table, and Dinah couldn't help notice that even though Allen seated himself at the head, he waited for Neil to finish his conversation before he began himself. Irritated that Neil had even unconsciously assumed command of the meeting, she sat as far away from him as possible and waited impatiently for him to realize they were all delayed because of him. He looked up finally, and with a casual wave of his hand that set Dinah's teeth on edge, indicated that the meeting could begin.

Dinah had to force herself to pay attention to the budget and schedule details Allen presented. Keenly aware of Neil glancing at her from time to time, she refused to look in his direction, pretending instead an intense interest in the vice-president's speech. It wasn't until Allen concluded that she realized she hadn't heard a word.

"So that's it for production so far," Allen finished. "Are there any questions before we get into the subject of a topic?"

"I have one," Dinah said.

Allen turned to her with an expectant smile. "Yes, Dinah?"

She took a deep breath, reminding herself that she had vowed to make a stand and that this was her chance. She had to let everyone know at the outset that she had no intention of taking a back seat to Neil.

"I'd like to know if Mr. Kerrigan and I are to have equal responsibility in this project," she said, and braced herself.

"Well, of course," Allen replied, his smile fading slightly as he began to sense trouble ahead. "I thought that was understood."

"I wanted to make certain it was," Dinah said evenly. "I'd prefer to clear up any misunderstandings now."

Allen glanced uncertainly down the table. "Neil?"

"That's the way I understood it," Neil said solemnly, but with a glint in his eye.

Visibly relieved that one hurdle had been overcome, Allen pressed on. "Let's move on to the discussion of the topic, then. Are there any suggestions?"

Dinah fought to disguise her surprise. She wasn't prepared for this. She'd assumed that several topics would already have been selected, and that they'd choose one. With Allen looking at her expectantly, she cast about in her mind for a suitable subject and was dismayed that she couldn't think of a thing. The suspicion that Neil would be amused at every idea she produced seemed to paralyze her, and she glanced involuntarily down the table at him, willing him to speak first so that she'd have some idea what to say in response.

Allen saw the direction of her glance and looked down the table, too. "Neil?"

Neil sat back. "Ladies first," he said casually.

As though they were spectators at a tennis match, four pairs of eyes swung back to her. Feeling as though she'd suddenly been spotlighted against a wall, Dinah knew she had to say something. Her mind a complete blank, she tried to think. Then she saw the gleam in Neil's eyes again and knew he'd been mocking her, and the thought annoyed her so much that she said, "As a matter of fact, I do have an idea or two."

Neil's lips quirked. "I was sure you would."

Suddenly Dinah did have an idea. She didn't know why she hadn't thought of it before. Smiling to herself in anticipation of Neil's reaction, she turned back to Allen, who was surreptitiously wiping his forehead with a handkerchief.

"I'm afraid I can't take credit for this," she said silkily, "but what about a program on the rising incidence of teenage alcohol and drug abuse?"

Allen's face cleared as he considered the idea. "That definitely has possibilities," he said enthusiastically. "What do you think, Neil?"

Dinah looked down the table again and almost grinned when she saw Neil's face. He knew why she had mentioned this; after all, he had challenged her about it just the other night. Hoping she had goaded him into a rash response, she waited expectantly.

"I'm not sure—" he began.

"But you were the other night," she said at once. "In fact, I believe you suggested a program on this very subject yourself."

He looked at her speculatively. "Yes, but that was in a different context."

"Oh, I see," she said, pretending disappointment. "Then you don't feel this issue merits your attention."

He frowned. "I didn't say that."

"Good. Then it's all settled?"

When Neil didn't answer, Allen asked hesitantly, "Neil?"

Dinah waited, not caring whether an explosion was imminent or not. She'd caught Neil off guard for the moment, but he was known for his quick recoveries, and she was prepared for anything from mild sarcasm to genuine anger. Nonchalantly she took a sip of coffee just as he said, "We can go with that."

Dinah was so surprised she nearly choked. She glanced quickly at Neil, sure that this was just another ploy, but he returned her look so blandly she didn't know what to think. It was obvious that for some nefarious reason of his own he had decided to concede her the point this time, but she knew it wouldn't happen so easily again. Oddly, she felt exhilarated, and dropped her eyes before Neil could glimpse her excitement.

"Well, I'm glad that's decided," Allen said, relieved, and then added a caution. "Provided, of course, that Mr. Rawlings approves."

"Oh, I think he'll approve," Neil said with that casual air of self-assurance that Dinah both envied and admired. Turning to her again, he asked politely, "Have you decided where we're going to tape this little project, too?"

Despite herself, Dinah flushed. It was clear that he was mocking her again, but this time she was a little more prepared. "As a matter of fact, I have," she answered coolly. "I think the program would have more impact if we taped in a small town instead of a large city. From the research I've done—" she threw him a significant glance; he didn't have to know that at the moment, her research consisted of reading that article in the paper "—the problem exists even in semi-rural communities."

"I take it you have one in mind," Neil said with a smile.

"Yes," Dinah answered, racking her brain for the names of towns she knew. Selecting one from thin air, she said, "It's called Willowset, and it's a few miles north of San Francisco...."

The meeting concluded some time later after hammering out the various details of when they would meet and where—subject to the head of programming's approval, of course. When they finally stood, Allen took the opportunity to ask Dinah to lunch.

"Lunch?" She looked at her watch, surprised to see that it was almost two. She'd been so intent that the hours had flown. "I'm not sure I have time. I have to catch a return flight at four."

"Oh, we'll make that easily," Allen replied. And then to her dismay, he called out, "Want to join us for lunch, Neil?"

Neil turned at the question, and Dinah held her breath. Disconcerted at the thought of spending even more time with him after the strain of the morning, she willed him to refuse, and was relieved when he finally shook his head. "Sorry, but I've got an interview this afternoon. How about a rain check?"

Allen didn't wait for him to change his mind. Grasping Dinah's arm, he hustled her out of the room and out to his car, and they were on their way almost before she could say goodbye.

The restaurant Allen chose was quiet and out of the way, near enough to the airport so they wouldn't have to hurry. He ordered champagne when they were seated and raised his glass.

"To friends," he said, his voice a little wistful, as though he wished they were something more.

Thrusting away memories of the last time she'd been offered champagne, Dinah smiled. "To friends," she acknowledged, and was glad they were. After taking a sip, she set her glass down. "I want to thank you for what you did today, Allen."

He looked surprised. "I didn't do anything."

"Yes, you did. I admit I was a little nervous going into that meeting—"

"You sure didn't look it."

"Thanks, but I was. I . . . I really didn't know what to expect. I mean, Neil has such a reputation—"

"He can be a little difficult at times," Allen agreed with an indulgent smile. "But he's not so bad when you get to know him."

"Isn't he?" she asked wryly. "You could have fooled me."

"He was on his best behavior today, wasn't he?"

"Yes, and that's what worries me," she admitted. "I'm not sure I can trust him."

Allen put a hand over hers. "If Neil says he's going to do something, he will."

"You sound like you've known him for a long time."

"I have. We were in the service together."

"Vietnam?"

"Yes."

Dinah saw the same shadow flicker in his eyes that she had seen so briefly in Neil's that day she'd mentioned his service record, and she was contrite. "I'm sorry. I shouldn't have asked."

"No, that's okay. It was a long time ago, and a lot of things have happened since then. I have to tell you, though, I admire the hell out of the guy. Not many men would have gone back as a correspondent after they'd been wounded twice in combat."

"No," Dinah agreed, feeling even more intimidated by Neil than she had before. She sighed. "It makes me wonder why he ever agreed to doing this special with me."

"Why wouldn't he?" Allen asked, surprised.

"Oh, come on, Allen. A man like that, a war hero, host now of one of the most popular programs on television? The only thing I can think of is that Daniel Rawlings talked him into it."

Allen smiled. "Maybe it was the other way around."

"Oh sure," she said disbelievingly. "I can just picture Neil Kerrigan marching into Daniel Rawlings's office and insisting on a time slot with me, especially when he detests my kind of show. He made that perfectly clear on one of his own programs."

"Yes, but that didn't have anything to do with you personally."

"It might as well have," Dinah said sourly.

"He just thinks you're capable of doing better, that's all."

Remembering that Neil had said the same thing, she looked at him sharply. "He told you that?"

Allen flushed. "Well . . . not in so many words."

She straightened. "Just exactly what did he say, then?"

Allen hesitated. When she continued to stare at him uncompromisingly, he sighed. "He, uh, said it would be a challenge."

"A challenge! For whom—him or me?"

"Why don't we order lunch?" Allen suggested hastily, grabbing the menus and shoving one into her hand.

"Allen," she said warningly.

Reluctantly he put his menu down. "Listen, I didn't mean to say that."

"So far you haven't said much of anything, but you know something I don't, and before we leave here, you're going to tell me."

He groaned. "Neil will kill me if I do."

"And I will if you don't," she said calmly. "Come on, Allen—what is it you're not telling me?"

"You're making a big deal out of this, Dinah—"

"It is a big deal! My reputation—not to mention my entire career—is at stake here, and if Neil plans to make me look like a fool, I want to know about it."

He looked shocked. "I never said that! Where in the world did you get that idea, Dinah? Neil would never do something like that—especially to you. He admires you!"

"He certainly has an interesting way of showing it!"

"But he does," Allen insisted. "Why else would he want to do this project with you? Do you know how many ideas he's turned down, how many people have approached him to do something just like this? He's refused every one... until you. Doesn't that tell you something?"

Dinah wasn't sure whether it did or not. She thought about it all the way back to San Francisco, and by the time she got home, she was even more uncertain about Neil's motives than she had been before.

Recalling how amiably Neil had accepted her suggestions, Dinah became more uneasy. He must be planning something, she thought, giving her just enough rope to tangle herself up in. Why else would he have been so agreeable?

She'd been relieved that the meeting had gone well, so grateful to have negotiated all the pitfalls successfully that she hadn't realized until she thought about it how little Neil had contributed. Frowning, she remembered the rumors she'd heard about how he conducted his own production meetings. It was said that he ruled with an iron hand, overriding any objections by the sheer force of his personality and authority. But he hadn't displayed any of that temperament today; he'd sat back and allowed her to run the whole show. It wasn't like him, and that unnerved her.

Dinah wished suddenly that she hadn't stated her own position so emphatically. It seemed presumptuous of her now, and she couldn't believe she'd acted so blithely sure of herself, so arrogant. She wouldn't have if he hadn't made her so angry that night at the restaurant, and recalling her behavior at the meeting today, her face reddened.

And I called him *pompous.* She winced. *What must he think of* me *now?*

NEIL WAS STILL at his office late that night when the phone rang. Glancing up from the background material on the senator scheduled for his next program, he frowned at the interruption and looked at his watch. Surprised that it was after eleven, he reached reluctantly for the receiver. The call was on his private line, and there were only a few people who knew the number and would call this late. One of them was his exwife, Elise.

"Well, I should have known I'd find you at the inner sanctum," Elise said. "I've been trying the apartment all night."

Neil sat back in the chair and rubbed his eyes. He wasn't in the mood for Elise right now; he had too much on his mind. Thrusting away the image of deep green eyes and fiery auburn hair that flashed into his thoughts just then, he said, "What is it, Elise? I've got work to do."

She laughed. Once he had loved the sound of her laugh because it was so musical. But it hadn't sounded that way for a long time. In the past few years it had become as brittle as Elise had herself. "You're always working, darling. Wasn't that the problem?"

Was it, Neil wondered. He had to admit it had been one of them. Elise had been right when she'd bitterly claimed he was obsessed with his work, but she had never understood that he didn't give a damn about his career. It was the work itself that was important to him, and he didn't care about the accolades or the honors or the status. What mattered to him was the power they gave him to do the kind of reporting he had to do. His work had always been uppermost in his mind; the fact that his "career" had developed along with it was just a dubious bonus.

"...so naturally I'm having all the bills sent to you. I just thought I'd warn you."

Aroused from his introspection more from the note of satisfaction in her voice than from what she'd said, Neil realized he hadn't been listening.

"Warn me about what?"

Elise gave an elaborate sigh. "Really, Neil, we don't talk that often. Can't you at least do me the courtesy of listening when we do?"

"I'm sorry. My mind was on something else."

"Your mind is always on something else," she said, her voice sharpening with that cutting edge he detested. Abruptly, he recalled another voice, a low contralto that was pleasing to the ears even when it was raised in temper. He thrust that away as Elise went on, "I just told you I'm having the kitchen redone."

"Again?"

"There's no need to be sarcastic. I know you don't think I even know how to cook."

"I never said that."

"Forgive me," she said mockingly. "I must have gotten that impression from all the meals you missed while we were married."

Neil took a grip on his temper. "Is that all you called to tell me?"

"As a matter of fact, it isn't," she said curtly. "Andy's birthday is coming up—"

"I'm aware of that."

"And I would appreciate it if you could manage somehow to fit him into your schedule. I know how busy you are," she continued spitefully, "so I'm calling to make an appointment. That seems to be the only way he ever gets to see his father."

"And who's fault is that?" he asked sharply, inevitably losing his patience as he always did whenever they talked about Andy.

When he and Elise had finally decided divorce was the only answer, Neil had asked for, then demanded, joint custody. But their marital situation had become so destructive by then that Elise had vowed to deny him any privileges, even visitation rights. Loving his son, then only twelve, Neil would have battled it all the way to the Supreme Court if he'd had to, but when he saw the effect their quarreling was having on the boy, he abruptly backed off. Andy had been too young to choose between his parents, and because Neil hadn't wanted his son to grow up feeling guilty for something that wasn't his fault, he'd finally worked out a compromise with Elise.

That had been some compromise, he thought, his mouth tight. Besides the huge annual settlement he'd agreed to give her, he'd also let her have the house, the cars, the savings accounts and everything else, even his beloved boat—all so he could have Andy one weekend a month.

It hadn't been the best solution, but it was the only one he could manage. His work took him away from home so much of the time that in his calmer moments, he had to admit that it really was best for Andy to stay with his mother. But he still missed having his son around, and sometimes he looked at Andy and wondered if he really knew him at all. This past year or so, Andy seemed to have become a stranger, and Neil tried to console himself by believing it was just some stage he was going through. Sixteen was a troubled time in adolescence; Neil could still remember the battles he'd had at that age with his own father. But he wished he saw more of Andy; he wanted to be more than a part-time father.

"...so for his birthday, I decided to buy him a car."

Neil bolted upright in disbelief. "You what?"

Piqued at his tone, Elise immediately became defensive. "I know we agreed that he should earn the money himself, but honestly, Neil, do you think that's fair?"

"I certainly do," he snapped back. "He'll appreciate it more, just as I did."

"Oh, please," she said wearily. "I really don't want to hear all those stories about how hard you had to work when you were growing up. It's not Andy's fault that your father couldn't afford to indulge you—"

"Whether he could afford it or not is beside the point!"

"That's exactly the point," Elise shot back angrily. "Just because you didn't have these things is no reason to deny your son a few privileges. It's the least you can do."

Deciding to ignore that thrust, Neil said warningly, "I don't want you buying him a car."

"I already did," Elise stated, and then added tauntingly, "I charged that to you, too. So don't be surprised when you get a bill for a Corvette."

Neil barely prevented himself from slamming down the phone when Elsie hung up. There was no way in the world he'd pay for that car, he thought irately. It wasn't the money, it was the principle of the thing. He was not going to have his son out joyriding somewhere, risking his neck just to prove how fast his car could go. He'd match whatever Andy earned himself if he wanted a car, but that was as far as he'd go.

Shaking his head angrily, Neil tried to return to work. But for once his formidable powers of concentration failed him, and finally he threw the folder on the desk and decided to go home. He was just reaching out to switch off the lamp when the minutes of that day's production meeting caught his eye. He paused, his mind suddenly flooded with recollections of

Dinah. He could almost smell the tantalizing scent of her perfume. It had been a light fragrance, but a lingering one; wisps of it had remained in the room long after she had gone.

Smiling to himself, he sat back in the chair again as he remembered the way she had acted during the meeting. She'd sailed in as though she owned the place, and in a way, it seemed she had. It wasn't only that she was a beautiful woman, which she certainly was, it was that she had such...presence. There hadn't been a man in that room able to keep his eyes off her, including him.

Chuckling aloud, he recalled how deftly she had boxed him in with that suggestion about a program on teenage drug and alcohol abuse. She knew he could hardly refuse when he'd brought up the idea himself, but he hadn't been able to resist giving her a hard time about it, just to see how she would handle it.

She'd handled it very well, he thought ruefully. For a minute there, he was sure she'd cut him down on the spot. Shaking his head, he wondered which intrigued him more: her quick temper or her even quicker tongue. It was almost worth provoking her into an argument just to see those eyes of hers flash; any exchange with her was definitely a challenge.

Just as the lady was herself, he admitted. He'd never met a woman like Dinah Blake. In addition to her sharp intelligence, she possessed the enviable ability to make assertiveness a feminine trait. He was fascinated by that, almost as much as he was by Dinah herself.

Smiling at the thought, Neil switched off the desk lamp at last and went home.

CHAPTER SIX

THE DAY BEFORE Dinah was scheduled to meet Neil and the crew to begin taping the special, she was in her office going over her own schedule. It was nearly evening and as she read over the list her secretary had prepared, she paused at the end of the second page to rub her eyes.

She'd been busy during the past four days since returning from Los Angeles. Because she was going to be away for at least a week working on the new project, she'd had to tape several segments every day to be aired during the time she was gone. It had been a strain: every one of the guests she'd interviewed had authored a book, and she had always made it a rule to read what a guest had written before the show. But that meant that she'd had to stay up until three or four every night this week to go over all the material.

So when she heard the knock on her office door, she looked up wearily. She'd just finished the second taping for the day, and she'd asked not to be disturbed for a few minutes so she could catch her breath. Unable to prevent a note of irritation in her voice, she called a curt permission to enter and immediately went back to her reading.

Several seconds later, she realized that no one had come in. Annoyed, she looked up again and jumped. Her office door was ajar, and waving gently in the air was a white handkerchief attached to a gold pen. The hand holding it was nowhere in sight, but she knew it had to be her secretary, so she smiled and said, "All right, Jackie. You can come in. I won't bite."

"Is that a promise?"

Dinah was too startled to answer. For a second or two, she thought she had imagined that deep voice, but when Neil poked his head around the door and grinned at her, she was so nonplussed that she just stared at him.

"Are you sure it's safe?" he asked, still waving that ridiculous little white flag. "Because if it's not, I can go away."

"No, please. . . ." Gesturing faintly, she tried to recover from her surprise as he opened the door fully and walked in. "What are you doing here?"

Still grinning mischievously, he came up to the desk and placed the flag in front of her before he took the chair opposite. "I came to call a truce."

"A truce?"

"Since we're going to be working together for the next week or so, I thought it would be a good idea to lay down our weapons in advance."

Dinah saw the glint of humor in his deep blue eyes and couldn't prevent a smile in return. "I see your point."

"Somehow I doubt that," he replied with another smile, "but I'll take it at face value for the moment. Are you free for dinner?"

Until a few minutes ago, Dinah had planned to go straight home from work, soak in a long, hot bath and fall into bed. She'd been too weary even to make a few notes to her secretary. It was amazing how quickly her energy returned at Neil's invitation, but she didn't want to appear too eager, so she murmured, "Didn't we try that once?"

Neil's mouth quirked again. "I'd hoped that this time we might make it through the first course, at least."

Suddenly exhilarated at the thought of spending an evening with him when he was in a mood like this, Dinah laughed and rose to get her coat.

Neil's glance followed her as she did, and she was suddenly glad that she was still wearing the green wool jersey she'd worn for the last taping instead of changing into something more casual. Unable to prevent the feminine thought that the sheath style flattered her figure, she turned to him as she held out the matching jacket.

"Maybe if we both try very hard, we might even make it to dessert," she said teasingly. "Do you have any particular place in mind?"

Neil took the jacket from her. "I thought I'd leave that up to you. This is your town, not mine."

Wondering if it was her imagination that his hands lingered a little longer than necessary on her shoulders as he helped her with the jacket, Dinah knew she hadn't imagined the thrill she felt when he touched her, and as they left the station, she was relieved they had agreed to take both cars. She'd never seen this side of Neil, but she was still wary, and as she drove to Fisherman's Wharf with Neil following behind, she reminded herself firmly to keep her distance. She couldn't allow this inexplicable attraction she felt to color her perceptions of the man; he was no less a power tonight than he had been a few days ago, and she still had to spend the next week or so working with him.

They went to The Mandarin in Ghirardelli Square, a restaurant Dinah liked not only for the excellent Peking-style food, but because it afforded a spectacular view of the bay. They were blessed that evening with a clear night, and Dinah turned from the view as Neil seated her and said, "Let's not order champagne tonight, shall we?"

"It never crossed my mind," he agreed with a twinkle in his eye. "This time you choose."

After they had autographed a napkin for an awe-struck waitress and ordered their dinner, Neil sat back and regarded Dinah thoughtfully. "I think I like this business of a truce."

"I think I do, too," she admitted, trying not to feel self-conscious because he was staring at her. "Was that really why you came tonight?"

"That, and the fact that I thought it would be wise to work out a few details before we get started tomorrow."

She immediately tensed. Neil saw the guarded look leap into her eyes and shook his head. "Truce, remember? I don't have any ulterior motives, Dinah."

Something about the way he said her name made her feel flushed. That, too, had almost been a caress, and she glanced away, telling herself she had to control her imagination. Why did she feel so disoriented with this man?

"What details?" she asked, hoping that if she kept her mind strictly on business, she could forget how attractive he was.

Neil seemed to be having a difficult time keeping his mind on business details, too. He looked blank at her question, and then shook his head again slightly, as if trying to recall what he had intended to say.

"Well...it's up to us to decide on our approach, and I'd like to hear your ideas," he said finally.

Dinah couldn't think of one at the moment; she was suddenly preoccupied with the way his black hair glinted in the subdued light. With an effort, she jerked her attention back to what he had said.

"My ideas?" she repeated, trying to give herself time to think. She'd asked her secretary to research some statistics on drug and alcohol abuse by teens when she'd returned to San Francisco, and she remembered reading them sometime during the past four days. Racking her brain, she tried to recall what she had read, but now she was distracted by the way his long fingers were resting on the table. Thinking fleetingly that he had graceful hands for a man, she forced herself to concentrate.

"Well, there are several possibilities," she said, willing her scattered thoughts into some order. Recalling at last some of the truly alarming details she had learned, she continued more strongly, "I think that the program would have more impact if we could get the kids to talk—honestly, I mean—about what they've experienced and how it's changed their lives. I know your forte is hard, factual reporting, but these children—and they are children, in some cases—aren't statistics. Neither are their families, and I—"

She stopped suddenly, embarrassed. Even to her ears her speech sounded flowery and sentimental, and she was sure he'd think so, too. "I think it's time to hear what you have in mind," she said faintly.

"Why? You're doing fine," he said, and looked amused at her skeptical expression. "Don't look so surprised. I'm not quite the ogre you think I am."

She was embarrassed again. "I'm sorry. It's just that I know this isn't the way you would approach it."

"No, but it's the way you would, and that's what I wanted to hear. That's why we're doing the program together, isn't it?"

She wanted to ask why they *were* doing it together, but she decided not to press her luck. She'd passed one trial successfully; she didn't want to attempt another.

The waitress came just then and after they'd been served, Neil said, "You've obviously devoted a great deal of thought to this project. But then, you seem to be a woman who's always prepared."

Dinah winced inwardly at that, thinking how ill-prepared she'd really been that day in Los Angeles. She'd just barely escaped making a fool of herself, and she had vowed that wouldn't happen again. She had debated about her approach to the special every spare minute since returning to San Francisco, determined to be ready with a well-thought-out presentation in case Neil asked her ideas. She hadn't expected him to; she was keenly aware that he was accustomed to making all the decisions. But after taking such a firm stand the other day, she had to be ready to prove that she was capable of holding up her end. It was more than a matter of pride. Dinah hadn't realized until after that meeting just how much she valued his opinion of her. She wanted him to accept her as a professional equal, whether they agreed or not.

Pleased now that she seemed to have achieved that goal, Dinah said, "I try to be. My father is a test pilot, and he always said one should be prepared for emergency landings whether they ever occur or not."

"Sounds like a smart man."

"He is," Dinah said fondly. "My mother died when I was twelve, and he's had to be both parents to me. I think he succeeded."

"I do, too," Neil agreed somberly. "It must have been difficult."

"Well, fortunately for me, he was progressive in his ideas about raising children. He never told me there were things I couldn't do just because I was a girl, and he encouraged me to be independent."

"He was obviously successful in that, too," Neil said dryly.

Dinah smiled. "I think it was his profession that made him think that way. Test piloting can be dangerous at times, and he wanted me to be able to take care of myself in case something . . . happened."

"Being a father myself, I can understand that."

"How is Andy?" she asked, glad of the opportunity to change the subject. She felt like she'd been talking about herself all night, and she grinned mischievously. "Has he come up with any more brilliant ideas lately?"

Neil sighed. "Well, it seems he's talked his mother into buying him a car for his sixteenth birthday."

"You don't sound too pleased."

"I'm not. She's promised him a Corvette, and I think that's too much car for a boy his age."

"He seems responsible," she suggested tentatively.

"So was I when I was sixteen, but that doesn't mean I was capable of owning a car like that."

"Well, I'm not really the one to judge," she said lightly, wishing she hadn't asked. "My first car was a beat-up old Volkswagen."

Neil made an effort to respond in the same vein. "Mine was a '41 Chevy," he said with a slight smile.

"I used to pray that it would just make it into town on Saturday nights."

"Did you live in the country?" she asked, intrigued.

He nodded. "Until a few years ago when he retired, my dad was a wheat farmer in Montana. They still own the farm, but they've moved to Arizona to avoid those hard winters."

"I always envied people who lived on a farm," Dinah said wistfully. "When I was younger, I would have given anything for a horse."

Neil grinned. "The only horses we had were the ones under the hood of a tractor."

Dinah smiled with him, thinking that she never would have guessed he'd spent his youth driving tractors and tinkering with an old Chevy. He seemed full of surprises, and she was pleased they had gone to dinner tonight. Her suspicions about him seemed unfounded now; she couldn't have asked for a more congenial dinner companion, and she was suddenly looking forward to working with him after all.

And then he said, "I'm curious about something, Dinah."

"What?"

"Are you really sympathetic with this problem of drug and alcohol abuse, or is that just the line you've decided to take?"

She was surprised at the question. "I'm not sure I understand what you mean."

"Well, you make it sound like drug abuse is an involuntary thing, something that should be excused because these kids don't know what they're doing."

Dinah frowned. "I don't think they do."

"I do."

She shook her head, unwilling to believe him. "You don't mean that."

"Yes, I do. You can't tell me that a kid who takes a handful of pills without even knowing what they are doesn't know what he's doing. He's trying to get high, and that's all there is to it."

She tensed, some of the warmth she'd been feeling toward him suddenly evaporating. "Don't you think your attitude is a little harsh?"

"No. I'm tired of all this permissive baloney. I think we are all responsible for our actions and should be held accountable for them."

"You're talking about adults," she protested. "I'm talking about children."

"Who will never become adults until they learn to accept the consequences for their behavior."

Abruptly feeling that she had entered a minefield without warning, Dinah tried to remain calm. She couldn't believe that the conversation had taken such a downward turn or that Neil had changed in the blink of an eye from a relaxed dinner companion to this hard-eyed inquisitor.

"Do you actually believe that a twelve- or thirteen- or even fifteen-year-old is capable of understanding the consequences of his actions?" she asked.

"If he's taught to, he will."

"Yes, but—"

"And if I could get through adolescence without resorting to using drugs or alcohol, so can these kids."

"But things were different then!"

"How?" he asked flatly.

Dinah felt that she was floundering. "Well, drugs weren't so prevalent then," she said, knowing it sounded lame.

"Alcohol was."

"Yes it was," she flared suddenly, tired of being on the defensive. "Are you going to tell me you never tried even beer when you were a teenager?"

"Sure I tried it," he admitted readily. "And I woke up the next day with a hell of a hangover, too. When my father found out what I'd done, he made me do a whole day's threshing. He didn't care that I had to stop several times to get sick—he said it served me right. And it did. I thought twice about doing that again."

"Not all kids have fathers like that."

"Didn't you?"

Squirming, she had to admit that her father probably would have done the same thing. "But that doesn't mean—"

"It means that the solution to this problem is teaching kids how to deal with problems effectively," he stated.

"But what about environment, background . . ."

He looked at her scornfully. "Don't tell me that you subscribe to the theory that 'society' is to blame for every ill."

Annoyed at his patronizing tone, she replied, "I believe that it has something to do with it."

"It shouldn't have anything to do with it at all," he declared. "Actions are either right or wrong. There's no excuse for not knowing which is which."

"And so that's the tone you want to take on this project?"

"I plan to be objective, yes."

"That's what you call objective? I'm sorry, Neil, but I don't believe any of these issues are as black and white as you'd like to make them."

"Good," he said, surprising her. "That's why we're co-hosts. You present one aspect, I'll give another and—" he couldn't prevent a cynical smile "—hopefully, our viewers will be able to make up their own minds."

"You really don't have much faith in people, do you?"

"No," he admitted. "Maybe you can make me change my mind."

Still annoyed with him, she asked coolly, "What makes you think I'd like to try?"

Neil had been amused at that, but when they left the restaurant directly after, he was quiet. As they walked the short block to the parking lot, Dinah glanced at him covertly, wondering what he was thinking. She wished now that she hadn't been so sharp with him, but she told herself he'd deserved it. The rationalization didn't lift her suddenly depressed mood, and she wondered how the evening that had begun with such promise could have fallen so flat at the end.

At first she had enjoyed matching wits with him. It had been exhilarating, a challenge she'd been eager to accept. But now she felt differently, and the thought that their relationship would always be based on this one-upmanship game they'd developed was discouraging. She didn't want to have to be always ready with a quick comment or a clever reply—she wanted something more.

And what was that, she asked herself irritably. She'd thought she'd learned long ago to separate her professional and her private lives. Mixing the two only led to complications; it had to be one or the other, and she'd decided after Ted left which it would be. She knew it had to be this way, so why was it so difficult now to heed her own advice?

Shooting another surreptitious glance at Neil, she was annoyed with herself again. He hadn't given her the slightest indication that he desired anything other than a working relationship, so what was she so confused about? For all she knew, he had a legion of girlfriends lined up outside his door, one for every day of the week. As far as he was concerned, she was just someone with whom he'd agreed to work.

And why *had* he agreed, she wondered suddenly. It obviously hadn't been because Daniel Rawlings had commanded it. She suspected that if Neil had really wanted to, he could have refused. He certainly had the power to do so. She'd seen herself the night of the awards dinner that his relationship with the head of programming was more that of equals than anything else.

"Why did you agree to do this project?" she asked abruptly, and then was horrified. She hadn't meant to voice her thoughts aloud, and she would have given anything to retract the question. They had reached her car by this time, and Dinah wanted to fling herself in and drive away before he could answer. Mortified, she put her hand on the door handle and felt even worse when she saw his smile.

"Why do you think?"

Dinah didn't know what to think. She had never felt so out of control and confused by a man, not even when she had first fallen in love with Ted. She still remembered those feelings of euphoria, but she hadn't thought she'd experience that again, at least not in the same way. She'd been so young then, and it had all been so new.

But there was something about Neil Kerrigan that struck a responsive chord in her, and without warning, she had begun to feel like that again, stirred by that same subtle excitement, tingling with that same anticipation. She didn't like these feelings; at times she wasn't even sure she liked Neil himself. They seemed to be so fundamentally opposite, their views so different, that she doubted they'd ever agree on any issue more important than the time of day.

Abruptly she realized he was still waiting for her answer. "I don't know why," she said, her voice unsteady because he was looking at her so intently. She had never been so aware of the compelling power of that gaze, and she wanted suddenly to reach up and touch his face. She tightened her fingers on the car handle instead, resisting temptation with an effort.

He hesitated for so long that she began to think she had offended him for some absurd reason. She was sorry if she had, but this was important to her; she had to know.

His voice was very deep, almost rough when he finally answered. "I don't suppose you'd believe me if I said I was just following orders."

She shook her head, her mouth suddenly dry. There was something about the way he was looking at her, something about the sudden tenseness of his body that was affecting her, too. She realized she was holding her breath, that the world seemed to be holding its breath with her. They seemed to be entirely alone; even the sound of a foghorn on the water only added to the spell they seemed to have woven about themselves.

"I've always admired intelligent women," he said at last. "And I knew when Andy suggested the idea that you'd be an asset to any project. That's why."

Absurdly, she was disappointed. He'd given her a compliment, and all she could think of was how much she had wanted him to say something else, something more personal, something...

Thrusting away those thoughts, she reached for the car door again. Feeling suddenly ridiculously close to tears, she muttered, "I see."

Neil's hand closed over hers, arresting the motion. "Those aren't the only reasons," he said huskily, and before she realized what he was about to do, he drew her into his arms and kissed her.

Dinah felt the impact all the way to her toes. For an instant she was swept with such force of emotion that it was all she could do not to surrender completely. Despite the damp chill of the night, his lips were warm, seeking, pressing against hers with such urgency that her own lips parted. Horrified at the depth of response he had evoked, she reared back.

Neil looked as stunned as she felt. The air seemed suddenly charged, and Dinah knew that if he touched her again, she wouldn't be able to resist. "I'm sorry," he said, sounding bewildered and disconcerted and unnerved at the same time. "I shouldn't have done that."

"I..." she began, and had to start over again because her voice was still choked with that torrent of emotion. Making a fierce effort at gathering the shreds of her composure, she managed, "I would appreciate it if you... if we... if that didn't happen again. Since we're going to be working together, we..."

"Yes," he said unevenly, and opened the car door for her.

Her legs were shaking as she climbed in, and she sank weakly onto the seat, wondering if she could drive home. Her hand was trembling so badly that she could hardly fit the key into the ignition, but at last the car started. Barely glancing back to see if the way was clear, she pulled out, not daring to look at him again.

The drive home seemed endless. She kept seeing Neil's face the instant before he bent down and kissed her; she could still feel the pressure of his mouth on hers. The power of her response frightened her. She had never felt such sweeping emotion, not even with Ted.

What was happening to her, she wondered desperately. She couldn't be this attracted to a man she barely knew, a man whose viewpoints and beliefs were so diametrically opposed to hers. It didn't make sense.

She couldn't deny he was extraordinarily handsome, with those broad shoulders and deep blue eyes and curling black hair. And she couldn't deny that she admired his quick mind and his obvious intelligence. He was sophisticated and urbane and charming when he chose to be, but then so were thousands of other men. What was it about Neil Kerrigan that made him stand out from all the rest?

Mortified that she'd acted like a schoolgirl tonight in the throes of some ridiculous crush, Dinah resolved that she wasn't going to make such a fool of herself again. She was a professional; she had a job to do. The fact that she'd be working with Neil so closely during the following week or two just made it a little more difficult, that's all. She was certainly capable of handling the situation. All she had to do was remember that this was her job, and that she was good at it. It was as simple as that.

But Dinah knew in her heart that it wasn't that simple at all. Arriving home at last, she unsteadily fixed herself a cup of tea before she went into the bedroom to pack. She had to meet Neil and the crew at Willowset tomorrow, but as she moved back and forth between her closet and the suitcase she had placed on the bed, her steps slowed more and more until finally she just halted in the center of the room. She couldn't forget that kiss, as brief as it had been, nor her response to it, and she was troubled. How was she ever going to keep her mind on business when the merest touch from him sent her into a tailspin?

Sinking down onto the edge of the bed, she told herself that she had to resolve this before she left or she'd be so mesmerized by the man that she would forget the reason they had gone to Willowset in the first place. She'd been agitating for months for an opportunity like this; she couldn't fall apart now when things were starting to move into place. She had plans, goals, and none of them included Neil Kerrigan.

All right, she was physically attracted to him, but what woman wouldn't be? But there was more to a relationship than that, and she doubted that they'd ever be able to understand or accept each other's viewpoints and beliefs. A relationship with Neil would eventually end in frustration and misunderstanding, and she just couldn't put herself through all that again.

No, it was hopeless, and the sooner she admitted that the better off she'd be. Once this project was finished, she probably wouldn't even see him again, except as their career paths crossed. They would be colleagues, nothing more.

But somehow that thought depressed her even more, and when she went to bed that night, it was a long time before she was able to sleep.

NEIL STOOD by the motel window, a half-finished drink in his hand, staring vacantly down at the empty streets below. It was after two in the morning, and he'd hoped the brandy he'd poured would relax him enough to sleep. It hadn't. He still felt as keyed up and tense as he had when Dinah drove off, and whenever he recalled how her lips had parted so briefly under his when he'd kissed her, he felt even more unnerved. It wasn't like him to pull such a stupid stunt; he still didn't know why he had.

Yes, he did.

Turning abruptly away from the window, he threw himself into a chair, glowering. Who was he trying to kid? He'd been wanting to kiss her from the moment he'd met her. But now that he'd acted out his childish impulse, he regretted it.

Because now he couldn't get her out of his mind. It had taken all this willpower to pull back. He'd wanted to hold her against him, to feel the slenderness of her body against his. He'd wanted...damn it, he had wanted a lot more than that. If she had given the slightest indication...

Cursing, he put the glass down and got up to pace. How the hell was he going to work with her every day, feeling like this? And why did he feel this way? He'd known beautiful women before—the world was filled with them. Why, suddenly, did they all seem pale imitations, not even worth a second glance?

This was ridiculous. He was acting like a schoolboy in the throes of some adolescent crush. He was more sophisticated than that; all it took was a little resolve. The breakup of his marriage had proved that he obviously wasn't capable of handling both his professional and personal commitments, and until he'd met Dinah, he had accepted that.

He *still* accepted it, he assured himself, and he'd prove it. This thing with Dinah was a momentary aberration, one he could control. When he met her tomorrow, he'd be professional and businesslike and courteous, nothing more. He'd put all this behind him, and refuse to be personally affected by her at all.

CHAPTER SEVEN

BY THE TIME DINAH ARRIVED in Willowset the next day, she had decided that the best way to handle what had happened between her and Neil was to ignore it entirely. If she was brisk and businesslike, Neil would believe that the "incident," as she was now thinking of it, had made so little impact on her that she didn't consider it worth mentioning.

At least, she hoped he'd think so, because if he even had a glimmer of what that brief kiss had done to her, she'd never be able to look him in the eye again. Whenever she thought about it, which was too often, she could feel her face growing warm and her entire body begin to flush. Hoping that if Neil mentioned it she'd be able to give some casual response, she drove into the parking lot at the Willowset Inn.

To her chagrin, Neil seemed to have forgotten the incident entirely. He and Chuck and Larry had already checked in, and when Neil met her in the lobby of the giant new motel complex just east of town, Dinah didn't know whether to be relieved or annoyed that his manner toward her was courteous but distant. Following the same suit after she'd registered and joined the three men in the small conference room reserved for their use, she noticed Neil's eyes on her several times as they went over the itinerary, but she forced herself to return his glance coolly. She was not going to make the same mistake again.

The first interview they had was with one of the local school officials, a pompous man named Gerald Perkins, who was clearly awed at the prospect of meeting the famous Neil Kerrigan, and flattered to have been singled out for such attention. Flattered, that was, until the camera was turned on him and he realized this was a little more attention than he'd bargained for. Instantly wary when Neil changed before his eyes from an affable visitor to a curt reporter, it was obvious that he soon regretted granting the interview.

"According to a recent survey," Neil began smoothly, ignoring Chuck as he moved into a better position with the minicam, and Larry as he adjusted the sound level, "the incidence of drug and alcohol abuse among high school students has increased dramatically in the past few years. More than fifty percent of students polled admitted trying marijuana, for example, and some twenty percent cocaine. The figures are even higher among high school seniors. Now, Mr. Perkins, my question is this. What is the school system doing about this increasing problem?"

With the ball dropped suddenly in his court, Gerald Perkins glanced nervously at the boom microphone Larry had swung over his head. Clearing his throat, he began, "I assure you that all school officials are aware of the facts..." and had to pause to wipe away a drop of perspiration that had trickled down his nose.

"Being aware of the problem and doing something about it are two different things, as I'm sure you will agree," Neil said suavely, and waited.

"Well, yes, of course," Perkins answered stiffly. "But I'm not responsible for what my students do outside school hours. We are not policemen, Mr. Kerrigan. We are educators."

"Yes," Neil agreed, too amiably. "So as educators, what are you doing to combat this problem? Do you have classes or seminars or discussions about drugs? Is there a course designed to teach your students about the dangers of drug and alcohol abuse?"

"Now that you mention it, we do have a course exactly like that on the agenda," the principal said, and looked pleased with himself until Neil raised an eyebrow.

"On the agenda, but not in effect?"

Nettled at Neil's tone, Perkins stiffened. "Mr. Kerrigan, if I thought that such abuses were taking place here, you can be sure I would act immediately. But this is not a public facility, it is a private high school. And one of the best in California, I might add!"

"So you're suggesting that the problem doesn't exist here," Neil said, his voice so deceptively low that Dinah glanced quickly at him. She knew that tone. It meant that he was getting ready for the kill.

Perkins drew himself up a little. The reputation of his school was at stake. "As I told you—"

"Because if you are, I'd like to inform you that the poll I'm referring to was taken right here, at this school."

Perkins blanched, but he pressed doggedly on. "Well, if any of our students are involved in such, er, activities, I can tell you with confidence that they aren't obtaining illegal substances on this campus. We monitor our students very carefully—"

"How?"

"How?" Perkins echoed blankly, and pulled out his handkerchief again. Mopping his face, he said, "Our faculty are all highly trained. We would certainly know if there were any, er, infractions here and deal with those involved immediately."

"I see," Neil said. "Then perhaps you'd better start with those students I saw on the front lawn as we came in."

"What—what do you mean?"

"Well, it was obvious to me that there were certain . . . transactions going on."

"That's impossible!" Perkins blurted, appalled.

Dinah wanted to say something at this point, if for no other reason than to give the poor man a chance to compose himself. Neil had him so rattled that he could hardly speak, but she was too fascinated by his technique to interrupt. She had seen him lure the guests on his programs into his verbal traps, but she had never observed the process at such close range, and she found it both intriguing and repelling. When they first arrived, Gerald Perkins had obviously been a man filled with a sense of his own importance; with a few well-chosen words, Neil had completely deflated him. She wondered what it would be like to take such liberties herself. She'd had a few guests in the past on her own program whom she would have loved to cut down to size, and the idea was tempting. Then she was ashamed of herself. She didn't enjoy humiliating people, no matter how pompous they were.

Wishing that they had defined their roles a little more clearly, she sat in silence as Neil continued to pursue and Perkins tried his best to parry. As the interview concluded, she wasn't sure which of them was more relieved: she or the hapless school principal. The man looked so unnerved when Neil finally stood that she could almost feel sorry for him.

"You were a little hard on him, weren't you?" she commented mildly when they left. Larry and Chuck were stowing the camera equipment in the rear of the station wagon they'd rented, while she and Neil walked to their own car.

"Was I?" he asked, sounding surprised. "No, I don't think so. Why?"

"Well, for one thing, the man was so nervous he could hardly remember his own name."

Neil shrugged. "That's his problem. He wouldn't have been nervous if he hadn't had something to hide."

Dinah realized that was true, but she still felt some sympathy for Perkins. She'd been on the receiving end of one of Neil's interrogations herself, and she knew that helpless feeling of trying to defend an indefensible position.

Wondering if she was really prepared for this after all, she climbed into the car and waited for him to go around the other side. Seeing Neil in action had been an eye-opener for her, and she wasn't sure she could be that aggressive when her turn came. She preferred a softer approach, one that set everyone at ease. It was one of the reasons she'd been such a success on her own show. Putting people on the defensive wasn't her style.

But it was obviously Neil's. During the hour they'd spent with the principal he had seemed so cold, so harsh. He had even looked different; his eyes had become a flat blue and it seemed that the planes of his face had sharpened. He had reminded her of a tiger stalking its prey, deadly and dangerous.

That image disturbed her even more, and she was silent on the way to their next appointment with a physician who specialized in treating addicted teens. She was aware of Neil glancing once or twice across at her, but she was too preoccupied with her own thoughts to wonder what he was thinking.

Disconcerted that she could admire his investigative techniques on the one hand and resent the killer instincts that prompted them on the other, she wondered if he expected the same thing of her. Recalling how haughtily she'd assured everyone within hearing distance that she was as much a professional as he was, she wished now that she hadn't made such an issue of it. After the way he'd handled that interview today, she knew that she'd never be able to match him.

"How would you have conducted that interview?"

Startled that he seemed to have been reading her thoughts, Dinah glanced at him and then quickly away. She couldn't see his eyes behind his sunglasses and she felt at a disadvantage. Stalling, she said, "Why do you ask?"

He grinned. "You've been too quiet since we left. It's not like you."

"I can be quiet at times," she protested.

"Only when you're gathering up a head of steam to blast someone. So go ahead—blast away."

"Well," she began warily, "I don't think I would have put Perkins on the defensive like that."

"Why not?"

"Well, it just seemed so—"

"Cruel?" Neil supplied. "Come on, Dinah. That man was a pompous fool. He didn't know what was going on in that school, and he should have. That's his job, just as it's mine to ask him questions he'd rather not answer." He glanced across at her again, that cynical smile curving his lips. "And that's how we find out things we're not supposed to. You can't be soft and sentimental when you're an investigative reporter or you'll never learn anything."

"But not every interview has to be an inquisition," Dinah objected.

"Ah. So you'd rather sit there and listen to someone telling you all the things they want you to hear, rather than chance hurting their feelings by demanding the facts."

Flushing, she said, "I didn't say that. But there is an old saying, you know, about catching more flies with honey than with vinegar."

"Not in journalism, there's not."

"Why are we arguing about this?" she asked. "Didn't we agree that you'd handle your interviews your way and I'd handle mine my way?"

"We did," he agreed, pulling into the parking lot of the clinic where they had their next appointment. "That's why I think you should take this one. This Dr. Mason we're going to see has a reputation of disliking reporters. We'll see if your honeyed approach works, all right?"

"Fine," she said haughtily, and sailed into the office ahead of the crew, looking more confident than she suddenly felt.

Dr. Mason was a tall, thin man dressed in jeans and sweatshirt and running shoes that had seen better days. Somewhat gruffly, he showed them into an office cluttered with medical journals and patient reports and stacks of folders from which the papers spilled and coffee rings were clearly visible on the covers. Without apology, he cleared space for them and then perched on the edge of his desk.

"So, what can I do for you?" he asked, and frowned as Chuck and Larry moved around taking sound- and light-meter readings.

Feeling her heart sink at the look on his face, Dinah wondered why he had consented to the interview. It was obvious he resented their presence, and she almost lost courage. But then she saw Neil watching her intently, and she became determined that this interview was going to be a success—with her approach, not his. So she gave Dr. Mason her brightest smile and said, "We're so pleased you agreed to give us your time today. I know how busy you must be."

Dr. Mason would have had to have a heart of iron not to be affected by that smile. Relaxing visibly, he waved his hand. "Anything I can do to help these kids is worth a little of my time."

"We feel it's worth some of ours, too," she replied warmly. "That's why we're doing this program."

Chuck gave her a thumbs-up signal then, indicating the equipment was ready, and she nodded slightly. "Dr. Mason, I think it would be helpful if you could first explain, in layman's terms, please—" another smile "—the physical effects of drug and alcohol abuse."

Thawed completely by that second smile, Dr. Mason paused a moment to gather his thoughts, then, ignoring the camera and the boom stretched out over his head, he began to tell them about the severe depression, paranoia, irritability and addiction that both substances can cause. He described the damage to the nervous system and told them about the intense "highs" of some of the drugs, where users can exhibit maniacal strength or total absence of pain on injury. Many of the substances distorted perception, anaethesized the inhibitory centers of the brain and produced hallucinations and delusions that were sometimes fatal.

"Whatever the kids want, it's available," he concluded somberly. "Uppers, downers, speed, crystal Meth, hash, heroine—you name it. A list of the things some of these kids have tried would make your hair stand on end. It's amazing so many of them avoid hospitalization. The physical assault on their systems alone is tremendous, not to mention the psychological effects. Fortunately, though, the human body is a wonderful machine, built to absorb a great deal of punishment. Many of these kids wouldn't make it otherwise."

"It's incredible," Dinah murmured, awed by the ghastly litany he'd just described.

"Yes, it is," he agreed. "And that's why the medical profession is extremely concerned by the increased use of all these different drugs. At high doses, some of them—cocaine, for instance—can produce a direct toxic action on the heart muscle, resulting in cardiac failure and immediate death."

"But what about the parents of these children?" Dinah asked. "Don't they realize—"

"I take it you're not a parent yourself."

She shook her head and looked at Neil.

"I am," Neil said. "I have a son, Andy."

"Do you think you would know if Andy was taking drugs or drinking?"

Neil looked offended. "Certainly."

"Don't be too sure. Too many parents don't."

"Well, I would," Neil replied stiffly. "I care about my son."

"So do the parents of these children. But it's difficult sometimes to accept. Either the parents don't recognize the effects of these substances, or they just don't want to believe that their son or daughter could be involved."

Seeing Neil's expression, Dinah said quickly, "So it's the parents, as well as the young people, who have to be educated."

Dr. Mason's glance swung back to her and immediately softened. "Yes, and that's why I agreed to talk to you today. I hope this program you're doing will help."

"So do we," Dinah replied, and then stood, sensing that the interview should end on this note. "Is there anything more we can do?"

Dr. Mason stood, too. "Just get your facts straight," he said. "And . . ."

"Yes?" Dinah asked when he paused.

"Maybe you'd like to go through the clinic," he said abruptly. "I've got a few minutes. I could show you around."

Dinah hid her reaction. She knew he'd agreed to this interview only on the condition that his clinic wouldn't be involved. He'd been adamant about the patients and their families not being disturbed, and the fact that he had actually volunteered to show them through was a surprise.

"I'd like that very much," she said, and smiled. Then, holding her breath, she asked, "Will you allow us to tape?"

He hesitated again, and she increased the power of her smile. Finally, he smiled, too. "As long as you get permission from the patients and their parents."

"Of course," she agreed, and couldn't prevent a victorious look at Neil as they followed the physician out of the office and down a short corridor to the clinic doors. Neil returned her glance with a raised eyebrow, but she saw the admiration in his eyes at her coup and was satisfied.

The doctor left them briefly to make arrangements, and as he walked away, Neil stepped close to her and murmured, "Well, that was a surprise."

"Do you think so?" Dinah asked innocently. "Why?"

"You must know that until now he's refused reporters access to the clinic."

"Oh, that. I didn't think we'd have any trouble," she said serenely, and vowed that he'd never know she'd been just as astonished as he.

Dr. Mason returned then, saying that he'd arranged for them to speak to a mother and her son, but only briefly. The boy, Dean Mathews, had arrived at the clinic just two days earlier after a three-month stay in the hospital. He'd been drinking the night he'd been involved in a car accident and had broken his back.

"He's one of the lucky ones," Dr. Mason said soberly as he led the way to the boy's room. "Some of them don't even make it to the hospital."

Feeling chilled by his words, Dinah glanced at Neil as they walked along and saw that he had paled, too. She knew he was thinking of Andy when he asked, "How old is Dean?"

"Seventeen," Dr. Mason replied. "He was the star quarterback on his football team until the accident.

His mother told me that he'd already received some offers by college scouts."

"Will he play football again?"

"He's going to have a hard time learning to walk again, Mr. Kerrigan."

Both Dinah and Neil were silent at that, and as Dr. Mason stopped before one of the closed doors, she felt herself tensing. She wished suddenly that she hadn't been so eager to see the clinic, but now that they were here, she could hardly refuse to go in. Smiling a little tremulously at Dr. Mason, she nodded when he cautioned, "Just a few minutes, now," and hoped no one would notice her hand was shaking when she pushed open the door.

In the end, it was Neil who managed better than she did. After they had introduced themselves and asked if Chuck and Larry could come in with the equipment, Dinah found herself so choked that she could hardly speak.

Dean Mathews was a good-looking boy with a shock of blond hair and blue eyes. As she summoned a smile for him, she could imagine that he'd starred off the football field as well as on it, for he had the kind of appeal the girls would find irresistible. He looked like everyone's vision of the all-American boy—until one saw the plaster cast that enveloped him from chin to hips. Feeling the sting of tears in her eyes at the sight, Dinah turned helplessly to Neil.

"Hold the camera for a minute," Neil said to Chuck. "I'd like to talk to Dean for a while without taping."

"Naw, that's okay, Mr. Kerrigan," Dean said, obviously thrilled at the presence of his visitors. His eyes sparkled, and his smile nearly broke Dinah's heart.

"I've been in this thing so long it doesn't bother me anymore. And it might do some of the kids out there some good to see me like this. I never thought it would happen to me, either."

Neil didn't patronize the boy with gratuitous remarks. He simply nodded and said, "Do you want to talk about it?"

Dean shrugged as best he could in the confining plaster. "What's to talk about? I did a stupid thing, and I'm paying for it. I'm just glad I was alone in the car. I sure wouldn't want to be responsible for anyone else ending up like this."

Dinah was watching Neil, amazed again at the transformation that had taken place. She had seen him this morning as a hard-eyed reporter who accepted no equivocation or excuse; she was seeing him now as a compassionate, almost gentle man, capable of communicating with this boy on his own level, and she realized that this was a part of him that he kept very private. Tears in her eyes again, she quietly slipped from the room.

Dean's mother was waiting in the hall, a small, round woman with graying hair and a tired look in her eyes. When Dinah introduced herself and asked if they could talk, Mrs. Mathews startled her by grabbing her hand and clutching it tightly.

"You don't know how much I appreciate your coming," Mrs. Mathews said, her voice breaking. "Dean was so excited when Dr. Mason said you wanted to interview him. He'll talk about this for months. It's given him such a lift."

Somewhat alarmed at the hysterical edge she heard in the woman's voice, Dinah gently led her to a nearby chair. "I know what a strain this must have been for you," she began. "But your son seems to be doing very well."

Mrs. Mathews fumbled in her purse for a handkerchief. "It just makes me so sad," she choked, beginning to cry. "If you could have seen him before—so tall, so handsome. He was always athletic, and now..."

Dinah wanted to comfort the woman, but she remembered what Dr. Mason had told them, and she couldn't make herself utter false reassurances. "I'm very sorry," she said at last, and winced at the thought of how inadequate that sounded.

"You know, I never knew Dean was drinking," the woman sobbed. "When they told me, I was sure it was a mistake. Not Dean, not my boy. He was such a good student, such a fine athlete...." Her voice broke again and she looked at Dinah with agonized eyes. "How could I not have known? I'm home for my kids. I take care of them. I love them. Why didn't I know?"

But Dinah had no answer for that, and she watched sadly as the woman excused herself and walked dejectedly away. Wishing that she could have found some words of comfort, she was just starting to go back to Dean's room when there was a terrible commotion at the front entrance. Startled, she looked around and was appalled to see two policemen and a boy burst through the doors with such force that one of the glass panes shattered. The youth's face was contorted, and he was fighting his captors so violently that his entire body heaved into the air. Screaming imprecations, he kicked and bit and clawed at the men trying valiantly to hold him. Dinah shrank back against the wall as Dr. Mason and several strong orderlies raced to help. Horrified at the sight of five men trying to subdue a boy who looked no more than fifteen, Dinah couldn't move until they finally managed to carry him away.

"What in the hell was that all about?"

Dazedly, Dinah looked at Neil, who had come running down the hall at the noise, followed closely by Chuck and Larry. "I . . . I'm not sure," she said shakily. "It happened so fast—"

"Are you all right?"

"Yes," she muttered, and then, more strongly, "Yes, I'm fine." With an effort, she pushed herself away from the wall. "I'm going to find out what was wrong with him."

"I'll do it."

Dinah looked at him. "I said I was fine," she repeated, and marched directly over to one of the officers, who was leaning against the reception desk, trying to catch his breath.

He was a big man, broad shouldered and thick waisted, and as she looked at him, she marveled again at the strength that boy had demonstrated. The officer looked as though he could wrestle an ox to the ground, and yet the youth they'd brought in had nearly broken away from him.

"Excuse me," she said. "My name is Dinah Blake, and I wonder if you could answer a few questions."

The officer immediately looked wary, and his glance flicked to his partner who had gone outside for a cigarette. It was obvious he wished he'd joined him and Dinah smiled, trying to put him at ease.

"If you have any questions," the officer said curtly, "maybe you should ask the doctor."

Dinah held her smile, but she was alerted by his defensive posture, and she decided to press him a little.

"I thought you might be able to tell me what was wrong with the boy, since you brought him in," she said pleasantly.

"Oh, no—not me," he glowered. "I know how it goes, lady, and next thing I know I'll be seeing myself on TV and somebody'll be screaming police brutality."

"You're the one who mentioned brutality, not I," she pointed out calmly, and then paused deliberately. "Should I have?"

The officer stiffened. "You saw what that kid was like. The two of us could hardly hold him. Hell, he damn near destroyed the patrol car while we were trying to get him here."

"Why did you bring him here, then?"

"Because this was the closest place, and I wasn't going to drive all the way downtown with a screaming maniac in the back seat, that's why."

"But isn't that your job, officer—" she glanced at his badge "—Officer Gentry?"

"Look, lady, it's not my job to chase after a bunch of stupid kids who've fried their brains on some drug or another."

"Oh, I see," Dinah said. "You have more important things to do, right?"

The officer frowned. "I didn't say that…exactly."

"Oh. Then you have less important things to do."

He flushed. "You're trying to twist my words around."

"I wouldn't want to do that," she said sweetly, and glanced at Chuck, deliberately motioning him closer. "It's all yours, Officer Gentry," she added, and stepped away as he eyed the camera balefully. "Oh, and you don't have to worry. I promise, we'll record everything you say—exactly.''

But the burly policeman declined to say anything at all. Shoving his peaked hat down over his eyes, he turned on his heel and strode out the door. Seconds later, they heard the screech of tires as the patrol car pulled away.

When they were driving away themselves after thanking Dr. Mason for his time, Neil burst into laughter.

"I don't believe it!" he gasped. "The look on that cop's face when you motioned to Chuck was priceless! Did you know he was taping the whole time?"

Dinah smiled without answering, pretending a sudden interest in the passing scenery outside the car window. *Let him wonder about that for a while,* she thought complacently, and decided that the score for today was a draw.

WHEN THEY ARRIVED at the motel, Dinah disappeared with the excuse that she had to finish unpacking, and left to themselves, the three men decided to play a few holes of golf before dinner. Neil was normally an excellent golfer, but it soon became obvious that he didn't have his mind on his game. When he found himself in a sand trap for the second time, the other men were amused.

"Something on your mind, Neil?" Chuck asked with a smile. They had all worked together on several projects, and he felt confident enough to tease the boss.

Neil glowered up at him from the sand pit. "My game's off a little, that's all."

"Right," Larry said, looking innocently up at the sky. "I guess that's why you went three over par on that last hole."

"It was four," Neil said grimly, blasting the ball out of the sand and so far out onto the green that he'd be over par on this hole, too. "But who's counting?"

"Not me," Chuck said, grinning. "I just needed a little exercise."

"And I wanted to work up an appetite for dinner," Larry put in.

Climbing up the fairway again, Neil dropped the club into his bag. "All right, so I'm a little preoccupied."

"It couldn't have anything to do with Miss Green Eyes, could it?" Chuck asked, trying to hide his sly smile.

Neil hefted the golf bag with such force that the clubs rattled. "It could not," he said loftily.

"Man, she's really something, isn't she?" Larry said. "She had that Dr. Mason eating out of her hand."

"Not to mention what she did to that cop," Chuck interjected. "I was laughing so hard I almost dropped the camera. She might look all peaches and cream, but she sure can pack a powerful wallop."

She could indeed, Neil thought as they walked to the next hole and he waited for Chuck and Larry to play. And right now he felt as though he'd been smacked right between the eyes. He'd known she had the ability to do this project; he just hadn't realized how talented she was. That combination of beauty and brains and charm could be devastating, and he knew that Dr. Mason hadn't been the only one to fall for it today—he'd been a little dazzled himself.

She could be tough, too; she'd proved it with that police officer. Smiling to himself, Neil knew that the man hadn't even know what hit him until it was too late. Dinah had finessed him right to the end. And with class. That's what he had admired most of all. She hadn't even raised her voice. She had just lured him in with that smile.

It was that smile he had to watch out for, he thought as he took his place and balanced the golf ball on a tee, that wicked, wonderful smile of hers. If he didn't watch it, he could lose himself in that smile, lured in just as those other men had been today. As Chuck and Larry seemed to be.

But not he, Neil thought, and swung the club in one lithe movement, arcing it down to meet the ball as he'd done hundreds—thousands—of times before. The two met with a solid crack, and he grunted with satisfaction as the ball flew into the air. Seconds later, when it fell into the shrubbery a good eighty yards to the left of the green, an image of amused green eyes flashed into his mind. As Chuck and Larry burst into laughter, Neil threw down the club and cursed.

CHAPTER EIGHT

THE NEXT DAY THEY WENT to a special school, a farm that had been established some distance from town for teens recovering from drug abuse. The place was a surprise, for in addition to regular classes, the students were expected to contribute to the farm's maintenance. The director of Get In Touch, as the program was called, was a cheerful, vibrant man in his late thirties named Mark Delaney, and as he showed Dinah and Neil around the grounds before they went to the main house, he almost crackled with energy.

Clearly proud of the program and the undeniable success he'd had with it, he pointed out the small herd of dairy goats, the giant vegetable garden cultivated at present with winter vegetables because it was still only mid-February, and several acres of experimental grapes. The farmhouse itself was a rambling affair, once built to house a large family, filled at present with fourteen youngsters ranging in age from thirteen to sixteen, both boys and girls.

With Chuck busily shooting everything in sight, Mark went on to explain that one of the reasons his school had been so successful was because the students were given so much to do. Chores were assigned on a rotating basis, and everyone was expected to begin his or her required task immediately after classes ended for the day.

"Idle hands . . . ?" Neil murmured.

Mark grinned again. "One of the problems is that these kids have too much time on their hands. At GIT we make sure they're too tired to think about getting into trouble."

Neil looked around, obviously recalling memories of his own days on the farm before he asked, "What kind of a staff do you have here?"

"Well, there's myself, of course. I'm here all the time. And then we have a couple who live in that cottage over there. They're our housekeeper and handyman. During the day, several tutors and counselors come, and that's about it."

"You're the only adult in the house at night?" Neil asked.

Mark looked amused. "If you're asking whether I sleep sitting next to the door, the answer is no. We don't have fences here, as you can see, except those required for the stock, and we don't have security guards. I've found that we don't need them."

Neil's expression was skeptical. "You trust them not to run away?"

Mark's gaze was direct. "How else are they going to prove they're trustworthy if they aren't given the opportunity to demonstrate it?"

Neil still looked doubtful, and Mark smiled again. "Let's go meet some of the kids," he suggested. "You can talk to them and see for yourself how the program works."

Dinah could hear a loud buzz of conversation as they approached the house, but as soon as they stepped into the huge living room, the din ceased. Almost as once, the six young people within leaped to their feet and stood waiting politely to be introduced.

As she acknowledged each one, Dinah found it difficult to believe that these teenagers had once been so
hard to handle at home that their parents had agreed
to hand them over to this young man's care. They all
seemed so clear eyed and freshly scrubbed that she
couldn't imagine they'd ever had any problems at all.
Mark Delaney seemed to have wrought a miracle cure.

"This is my graduating class," Mark said proudly.
"They've all agreed to talk to you because they want
everyone to know that you can take charge of your
life, if you have a little help doing it, right?"

"Right!"

The shout was unanimous, and as the group got
settled, the young administrator murmured that he'd
be in his office if they needed him. Dinah didn't think
they would. As soon as he'd gone with a cheery wave
of his hand, she turned to the young people and said,
"We'd like to tape this interview, unless you have any
objections."

"Naw," one boy said. "I've always wanted to see
myself on TV. This is going to be on TV, isn't it?"

"Yes, it is," Dinah answered. "We're—"

"I used to watch *Personalities* every chance I got,"
a girl spoke up, her eyes shining as she gazed at Dinah.
"I think you're just wonderful!"

"Well, thank you. But now—"

"What's it like to blast all those government guys,
Mr. Kerrigan?" a new voice asked, a boy who looked
about sixteen. "My dad says you've really got guts."

Neil looked amused at that, but before he could respond, several other voices were raised, the questions
flying at both Dinah and Neil so fast that they looked
at each other helplessly and laughed. Neil finally
raised a hand in mock protest.

"Hey! I thought we were the ones who were supposed to be asking the questions."

"We can all ask questions here," a shy-looking blond girl said. "That's the rule."

"Oh, I see," Dinah said solemnly. "Well, we certainly wouldn't want to break any rules. I'll tell you what. You ask a question, and then we'll ask one. Is that fair?"

It was fair. Enjoying herself immensely, Dinah accepted the space on the couch that had been made for her and looked up at Neil as he took a place beside her. Their eyes met, and she was pleased to see that he was enjoying this, too. A few minutes later, they looked at each other again in shared amusement. The lively young people surrounding them seemed to have completely forgotten the agreement. The questions flew at them again, but the teenagers were so obviously excited that neither Neil or Dinah could deny them the opportunity to ask what they liked.

"Did you go to college, Miss Blake?" a girl, Mary, asked.

"Yes, I studied at UCLA in Los Angeles."

"Do you get to travel all over the world for free?" a boy, whose name was Tony, asked Neil.

"If I'm on assignment, the network pays my way," Neil answered, and then grinned. "But if I'm on vacation, I have to buy my ticket just like everybody else."

"What's it like being on TV, Miss Blake?"

"Well, most of the time it's exciting, but usually it's hard work, just like any job you want to do well."

"Do you call the president by his first name, Mr. Kerrigan?"

"No, I call him Mr. President—unless we're on the tennis court, and then I call him the winner."

The kids laughed at that, and then Neil tried to ask a question himself. "All right, it's our turn. We did come here to talk to you about—"

"Oh, who wants to talk about that?" Hal said. "That's old stuff. We're all done with that."

"We know you are," Dinah said. "But don't you want to help other kids who are trying to deal with the same problems you've overcome?"

"Sure, but we can tell them in two sentences about that."

"What would you say?" Dinah asked curiously.

"We'd tell them to stay away from the stuff in the first place," the shy girl, Jessie, answered. "It's just not worth it."

"And then?"

"And then we'd tell them that if they were stupid enough to go ahead and think they could handle it, to beg Mark to Get In Touch."

There was a general, heartfelt chorus at that, and then one girl, who hadn't said much until now, spoke up. "Are you two married?"

"Married!" Dinah exclaimed, startled. "To each other, you mean?"

"Yes," the girl, Sarah, said with a sigh. "You look like the perfect couple."

As Dinah tried to think of a response to that, Neil leaned over and murmured, "This one's all yours."

She shot him a sideways glance. "Thanks a lot," she muttered, and then looked at Sarah again. "No, we're not."

"Not what?"

"Not married," Dinah said, and knew she was only making it worse when she added, "To each other...or to anyone else..."

As the kids started to laugh at her fumbling response, Dinah felt her cheeks flame. Not daring to look at Neil, who she was sure was laughing, too, she glanced up and saw that Chuck had turned the camera on her. Realizing that by now her face was probably beet red, she signaled him frantically to cut away from her and then looked pointedly in Neil's direction. Grinning behind the camera, Chuck obediently swung that way.

Neil's voice sounded choked when he answered, but with laughter or surprise, Dinah couldn't tell. "Sorry to disappoint you, Sarah," he said, "but at present, there are no plans for marriage."

"Does that mean there will be in the future?" Jessie asked eagerly.

This time when he replied, Dinah knew with certainty that he was laughing. "You'll have to ask Miss Blake about that."

Dinah glanced at him quickly, wondering why he had couched his reply in those terms. But he looked ingenuously back at her, and she had no choice but to turn to the group again.

"What Mr. Kerrigan means," she said firmly, "is that we're both too busy to get married right now—to anyone, least of all to each other."

"Aw, gee, that's too bad. Then you could do a show together."

"We are doing a show together," Dinah pointed out, trying to guide the conversation into a safer channel.

"No, I mean a weekly show."

Startled at the suggestion, and even more surprised at the quick thrill she felt at the thought of it, Dinah said quickly, "I'm afraid that would be impossible. You see, I live in San Francisco, and Mr. Kerrigan lives in Los Angeles—"

"But other couples live in different cities and work something out."

Wishing she had never agreed to this question-and-answer forum where she seemed to have become the subject of the interview, Dinah muttered something about that being a network decision, and stood, indicating that the session was over. Feeling that her smile was merely pasted on her face, she managed to escape a short while later with a little of her dignity intact, and her expression dared Neil to laugh when they finally climbed into the car.

But Neil seemed as preoccupied as she as they drove back to town, and they had almost reached the motel before he spoke. Glancing at his watch, he asked, "How about having dinner with me?"

"Tonight?" she asked faintly, and immediately came up with several reasons why she couldn't before she realized how ridiculous they would all sound. She had escaped yesterday with a manufactured excuse, but she couldn't avoid him forever. He'd begin to think that she didn't trust herself to be alone with him, and that was absurd. Just because she had lost a little control that one night didn't mean that it would happen again. Hadn't she insisted that their relationship be strictly professional from then on?

Neil certainly seemed to have taken her at her word. Except for those few teasing moments today, he'd been the perfect gentleman, the consummate professional, intent on his work, nothing else. And it was only dinner, after all, she reminded herself. What could possibly happen in a public place like a restaurant?

"All right," she agreed, hoping she sounded more calm than she felt. "But if you don't mind, I'd like to eat at the motel restaurant. I've got some reading to catch up on for tomorrow."

He glanced across the seat at her, and for an instant she was sure that he'd see through her transparent excuse for an quick escape and be amused. Instead, he said, "So do I. We'll make it an early night, okay?"

Contrarily, now that he'd been so agreeable, she felt disappointed. Wishing she'd make up her mind about what she wanted, she went directly to her room when they arrived at the motel and threw herself onto the bed. Staring up at the ceiling, she told herself that she couldn't have it both ways, but that rationalization didn't seem to help, either. Finally she dragged herself off the bed and went to take a bath before she got ready for dinner.

Dinah had always been careful about her appearance, even before she became something of a celebrity. But tonight as she debated what to wear, she realized that she was paying more attention to detail than usual, hesitating between a feminine, elegant paisley silk dress and the casual cinnamon-colored evening pants with a matching overblouse. Annoyed, she grabbed the pants outfit and then immediately threw it down on the bed. Snatching up the dress defiantly, she told herself that a dress was just a little more...dressy, that's all; it certainly didn't mean that she was trying to impress anybody.

But Dinah wasn't sure that was true as she took the elevator to the lobby and then headed in the direction of the restaurant. After seeing Neil at work these past few days, she was filled with even more conflicting emotions about him than before. He was like a chameleon, one minute the tough reporter, the next trading jokes with a group of teenagers or showing heartfelt compassion for a boy who'd been injured in an accident. The things he said seemed at odds sometimes with the things he did, and just when she was beginning to think that she knew him, he'd surprise her again.

Neil was waiting in the restaurant's foyer when she entered, his back to her as he studied an antique grape press on display. Her steps slowed when she saw him, and even before he sensed her presence and turned to look at her, her heart had begun to beat a little faster. He had dressed in a sport coat and slacks for the evening, but he wore those with the same casual elegance that he might have donned black tie and tails. Reminding herself again that she was in control of the situation, Dinah walked briskly up to him.

Neil's eyes lit with appreciation when he saw her, and suddenly she was glad she had chosen the dress after all. Graciously tilting her head in acknowledgment to his murmured compliment, she was dismayed to find her control slipping a little when he took her arm. Even that casual contact sent a thrill through her, and she deliberately moved in front of him as a gawking hostess led the way to their table.

"You certainly don't look as though you've spent the day fielding awkward questions from inquisitive teenagers," he said admiringly when they were seated.

"Thank you," she said lightly, "but I enjoyed it."

"I wasn't sure you did. You were so quiet on the way back."

"Was I?" she asked, and began to busily study the menu she'd been given. Why was it that even though she'd been with him all day, she still felt this tingling sense of anticipation? They were colleagues, she reminded herself firmly, nothing more, and on that thought, she put the menu down.

"You were quiet yourself," she said, hoping that if she kept the conversation safely on a business level, she wouldn't feel this subtle excitement every time she looked at him.

He shrugged. "You seemed so preoccupied I didn't want to bother you."

Dinah forced a laugh. She would have died before admitting that she'd been preoccupied with thoughts of him, so she said, "I was thinking the same thing about you."

The waiter came then, and after he had left, Dinah watched Neil in silence for a moment before she said, "You still seem preoccupied, Neil. Is something bothering you? Are you dissatisfied with our progress so far?"

He looked surprised. "Why do you ask that?"

"Well, you haven't said one way or the other, and I wondered if something was wrong. If there is, I think we should talk about it. It's not too late to change the thrust of the program, if you have another slant you want to take."

He shook his head. "No, no. I think it's going just fine. I was just thinking about Mark Delaney and his Get In Touch program."

Dinah smiled. "He's certainly achieved remarkable results, hasn't he?"

"Has he? It seems to me those kids were enjoying what amounted to a long holiday from responsibility."

Her smile faded. "How can you say that? They have to attend classes. They're required to help with the maintenance of the farm—"

"It's still a vacation," Neil said flatly. "What are they going to do when they have to return to reality?"

She was dismayed by his attitude. "They'll be better equipped to deal with their problems, for one thing."

"Do you really think so?"

Trying to quell her irritation, she replied, "Yes, I do."

"I hope you're right," he said, and then smiled suddenly, catching her off guard. "Let's not argue about it, shall we?" he said persuasively. "I have to admit that interviewing those kids today was an experience."

Dinah decided to let it go. She didn't want to quarrel with him, not when they'd been getting along so well, so she forced a smile and said, "You mean when they interviewed us."

He grinned. "That was cleverly done, wasn't it?"

"A little too clever, I think," Dinah said. "Some of them are going to make excellent investigative reporters. They certainly knew how to ask a leading question."

"Yes, like all that business about marriage."

Despite her irritation, Dinah felt her cheeks reddening. "Oh, that," she said, praying he wouldn't notice her sudden flush. "Well, of course, we both know how absurd that is."

"Of course."

The waiter mercifully appeared then, and Dinah silently blessed her foresight in ordering an entrée that required preparation at the table. She was aware of Neil watching her instead of the elaborate ceremony with chafing dishes and flames and various liquors, but she pretended to be enthralled with what the waiter was doing so that she could compose herself. Still disturbed by Neil's criticisms of the Get In Touch program, she couldn't imagine why his remark just now about marriage had unnerved her.

She'd been even more unnerved today when those teenagers had questioned her about her marital status. That seemingly innocent inquiry had caught her so off guard that she'd floundered for an answer when the obvious response would have been a simple denial. She should have laughed and turned it back with a joke that indicated her amusement at the thought that she and Neil were married.

But she hadn't done that, and she didn't know why. It wasn't as though she'd been secretly thinking about marriage—to anyone, least of all to Neil. Hadn't she already decided that any relationship with him, professional or otherwise, simply had no future?

"Is something wrong?"

Dinah started. "No. Why?"

"Well, you've hardly touched your dinner."

Surprised, Dinah looked down at their plates. She realized that Neil was finished, while she had barely taken a mouthful. "I guess I'm just not hungry."

"Any particular reason? Maybe you're the one who isn't happy with the progress we've made so far."

"Oh, no. I'm really pleased with the interviews we've done."

"Including the one today?" Neil asked with a smile.

Dinah forced a laugh. "Even that."

Suddenly serious, Neil leaned forward slightly. "You mentioned that some of those kids would make good investigative reporters, Dinah, but I don't think you're so bad yourself."

Taken aback by the compliment, she murmured, "Thank you."

"No, I mean it. You handled that police officer very well yesterday, and it was obvious that Dr. Mason would have turned the clinic inside out for you."

"Oh, I'm sure if you had been doing the interview, he would have made the same offer."

"I don't think so. You have an...effect on people."

Uncertain whether she had imagined that suddenly husky tone in his voice, Dinah wasn't sure how to respond. Laughing nervously, she said, "That's my job."

"I wasn't only talking about your job."

Slowly, she raised her eyes to his. When she saw his expression, she drew in a breath, wondering what was happening. The air seemed electric, and she wanted to say something to break this vibrating silence, but the words wouldn't come. She could only stare helplessly into those eyes, drawn into something that somehow seemed inevitable.

"Dinah..." he began, and stopped. Reaching across the table, he gently placed his hand over hers, holding it lightly, as if he was afraid she might snatch it away.

The touch sent a jolt through her. It took all her control not to turn her palm up and lace her fingers with his, but she knew if she did, she wouldn't be able to stop there. His face was only inches away from hers, and the power of those blue eyes was so compelling that she dropped her gaze to his mouth, that strong, sensual mouth that had once so briefly claimed hers. With an effort, she jerked her eyes away from that, too.

"Dinah, we have to talk about it," he said softly.

"There's nothing to talk about."

"I think there is. I can't go on pretending that that night never happened."

"Nothing happened that night!" she protested, and knew she was lying to herself, and to him, too. Something had happened, something so powerful that she knew she'd never be the same. "Nothing happened," she repeated almost fiercely.

His hand tightened over hers. "We both know that isn't true."

"It is!"

"Why don't you look at me, then?"

But she couldn't look at him because then he'd know that she'd never forgotten that night, either. She tried to pull her hand away, but he held it fast.

"I've tried, Dinah," he said hoarsely. "I've tried to keep our relationship strictly professional. I thought I could do it; I told myself I could. But that was before we started working together, seeing each other every day—"

"Neil, please!" she said desperately. "This is crazy!"

"Yes," he said harshly. "It is crazy. So why don't we do something about it?"

She did look at him then, and instantly knew it had been a mistake. She had seen many expressions on his face before, but she had never seen this pleading look in his eyes, and it was her undoing. He wanted her as much as she wanted him, and it was foolish to pretend otherwise.

As if in a daze, she got to her feet. Neil scrawled his name across the check, and then they were walking out of the restaurant toward the elevator. When he took her arm, she wasn't surprised to discover that he was trembling as badly as she.

CHAPTER NINE

NEIL'S ROOM WAS IN SEMIDARKNESS when they entered, illuminated through the open window by the lights from the pool below. The movement of the water cast wavering shadows on the walls and the ceiling, giving the room an almost ethereal atmosphere that was enhanced by the scent of the after-shave he had used. The tangy fragrance filled Dinah's nostrils, conjuring up images of him standing with only a towel wrapped around his waist after a steamy shower, and when she felt him reach for the light switch, she grasped his arm.

"Not yet..." she murmured. She wanted to enjoy this intimate, scented darkness and the fantasies it evoked.

But Neil wasn't a fantasy. His hands were very real when he placed them on her shoulders; she could feel him beginning to tremble again with the same rising emotion she felt. His face was in shadow when she looked up at him, the strong planes and angles softened by the flickering light from the pool. But his eyes weren't soft at all. They burned in that half light as he gazed down at her.

"Tell me now," he said huskily. "Because if I kiss you again, I won't be able to stop...."

She looked up at him, realizing that she'd been waiting for this moment, been denying the power of her attraction to him, denying her need...and her desire. Because she now knew that, having had a taste of what could be between them, she had yearned for more. He had possessed her thoughts; he had invaded her dreams; he had become a presence in her life even when they were apart.

And now that this moment had come, she couldn't remember why she'd had any doubts about him; she couldn't recall the things they'd argued about. Suddenly they all seemed insignificant.

"Kiss me, then," she whispered, and raised her arms to wind around his neck. "Because I never want you to stop...."

A low moan escaped him, but still he held back, his hands moving to her waist to hold her slightly away from him, as if he was afraid to get too close. "Are you sure?" he choked. "We won't be able to go back...."

Smiling, she drew his head down to hers.

There was nothing tentative about the first touch of his lips. It was as though all the pent-up longing and desire burst in him at once, and he abandoned himself totally to the sensation. Dinah responded in kind, returning the pressure of his mouth fiercely, pressing against him even as he tightened his arms around her. A flame lit inside her, fanned instantly to a raging blaze, and so powerful was that first coming together that they both swayed.

Then Neil was kissing her even more deeply, his tongue exploring her willing mouth, his hands hot against her back as he held her pliant body to his. When he brought one of his hands up to caress her throat, and then down, into the V of her dress, she wanted to rip the garment off. The silk seemed to rasp against her skin, a barrier between them when she was longing to tear down the walls that had kept them apart. Her hands shaking, she pushed his sport coat off his shoulders and to the floor, then slid her fingers between the buttons on his shirt to the warm flesh underneath.

He uttered a sound deep in his throat when she slowly began to undo the buttons, one by one, until finally the shirt fell to the floor, as well. Her fingers splayed against his skin, she kneaded the hard muscles that contracted as he tightened his arms around her again.

"My God, woman. What you do to me..." he groaned, and buried his face in the sweet fragrance of her hair.

His chest was smooth under her lips, and she had the fleeting thought that she was glad. She had never liked hirsute men, and this tanned, glorious body of his was as smooth and hard as a youth's. But it was no youth who put a hand in her hair and gently pulled her head back to look at him. Neil kissed the fluttering pulse in the hollow of her throat. The sensation was so exquisite that she arched away from him, her head falling back even farther, her eyes closing as she abandoned herself to his seeking mouth and hands.

As if it were tissue, her dress whispered to the floor. The breeze from the open window caressed her tingling skin, and then she felt his lips on the swell of her breasts and she arched even higher as he pulled away the lacy wisp of her bra. His tongue encircled one swollen nipple and then the other, and the renewed fierceness of her desire for him made her weak. Legs trembling, she pressed against him, and the sensation of her bare breasts against his chest was torture.

"Oh, Neil..." she moaned, clinging to him. She could feel the hardness of him against her thigh, feel the response of her own body to his in the rush of moist heat that erupted at that contact, and she moaned again. She lifted his head to hers, and mouths locked hungrily once more, they fell onto the bed.

As his weight pressed her down, Dinah thought that she had made love before but never like this, never with such fierce hunger or intensity. It seemed that every nerve in her body was exposed; wherever he touched her he left behind a burning, aching desire to be touched there again. Almost frenziedly, she ran her hands over his chest, down to his belt, which she unbuckled, and then below. He groaned as she cupped him in her hand, and with one quick movement, he pulled away her lacy bikini panties and then stood to shed the rest of his clothes.

The flickering kaleidoscope of reflected light from the pool illuminated his body as he paused to look down at her, and Dinah's lips unconsciously parted as she stared at him. He seemed to be that bronze statue of the Roman warrior she had seen once, now come to life, and her breath caught. She drank in the proud lift of his head, the virile stance of his body, the quintessential maleness of him. When he made a move to join her again, she sat up.

"Wait..." she whispered, and came to him.

Kneeling, her head was level with his broad chest. He drew in a sharp breath as she pressed against him, her breasts against his flat belly, running her hands down his back to his tight buttocks, to the strong thighs whose muscles quivered at her touch. Pulling back a little, her lips followed the valley of muscle down his torso, and she took him in her hand again, aroused even more at the throbbing evidence of his desire for her. When she looked up again, his eyes were afire.

"Dinah..." he choked, and buried his hands in her hair. Uttering a helpless sound, he bore her backward to the bed, spreading her legs with his thigh, cupping one breast in his hand, reaching down with the other to caress the pulsing valley between her thighs.

His touch aroused her to fever, and she wrapped her legs around him, almost desperately seeking release from the excruciating desire he had evoked. She was bombarded with sensation: his hand kneading one breast, his tongue moving over the nipple of the other, was torture of the sweetest kind. She raised his head to claim his hot, seeking mouth with her own. Her hips began to move in the unconscious, ancient rhythm of all living things in the heat of passion, and Neil groaned again. She arched upward as he slid his hands under her, cupping her buttocks, bearing down with the weight of his body, a weight she no longer felt.

"You're incredible," he gasped, but Dinah barely heard him. Her body was no longer her own; she was possessed by him, filled with him, being swept away by such a flood of sensation that she could no longer hold back. Pleasure began as a pinpoint, expanded swiftly and then exploded inside her.

He cried out at the same time, his own body straining as he went with her, shuddering with the force of that exquisite release. They clung mindlessly to each other as the waves battered them, until eventually the last wave receded with a quivering sigh and they collapsed in exhaustion.

Some endless time later, when Dinah was still drifting in that luxurious aftermath, Neil lifted his head. "Am I too heavy for you?"

Dinah opened her eyes. His face was only inches from her own, and she smiled at his faintly anxious expression. "What do you think?"

He laughed softly and kissed the tip of her nose. "I don't think we should have waited so long. If I'd known it would be as glorious as this, I would have ravished you the moment I met you."

He was still lying on top of her, and she ran her hands lightly down his back. "Ah, yes, but anticipation has its own reward, don't you think?"

"To hell with anticipation," he said, and lowered his head to nuzzle her breast. "I believe in action...."

"I can see that," she murmured, feeling the evidence of his arousal growing inside her again. Running her tongue around the curve of his ear, she whispered, "Second time's the charm."

His lips were warm and soft, exploring hers. "You mean the third time..."

"That too," she answered, and laughed at his expression before he rolled to his side, pressing his length against her, holding her close to him.

The contact of his body excited her; she lifted her lips to his. But instead of kissing her, he began to whisper of the sensations she was causing in him and the ways in which he wanted her.

His hands and mouth began to rove over her body, gently at first, and then with increasing passion as she responded with caresses of her own. Deliberately prolonging the anticipation, he spoke of the soft fullness of her breasts and how smooth her skin felt under his mouth; kissing her eyelids, he told her how beautiful her eyes were. He whispered things she had never heard from a man before, and with each word, with every touch of his lips, they both began to tremble with desire, until finally neither of them knew which had inflamed them more, the murmured words he spoke or the responses of their own flesh.

She hadn't believed it could be better the second time, but it was—for both of them. With words and touches and caresses, he took her to heights she had never attained before, and this time it was she who cried out in glorious abandon at the last. He came with her, and she laughed exultantly as he surrendered, too, to that exquisite, indescribable sensation that had fallen like an avalanche, claiming them both.

When Dinah finally opened her eyes, Neil was lying beside her, one arm flung across his eyes. His breathing still ragged, he muttered, "What happened?"

Dinah laughed as she nestled close to him. "You tell me. You're the man of action."

He groaned. "That was before you got a hold of me."

"You weren't so bad yourself."

"What time is it, anyway?"

"Why, do you have a date?" she asked with a grin, and looked toward the beside clock. It was then that she saw the red light on the phone. "Did you know you had a message?"

"No, and I don't care. If it's important, they'll call back."

"Maybe they did and we didn't hear it."

He raised his head to look at her. Returning her grin, he said, "We were a little preoccupied, I admit."

"You'd better see what it is."

"Now?"

Still lying atop his chest, she reached over and lifted the receiver. Handing it to him, she said, "Now."

With a mock glare, he took the phone. "You're a hard woman, Dinah Blake," he muttered as he dialed the desk.

"You didn't seem to mind a few minutes ago," she teased.

"That was when..." He was interrupted as the desk clerk answered, and Dinah was dismayed when she saw him frown. "I see," he said, and hung up the phone again. "I knew I shouldn't have answered that," he muttered. "It's a message from Elise."

"Is something wrong?"

"I don't know," he answered, sounding annoyed. "She says it's urgent, but with Elise, you never know. Wait a minute. Where are you going?"

Dinah had started to get out of bed. "I thought you'd like some privacy."

Sliding across the bed, he put an arm around her waist and nuzzled her back. "I'll call her later," he murmured.

Dinah closed her eyes against the tingling sensations his mouth produced as his lips left her shoulder and pressed against the nape of her neck. "She said it was urgent," she reminded him, her breath catching as he reached up to fondle her breast.

"With Elise, that could mean anything from a broken faucet to an outbreak of war," he said, and began tracing the curve of her spine with slight brushes of his lips that made Dinah shiver. "You have the most beautiful back," he said huskily.

Suddenly Dinah didn't care whether his call was urgent or not. Aroused by his caresses, she started to turn toward him. "And you..." she began, and was interrupted by the chiming of the phone.

"Ignore it," he said, pulling her toward him.

But the phone was impossible to ignore. Neil swore on the fourth ring and, holding Dinah with one arm, snatched the receiver, barking a hello. Lying next to him, Dinah watched his eyes darken.

"Damn it, Elise," he said abruptly. "I just got in."

Not wanting to listen to his conversation with his ex-wife, Dinah started edging toward the side of the bed. His ear to the receiver, Neil gestured at her, indicating that he wanted her to stay, but she shook her head. The mood was definitely broken now, and she was just buttoning her dress when he bolted upright in the bed, shouting, "He did *what*?"

Dinah was so startled that she said quickly, "What is it?"

He made a just-a-minute gesture, listening intently to whatever Elise was telling him. After a moment, his face grim, he demanded, "Were they hurt?"

Alarmed, Dinah sat down on the edge of the bed, her high-heeled sandals in her hand. She knew she should quietly leave, but something in Neil's expression held her there, and she waited anxiously, wondering what had happened. When Neil's expression changed from one of concern to anger, she didn't know whether to be relieved or not.

"That's impossible," he said curtly to Elise after listening a moment more. "I'm on assignment—"

Whatever Elise replied to that seemed to anger him even more. "I can't just drop what I'm doing right now! Besides, he has school. What about that?"

Dinah knew it was time to leave. Slipping her heels on, she was searching for her purse when Neil said furiously, "Of course I think this is important enough for him to miss a few classes! Send him up here then, but warn him that he's going to have some explaining to do when he gets here!"

The phone crashed down as she was retrieving her bag from behind a chair where she had heedlessly dropped it. She turned questioningly as Neil cursed again and snatched a robe from the foot of the tangled bedclothes. "Damn kids!" he muttered.

"Is Andy all right?" she asked in concern.

"I told her not to buy him that damned car!"

Alarmed again, she blurted, "Andy was in a car accident?"

He looked at her furiously, as if she were responsible. "Yes," he said curtly. "He and a friend of his were out joyriding. *Joyriding!* They're lucky they didn't kill themselves."

"Were either of them hurt?"

He ran a hand through his hair, obviously trying to control himself. But his voice still shook with fury when he said, "Not a scratch."

"Thank God!"

"It would have served them both right if they'd ended up in the hospital!"

She was shocked. "Oh, Neil, you don't mean that."

"Yes, I do," he shouted. "To think that a son of mine—"

She could see that he was working himself into an even greater state of rage, and so she said quickly, "Calm down, Neil."

"Calm down! My son rolls a brand-new Corvette with another person in the car and you tell me to calm down?"

"I just meant . . ."

There was a wet bar in one corner of the room, stocked with bottles and ice and glasses. He went to it and poured himself a stiff shot. "I think you'd better leave," he said without turning around.

"Neil . . ."

He did look at her then, his eyes so cold that she actually shrank back. He saw her recoil and made an effort to apologize, saying harshly, "I'm sorry. I'm just not good company right now."

"I understand—"

"Do you?" He took a swallow of the drink. "Well, it's beyond my comprehension!"

"He's young, Neil. It was a mistake."

His expression became even more grim. "A mistake he's not going to have a chance to repeat, that's for sure."

"Neil—"

He looked at her fiercely. "I don't want to discuss it anymore."

Dinah saw that it was futile to talk to him now. He was upset; he had every right to be. But his attitude was so harsh and unyielding that she despaired. What had happened to the closeness they had experienced only a short while before? Why wouldn't he just share his feelings with her?

Wondering if their intimacy had only been an illusion, Dinah said a quiet goodbye and went down the hall to her own room, fighting tears. Throwing herself onto the bed, she pressed her hands over her eyes.

How could things have gone so wrong? It didn't make sense; it wasn't fair.

Angrily brushing the tears away from her cheeks, Dinah sat up. Fair or not, she couldn't spend the rest of the night crying over a foolish mistake, which was exactly what it had been. She'd believed that there was more between them than physical attraction, but it was obvious she'd been wrong. If he could shut her out so easily, it was clear that she'd been willing to invest more in their relationship than he'd been, and she wasn't going to put herself through a situation like that again. She knew from bitter experience how difficult it was to mix marriage and a career, and without communication, it was impossible. So if Neil was too private a man to share his thoughts and feelings with her, there was just no future for them.

Writhing at that last thought, Dinah grabbed one of the pillows and clutched it tightly. The sensations he had evoked in her tonight flooded her mind until her entire body felt flushed. She had never been made love to like that. It was something out of a fantasy, a dream. The thought that she'd never feel his lips on hers again, or know the sure touch of his hands, or feel the fire of his body, was devastating.

But she couldn't allow what had taken place tonight to happen again. She had to be on her guard against it because despite all her rationalizations, she was still dangerously close to becoming involved with him. She couldn't give her heart only to have it crushed once more; she'd been through enough pain and disillusionment to last a lifetime. When she saw him tomorrow, she'd pretend that this night had just been a fleeting thing, brought on, perhaps, by too much wine. She could carry it off if she had to; all she had to do was think of her career. She'd be business-like and professional, as she had vowed before, and Neil would never know how much it was costing her to close her mind and her heart to him.

DINAH FELT HAGGARD and exhausted when she went down to the motel coffee shop the next morning for breakfast. Not surprisingly, she hadn't slept well, and she'd had to spend extra time in front of the mirror repairing the damage before she left her room. Thankfully, Neil wasn't there when she arrived, and she took a table at the far end of the room, ordering coffee as she began to read the material she'd ne-glected the night before. They had several interviews scheduled today, and she forced herself to concen-trate. The last thing she wanted was to be ill-prepared; she couldn't allow Neil to suspect how much last night affected her.

But the lines blurred again and again before her eyes, and finally she just closed the folder. How was she going to get through this day and the ones follow-ing when she felt like bursting into tears every time she thought of Neil?

"Do you mind if I join you?"

There was no mistaking that deep voice, and she forced herself to look up at its owner. She'd wanted more time to prepare herself for this first meeting, but when she saw Neil standing there, looking down at her with a somber expression, she knew that years wouldn't have made any difference. Her heart had leaped at the sound of his voice, and when she saw the shadows under his eyes, she wasn't surprised. Ob-viously he hadn't slept well, either, but she wasn't so foolish to think that had anything to do with her.

Longing to ask about Andy, she said instead, "Please do," and managed a faint smile. "I wanted to talk to you anyway, about the appointments we—"

"There's something I'd like to say first, if I may."

Instantly wary, she nodded. "All right."

He leaned forward, his eyes suddenly bleak. "I acted like a jerk last night, and I'm sorry."

Dinah didn't know what to say. She hadn't expected him to apologize, and she was caught off guard. "Oh . . . well . . ." she said faintly. "I know you were worried about Andy."

"That's no excuse. I shouldn't have said any of those things. I don't know why I did. You were only trying to help."

"No, you were right," she said, willing herself not to be moved by the expression in his eyes or the fact that he genuinely seemed to be sorry. His hand rested on the table, and remembering the things his hands had done to her last night, she jerked her glance away and said, "It was none of my business. Now, about these interviews—"

"Dinah. . . ."

She faltered to a stop at the way he spoke her name. The word held such longing and regret that despite her resolve, she couldn't help but be affected by it. "Neil, please," she said, and hoped she didn't sound as desperate as she felt. "We really don't need to discuss it anymore. As far as I'm concerned, it . . . it never happened."

His eyes held hers. "And last night?" he said softly. "Do we pretend that never happened, either?"

"Last night was a mistake," she said unevenly, and tried to distract herself by taking a sip of coffee. Horrified when her hand started shaking so badly that some of the coffee sloshed out of the cup, she hastily put it down.

Without comment, Neil handed her a napkin. Their hands touched as she took it, and she despised herself when she felt the impulse to twine her fingers with his. What had happened to all those firm promises to herself last night? Was she so weak-willed that she couldn't even remember them in the light of day? Was even the fact that he was sitting opposite her enough to make her forget all her resolve?

Apparently it was, for when he looked at her again, her heart turned over. "I am sorry, Dinah," he said softly. "I didn't intend for the evening to end that way."

Summoning every ounce of control, she returned his glance. "Perhaps it's best that it did. I thought we had agreed—"

A movement at the corner of her eye caught her attention just then, and she looked up. Startled to see someone standing a few feet away, waiting for a break in the conversation before he interrupted them, she exclaimed, "Andy!"

The teenager came forward, his face pale as he glanced at his father, who was just turning around to look at him. "Hello, Miss Blake," he said nervously. And then, "Dad?"

Dinah glanced quickly at Neil. Seeing the ominous darkening of his expression as he looked at his son, she began to gather her things. "Excuse me," she murmured. "I think I'd better leave you two alone."

"Please don't go, Miss Blake!" Andy blurted.

"Well, I don't think—"

"Maybe you'd better stay," Neil said, obviously trying to control himself. "We might need a referee."

"Oh, Neil, I really—"

"It wasn't my fault, Dad!" Andy cried just then. His voice was so high-pitched with nervousness that it rang out in the coffee shop and several heads turned their way. Andy didn't notice; he was too intent on explaining to his glowering father. "It wasn't my fault, honest! I wasn't even driving, Gary was. He said he'd be careful, but ... but ..."

"Sit down," Neil commanded, and before Dinah could move out of the way, Andy had leaped to obey. He slid into the booth beside her, effectively blocking any escape, and she closed her eyes briefly, wishing she was anyplace but here.

"Dad, please listen to me," Andy begged.

Neil's expression became even more grim. "I'm listening. But first I want to know how you got here. You were supposed to call when your flight got in. Your mother and I agreed I'd pick you up at the airport."

"I didn't want to bother you, so I took an express bus and then a cab," Andy said anxiously. "Look, Dad, I didn't even want to come here. I know you're working, and I told Mom I'd only be in the way."

"You're never in the way," Neil said heavily.

"But I know how busy you are ..."

Dinah's glance traveled from Neil's face to Andy's and back again as they talked. The resemblance between them was uncanny, but as Andy earnestly tried to convince his father of his innocence in the joyriding incident, Dinah began to realize that while their physical characteristics were so similar, their personalities appeared entirely different. Andy seemed much more open with his feelings, far less stubborn in his outlook, and after listening to him for a few moments, Dinah wasn't sure that was totally due to his youth.

Unwillingly, her glance strayed to Neil again, and she couldn't help wondering if Neil had always been so harsh and demanding or if something had happened to make him so mistrustful of his feelings, so determined to hide behind that protective wall.

An image of him talking to Dean Mathews flashed into her mind just then, and she remembered thinking that day that she was seeing a glimpse of the man Neil kept so hidden. He'd been gentle and compassionate with that boy; he hadn't even remotely resembled the stern and unyielding man he was today. Which was the real Neil Kerrigan?

"I didn't even want that car, Dad," Andy was saying desperately as Dinah came out of her reverie. "But I couldn't hurt Mom's feelings, could I? Jeez, I didn't know what to do!"

"So playing chicken on the highway was your way of resolving the problem?"

Andy winced at that. "I told you I wasn't driving, Dad. If I'd known that Gary was going to...to..."

"You could have both been killed."

Cringing again at his father's tone, Andy stared down at his hands. His voice low, he said, "I know. I promise it won't happen again."

Neil still wasn't ready to forgive him. "I should think not," he said evenly. "Since you totaled the damned car."

Andy's head sank even lower on his shoulders at that, and he looked so woebegone that Dinah felt sorry for him. She almost said something to comfort him, but she didn't dare intrude. This was a private matter and she shouldn't even be present. Wishing again that she had escaped before Andy had boxed her in, she dared a glance in Neil's direction.

Neil didn't see Dinah looking at him. He was regarding his son's bowed head with a mixture of exasperation and relief. He'd been furious last night; the thought that his son could have been killed because of his foolishness enraged him, and he hadn't realized until Dinah had gone that his anger hadn't been directed at Andy, but at himself. When Elise had called and told him about the accident, his first reaction had been a paralyzing fear. An image of that boy in the clinic had flashed into his mind, and he'd pictured Andy in the same condition. Then, when Elise had told him that both boys were unhurt, he'd felt a terrible guilt. He'd blamed himself because he hadn't been there to make sure that things like that didn't happen, and he'd been angry because he felt he'd failed Andy somehow.

Now, seeing how sorry Andy was, how anxiously contrite, he couldn't be angry with him any longer. By some miracle, Andy had escaped, and the wave of love he felt for his son made him want to reach out and touch the boy's tousled hair.

But he couldn't make himself do that, and so he said gruffly, "I hope you've learned your lesson."

Andy looked up. "I have, Dad," he said fervently. "And I'll...I'll pay for the car out of my allowance."

Neil couldn't prevent a smile at that. If he held Andy to his promise, the boy would be paying for that car the rest of his life. "I think it will be sufficient if you pay what the insurance doesn't cover."

Andy's face cleared. "Thanks, Dad!"

Neil had to give one last warning. "But no more joyriding."

"No, sir!" Andy promised vehemently, and then grinned. "Have you had breakfast yet? I'm starved!"

So they ordered, Dinah just having a refill on her coffee, amazed at the quantity of food a famished teenage boy could put away. As Andy polished off a second order of pancakes drowning in syrup and butter, her eyes met Neil's across the table in shared amusement, and she was glad she'd been forced to stay.

Then she realized that nothing had changed. Neil had apologized to her, but he was still the same man as he'd been the night before, and even an apology couldn't change that.

"Andy," Neil said, and then paused while his son signaled the waitress to bring him a piece of apple pie with ice cream. Gazing disbelievingly at Andy as he began to eat that as if starved, he went on. "Dinah and I have some appointments today, but we're ahead of schedule, and I think I can manage a day off tomorrow. How would you like to go skiing?"

Andy paused with a forkful of pie halfway to his mouth. "Skiing? That would be great! But are you sure you can take the time?"

Neil glanced at Dinah inquiringly. Seeing the rapturous expression on Andy's face, she couldn't refuse, and so she laughed. "I can manage by myself tomorrow. We only had some street interviews scheduled anyway."

"But you have to come with us!" Andy exclaimed, sounding dismayed. He turned to his father again. "Doesn't she, Dad?"

"Oh, no," Dinah said quickly, before Neil could reply. "I—"

"Why? Don't you ski?" Andy asked anxiously.

"Well, yes, but—"

"Then you have to come. It wouldn't be fair if we went and you didn't. Isn't that right, Dad?"

Neil nodded solemnly. "That's right. If Dinah doesn't go, I guess we shouldn't, either."

Neatly boxed in again, Dinah gave Neil a quelling look. He knew as well as she did that if she refused now, Andy would be crushed. But when she thought of being alone with Neil at a ski lodge, she knew she'd never be able to trust herself. She wouldn't put herself in that position, and she was just starting to make some excuse when Andy turned to her again.

"Oh, please, Miss Blake," he said pleadingly.

How could she refuse after that? Gazing into those deep blue eyes so like his father's, Dinah knew she was doomed. Sighing, she nodded, and then had to smile when Andy gave a whoop of delight and ordered another piece of pie.

CHAPTER TEN

DINAH HAD ALWAYS LOVED Lake Tahoe—the area was such a beautiful ski resort.

"Wow!" Andy exclaimed, leaning over the back seat as they crossed the summit and caught their first glimpse of the magnificent lake. "That's really something!"

"Haven't you been here before?" Dinah asked, pleased at his reaction because she always felt that way herself.

"No, we usually ski Mammoth, or sometimes Aspen or Vail," Andy answered, and added, "when Dad can take the time."

"Which isn't as often as I'd like," Neil said regretfully. "I don't think we've been skiing since last year, have we, son?"

Andy shook his head, and Dinah smiled. "Well, don't feel alone in that crowd," she said. "I'm probably so rusty I'll have to stay on the bunny slopes the whole time."

"Somehow I doubt that," Neil said dryly. "Didn't you compete when you were in your teens?"

Dinah looked at him in astonishment. "How did you know about that?"

He smiled. "I told you I had a good research department."

"Did you really compete, Dinah?" Andy asked eagerly. "Did you win anything?"

"Only in the slalom and the downhill," Neil said with another smile.

"Jeez!"

Slightly embarrassed by the reverence in Andy's voice, Dinah laughed. "That was a long time ago, Andy. And I just ski for fun now."

"Why didn't you go into the Olympics?"

"Oh, I don't know," Dinah said lightly, remembering how torn she'd been. The choice had been either to dedicate herself to a sport that might not yield her anything or opt for college. She knew she wouldn't be able to do both, and she'd agonized over her decision for months. "I finally decided I'd rather get my degree."

"Are you sorry now?" Andy asked curiously.

"No," Dinah answered, and knew she wasn't. The choice had been right for her, and now she was competitive in a different way.

Andy was silent after that, and Dinah was preoccupied herself as they drove into the South Shore. They'd heard on the car radio that the skiing was good, and Dinah promised herself that she'd spend so much time on the slopes that she'd be too tired tonight to do anything but fall asleep.

She'd been acutely aware of Neil sitting just across from her during the entire drive, and even though she'd vowed to keep her distance, she could still feel that powerful attraction. It had been a mistake to come, she thought gloomily, and wished that Chuck and Larry hadn't been so enthusiastic about having a day off. If they had offered even a token protest, she would have had an excuse to stay behind. But they'd been thrilled at the opportunity to try out the numerous golf courses around Willowset and had practically pushed her into the car.

So now here she was with Neil and his son. She'd hoped that Andy's presence would distract her from his father, but it hadn't worked that way. She was still sensitive to every nuance in Neil's voice, alert to every shade of his smile, and when once he had reached across the seat to touch her casually on the arm, she'd had to force herself not to return the slight pressure of his fingers.

It was hopeless, she thought, and felt utterly depressed as they finally pulled up at the giant hotel where Neil had made reservations.

But an hour later, after they had registered and changed into the ski attire they'd all hastily bought for the trip, Dinah began to feel exhilarated. Even though it was already late afternoon and they'd only have time for a few runs, actually being on the slopes again after such a long absence immediately lifted her spirits.

The snow glittered in the sunlight, the air was crisp and clean, and she smiled to herself as she and Neil rode up in the chair lift together. Andy was in the chair in front of them, and as they were drawn smoothly up the mountainside, he turned and waved so vigorously that the chair began to sway. As he turned around again and began swinging his skis to make the chair sway even more, Dinah laughed and commented that he looked like he was already having a good time.

Neil smiled fondly at his son's back. "He loves to ski. It's a shame we can't do it more often."

"He was thrilled when you let him have a room by himself," she said, and then winced inwardly. She'd promised herself that she wouldn't read anything into that, but as soon as she'd said it aloud, she wondered why Neil hadn't insisted Andy stay with him.

"I thought he'd get a kick out of it," Neil replied calmly, and then looked at her. "Is your room all right?"

"It's fine," Dinah replied dryly, thinking of the huge round bed and the heart-shaped Jacuzzi. There was even a television set mounted on the wall in the bathroom and a phone extension in case she felt like making a few calls while she luxuriated in the bath. "I feel like visiting royalty."

"You've been working hard on this project. I thought you deserved it." He hesitated, and then asked, "Are you glad you came?"

Dinah looked over the sparkling expanse of snow, at the pine trees whose boughs were laden with great puffs and then down at the few intrepid skiers who had dared this advanced run. The lift was so high above them that they seemed like colorful dolls skimming along. She looked at Neil again and knew he was waiting intently for her answer.

"I didn't want to," she admitted finally. "I know you don't see Andy as often as you'd like, and with a third person along..."

"Andy wouldn't have invited you if he didn't want you here," Neil pointed out with a smile. "In fact, as I recall, he was rather insistent. I think you've made a conquest."

"Oh, you know boys at that age," she said lightly, and wondered why she suddenly felt self-conscious. Was it because that wasn't quite the conquest she would have preferred to make?

"Andy's not your only admirer, you know," he said casually, as Dinah's heart gave a great leap. "Chuck and Larry seem to have fallen under your spell, too."

Dinah hid her disappointment by becoming angry with herself. Had she actually hoped that Neil would confess that he'd become even more entranced than his son? She made some noncommittal remark and was relieved to see that they had arrived at the summit. As they prepared to leave the chair, she sensed Neil was watching her, and she distracted herself by waving gaily at Andy.

Andy returned the gesture with a grin and a lift of his ski poles. "Last one down buys cocoa!" he shouted, and was off.

Laughing, Dinah and Neil exchanged glances. "Are you up to this?" he asked.

Dinah's chin lifted. "Try me!" she said, and dug the tips of the poles hard into the packed snow.

Neil caught up to her seconds later, and as they started down the steep slopes, Dinah laughed in sheer delight when he stayed with her. Side by side they skied that treacherous mountain, and they weren't halfway down before Dinah knew it was going to be one of those rare things, a perfect run. Glancing behind her, she saw that the tracks made by their skis were absolutely parallel even through the turns, and when she gestured to Neil and he saw it, too, they both laughed again and tucked deeper for even greater speed.

They skied like that all the way down, and it was as though they moved with one mind, one body, tied together by an invisible cord. She never noticed when they passed Andy; she didn't care who won. With the wind whistling in her ears and Neil by her side, she wanted that run to last forever.

It was over too soon. Ending in a flying spray of snow just inches from the racks of skis stacked in front of the lodge, Dinah whipped off her wraparound glasses and cried exultantly, "It's a tie!"

Neil didn't answer. She looked his way and saw him hunched over his ski poles, gasping. He looked as if he was about to collapse.

"Neil!" she cried, and kicked off her skis so that she could run over to him. Pulling off her gloves, she grasped his shoulder. "Neil, what's the matter? Are you hurt?"

He grabbed her then, and they both fell into a snowbank, his weight on top of her. Thoroughly frightened now, she tried to lift his head. "Neil! Answer me! Are you..."

Then she realized he was laughing. Pulling off his glasses, she saw the merriment in his eyes and said accusingly, "I thought you were hurt!"

"Only my pride," he gasped, still breathing hard from exertion. "I thought for a while there you were going to beat me."

Embarrassed that she'd fallen for his trick, she tried to struggle out from under him. He was too heavy for her, and she looked up at him as haughtily as she could under the circumstances. "Well, I could have, if I'd tried."

His grin broadened. "I'd rather you didn't, if you don't mind. You almost gave me a heart attack, woman."

And suddenly, with the way he said that last word, the atmosphere changed. They both became aware that he was lying full-length on top of her, and even through the quilted ski clothing each wore, the contact was achingly intimate. Dinah looked up into the eyes that were so close to hers, and when she saw the desire he couldn't hide, her entire body seemed to come alive. It seemed forever before he lowered his head and kissed her.

Despite the late-afternoon chill, his lips were warm as they touched hers, and without volition, her own lips parted. Raising one hand as their kiss deepened, she buried her fingers in his hair, holding his head to hers.

A self-conscious cough from somewhere above them made her eyes fly open, and when she saw Andy standing there, she was mortified. Instantly struggling to a sitting position, she pushed Neil away and said faintly, "Andy..."

Andy grinned as they both got to their feet. Saluting them with a ski pole, he started for the chair lift again, but couldn't resist turning back. "I guess that's better than a cup of hot chocolate, huh, Dad?" he said, and sped away toward the lift before Neil could grab him.

They made two more runs before the lifts closed for the night, both Dinah and Neil being careful to include Andy as they skied at a more leisurely pace. Halfway through the last run, Dinah stopped on the crest of a hill to watch Neil and his son weave their way down the slopes, and as her eyes followed the streak of midnight blue that was Neil, she knew that whatever happened between them in the future, she would always remember that first exhilarating run.

She had never felt so close to him as she had then, not even when they'd made love. They had experienced a meeting of the minds on that run; it was as though they were so attuned to each other's thoughts that without even touching, they had moved as one.

Why were moments like that so fleeting and so rare, always so tantalizingly out of reach? She almost wished that it had never happened, because now, having glimpsed the way it could be, she felt bereft. She knew she'd never experience that profound closeness with Neil again. Too many obstacles stood in the way for them, and once they left this sparkling white paradise, reality would intrude. They'd be on opposite sides once more, driven by their differing goals, preoccupied with separate ambitions. Neil would go his way and she'd go hers, and when—or if—they met again, that perfect moment they'd experienced would only be a memory.

She realized that Andy and Neil had stopped to look back, obviously wondering what had happened to her. With a determined effort, Dinah shook off her sudden depression and made herself wave gaily, as though she'd just stopped to catch her breath.

"Are you all right?" Neil asked when she caught up to them.

Grateful for the dark glasses that hid her eyes, Dinah forced a laugh. "Of course. I just wanted to watch you two hotdog it down the hill."

Andy laughed at that, obviously pleased that she'd been watching his form. Dinah glanced at him, frowning slightly when she realized his form had been a little erratic on this last run. Then she dismissed it. He was probably showing off for them, even though his exuberance had caused him to take a bad spill a few minutes ago. He'd bounced up unhurt, laughing when she'd asked him if he was all right, and he certainly seemed to be as he skied off now.

Realizing that Neil was looking at her questioningly, Dinah summoned a smile before she skied after

Andy. When they got back to the hotel, she refused
Neil's offer of a hot rum, escaping to her room with
the excuse that she had to have a nap before they met
for dinner.

Finally alone, Dinah took off her heavy ski clothes
and put on a robe. But even though she was tired, she
was too restless to lie down, so she started a fire in the
stone fireplace and curled up on the hearth. Gazing
vacantly into the growing flames, she tried to tell herself there was no reason to feel so disheartened. She
knew she'd made the right decision not to become
emotionally involved with Neil, but it seemed now that
deciding that and carrying it out were two entirely
different things. When he'd kissed her today, she'd
totally forgotten all her promises to herself; the instant his lips touched hers, she had forgotten everything but him. What had happened to all her resolve?

Suddenly she wondered why it was so important to
her. What was so wrong with having an affair with a
man who attracted her? Who would it hurt?

But she knew who would be hurt, and the knowledge depressed her again. Besides, she just wasn't the
kind of woman who engaged in casual sex, no matter
how attracted she was. The idea of making the most
of a torrid affair until it inevitably fizzled disgusted
her, and she'd never been able to understand women
who expected no more from a man than what his body
could give them.

Neil had never indicated that he wanted anything
more than a physical relationship with her, and if she
surrendered to her own attraction to him, she would
have to accept the consequences. Was she prepared to
do that, knowing the heartache that would inevitably
follow?

Resting her forehead on her drawn-up knees, Dinah almost thought she would accept it. She wanted him; she couldn't deny it. Whenever he looked at her, or smiled at her, or touched her, even in the most casual way, it was as though she had no will of her own; he seemed to have cast some spell upon her.

But wanting Neil and having him were not the same. If they had nothing more between them than desire, their passion would inevitably die, and she would be left with nothing but the bitter knowledge of what a fool she had been. Was she willing to accept that, too?

Lifting her head again, she stared somberly at the leaping flames. Was it worth the price, she wondered, and knew as soon as she asked herself that it wasn't. If she was determined enough—and she was, she told herself firmly—she could conquer this. If she weakened, all she had to do was remember what was at stake. Resolved again, she went into the bedroom to dress.

They met at the restaurant, high atop one of the casinos, and at first Dinah was so preoccupied with maintaining a gay facade that she didn't notice Andy wasn't eating. Eventually realizing that he'd hardly touched the steak he'd ordered, she asked in concern, "Aren't you hungry, Andy?"

"What?" He looked down at his plate. "Oh, I guess I'm just tired, that's all."

"Too tired to eat?" Neil said in surprise. "That's a first."

"Well, you guys did give me a pretty rough time on the slopes today," Andy said with a grin. He picked up a spoon and began tapping it against his water glass. "Man, when you went down the first time, you passed me like I was standing still. You sure can ski, Dinah."

"Thank you," she said, but her eyes were on the spoon he held. He was tapping it against the tabletop now, and something about the way he was doing it disturbed her. Then she realized that there was no rhythm to it. It was as though he was agitated for some reason, and this was the only way to expel his excess energy. With a start, she saw that his hand was shaking, and that he was using the tapping of the spoon to cover it. "Andy, are you feeling all right?" she asked.

"Sure," he said, tapping even louder. "Why?"

Had she imagined that feverish look in his eyes? She must have, for an instant later he had dropped the spoon and had picked up his fork. "Guess I'm hungry, after all," he murmured, and speared a generous piece of steak. "What's for dessert?"

Puzzled by his erratic behavior, Dinah noticed that when the waiter came to clear the table, Andy hadn't finished his meal after all. Odd, she thought, for a boy who had wolfed down that huge breakfast the other morning. Was something wrong and he didn't want to tell them? Was he afraid that if he confessed to not feeling well, his father would cut short the trip?

She looked covertly at Neil as he began to talk to Andy about skiing tomorrow morning before they left, but he didn't seem to notice anything amiss, and she thought then that she was mistaken. Neil didn't appear concerned; she must be imagining things.

But she wondered again when Andy excused himself a short while later without ordering dessert, and as she watched him leave the restaurant, she turned to Neil. "Do you think Andy is feeling all right?"

Neil looked surprised. "That's the second time you've asked that tonight. He told you he was. Why don't you believe him?"

"It's not that I don't believe him," she said cautiously. "It's just that he seemed so . . . so nervous."

Laughing indulgently, Neil replied, "Excited is more like it, I think. Don't you recognize a teenage crush when you see one?"

She didn't laugh with him. "I don't think it was that."

"What, then?"

But she couldn't tell him that she wondered if Andy had taken something; the idea sounded preposterous, even to her. And how could she justify such a horrible suspicion? By pointing out that Andy had tapped a spoon against a water glass? If Neil didn't laugh at her outright, he'd think she'd lost her mind.

But then she remembered how erratically Andy had skied that last run. They had taken a short break at the lodge before, and Andy had gone off somewhere by himself for a while. When they had all returned to the slopes again, Andy had been . . . different. She'd noticed it, but she'd been too preoccupied with thoughts of Neil at the time to pay much attention.

Now that she thought about it, she was disturbed. There had been something almost frenetic about him, and the good form he'd displayed before had disappeared. He'd taken a nasty spill on a simple mogul, and when she'd skied up to him, he'd laughed shrilly, his eyes feverish as he struggled to his feet. She'd thought that he was embarrassed that she'd seen his fall, but after observing his behavior tonight, she wasn't so sure.

"Do you remember those kids we interviewed at that school before we left?" she asked carefully.

"The Get In Touch program?"

"No, the high school. We talked to a group on their lunch hour."

"Yes," he answered, obviously puzzled. "Why?"

She took a deep breath. She didn't want to say it, but her concern for Andy overrode her reluctance to confront Neil. "Do you remember what they said about their parents not knowing when they were high?"

"Yes, but what does that have to do with—" He broke off, frowning. When he looked at her again, his expression was guarded. "Are you suggesting that Andy is on drugs?"

Wishing that she'd never broached the subject, Dinah forced herself to meet his eyes. "I don't know, Neil. But his hands were shaking tonight, and after the way he skied today—"

"There was nothing wrong with the way he skied today," Neil said flatly. "I told you he was just showing off for you."

Feeling a little desperate, she said, "Yes, but he took that bad fall—"

Neil's eyes had darkened angrily. "I suppose you've never taken a fall?"

"Well, of course," she said, trying not to quail before his expression. "But when I asked him if he was all right, he acted so strangely..."

Neil's voice dripped sarcasm. "Did it occur to you that he might have been embarrassed?"

"It wasn't that," she said wretchedly. And then she added, "Neil, I don't want to fight about this. I only mentioned it because I'm concerned."

"Then your concern is misplaced," he said angrily. "Andy is an honor student and captain of the basketball team. A boy like that doesn't take drugs or anything else. And certainly not a son of mine!''

"I'm not accusing him, Neil," she said pleadingly. "It's just that I keep remembering what those kids said about their parents not knowing—"

"Are you trying to tell me I don't know my own son?" he demanded. "Because if you are, I can assure you you're mistaken. I might not spend as much time with him as other fathers do with their sons, but I'd know if he were on something. What kind of father do you think I am?"

"Neil, please . . ."

"I think this conversation is over, Dinah," he said coldly. "Obviously, this program we've been working on has gone to your head. Just because you've gone out on a few interviews doesn't mean you're an expert, and I'll thank you to keep your amateur opinions to yourself!"

Dinah's eyes flashed at that. "I'm not the only amateur around here," she snapped. "And if you can't see what's going on under your own nose, maybe you should talk to some of the parents of these kids, like I have. You might not feel so superior then!"

Neil was just as angry. "I don't need to talk to anyone. I know my son, and I'm telling you for the last time that he'd never take anything. He knows better!"

Dinah rose from the table, so infuriated at his stubbornness that she was nearly inarticulate. "I certainly hope you're right," she said. "For Andy's sake, if not for yours!"

And before he could reply, she whirled and stalked out.

Only her pride prevented her from bursting into tears of pure frustration as she took the elevator back to her room. Oh, she'd been right all along, she thought angrily. He was the most narrow-minded, smug, infuriating man she'd ever had the misfortune to meet. She must have been out of her mind to contemplate having a relationship with him, and the thought that she'd succumbed to this inexplicable attraction to him even once enraged her all over again. If this project wasn't so important to her, she'd walk out right now.

Outrage propelled her all the way to her room, and as she shut the door behind her, she was still seething. Well, she wasn't going to walk out, and she wasn't going to allow this ... this girlish infatuation to affect her work. Her career was certainly more important to her than any fantasy about a relationship with Neil Kerrigan.

And that's exactly what it was, a fantasy. What a fool she'd been to think it could be anything else!

She could conquer this maddening attraction, she thought grimly; she would conquer it. And if for any reason she felt herself weakening in the future, all she had to do was remember the quarrel they'd had tonight.

CHAPTER ELEVEN

NEIL RETURNED FROM WILLOWSET in a foul mood that didn't improve when he learned that he had to fly immediately to Washington to interview a Pentagon official. The trip was a disaster. Although he'd promised himself he wouldn't think about Dinah, he kept imagining the entire time how differently she would handle the interview. Even though he grilled the general into a cold sweat, he wasn't satisfied with the responses he was getting. It was galling to realize that with one smile Dinah would probably have gotten more out of the man than he had with a dozen facts and figures, and by the time he left Washington, his foul mood had turned black.

He compounded the disaster by calling Elise from the airport as soon as he arrived in Los Angeles. He insisted on coming over to talk to her about Andy, but the instant he walked into the house, he knew he shouldn't have come. Elise was hostile and defensive, and the conversation got off to a rocky start and rapidly worsened.

He knew it was partly his fault. He should have left it for a time when he wasn't in such a disagreeable mood. But in addition to everything else, the things Dinah had said about Andy had been preying on his mind, and despite his vehement denials to her and another scene before they parted, he couldn't dismiss her concerns. So he had insisted on coming over, and now he wished he hadn't.

"What do you mean, has Andy shown any behavior problems lately?" Elise screeched at him. "Are you implying—"

"Keep your voice down!" Neil commanded, aware of Andy upstairs. His son was supposed to be asleep, but he didn't want to take the chance that Andy would overhear.

Elise flung up her blond head. "Why, are you afraid your son will hear you accusing him of being a . . . a juvenile delinquent?"

Neil was trying his best not to lose his temper. Sometimes he marveled that he'd managed to stay married to this woman for thirteen years. It seemed a lifetime ago that they had loved each other. They'd even managed to be reasonably content during the first few years of their marriage, when Andy had been small and he had just returned from Vietnam.

Thrusting away still-vivid memories of that nightmare time, Neil paused before he replied. He'd once thought Elise beautiful, with her pale skin and wide, light blue eyes. Her hair had been honey-colored when he met her, and so soft it was like silk. But like everything else about her, she had changed that, too. Her hair was bleached now to a white blond that looked stiff to the touch, and her skin had lost its youthful bloom from years of rigorous dieting. She was still a beautiful woman, he supposed, but she seemed hard and brittle to him now, and the look she gave him made him wonder if they had ever loved each other at all.

"I'm not accusing Andy of anything," he said evenly. "But I don't think it's an unreasonable question. After all, he was involved in that stupid stunt with the car."

"I told you he wasn't driving!"

"So did he. Does that make him any less responsible?"

"It wasn't his fault!" Elise cried. "Why do you always blame him when something happens? You're so hard on him. You expect so much!"

"I expect him to act responsibly."

"He's too young—"

"He's sixteen years old, Elise," Neil said harshly. "He's no longer a little boy."

"Sixteen doesn't make him a man!" Elise flung at him. "And you'd understand that if you spent more time with him!"

Neil took a deep breath. He could see where this was going, and he said, "Let's not stray from the point, shall we?"

Elise's eyes flashed. "I think that's exactly the point, Neil. You take him for a few days here and there, and you think you know all about him. Well, you don't. I'm his mother, and I know him better than you do. I'm the one who takes care of him!"

Neil thought of all the bridge parties and the golf games and the country-club activities—not to mention the endless hours of shopping—that she involved herself in, and just barely prevented himself from making a sarcastic remark. But he hadn't spent as much time with Andy lately as he would have liked, so he could hardly accuse her of being lax when he was guilty of the same thing himself.

"I'll be glad to take over whenever you say," he said, his voice tight. "You know I've always wanted Andy to live with me."

"And just when would you have time for him?" she demanded sarcastically. "Between assignments? Is he supposed to take care of himself while you're off gallivanting around the world in search of that elusive interview? Look at you now. You've been gone a week this time. The next time it might be a month, or six. Is he supposed to stay by himself in your apartment until you decide to come back?"

"I could work something out."

"Like you did all those years he was growing up? I used to have to show him pictures just so he'd remember what you looked like."

Neil gritted his teeth. "I know you resented my being gone so much—"

"Resented it!" Elise laughed shrilly. "How could I resent it? That's why our marriage lasted as long as it did. We never saw each other long enough even to have a decent fight!"

Taking another grip on his temper, Neil said, "I don't think we need to discuss our relationship—or lack of it. I do think we need to talk about Andy."

"There's nothing wrong with Andy! Are you going to hold this...this joyriding incident over him the rest of his life?"

"It's not only that, Elise. There are a few other things I've noticed."

"What things?" she demanded.

Neil thought of that night at Lake Tahoe when Dinah had suggested Andy might have taken something; he'd categorically refused even to consider such an outrageous idea. But when he'd tried to awaken Andy the next morning, his son had seemed so groggy, so disoriented for a few minutes that he began to wonder. He'd dismissed his suspicions again when

Andy had seemed his usual self on the drive back from Tahoe, but then on the way home from Washington, he recalled Dinah's statement about parents not knowing when their children were taking something, and he began to wonder for the first time if it was possible. Had Dinah been right all along?

Cursing the doubts she'd planted in his mind, Neil tried to explain to Elise and was infuriated when she laughed at him.

"You're accusing Andy of taking drugs just because he wouldn't eat his dinner and slept in one morning?" she asked caustically. "Well, it's obvious that you don't know your son at all, if you think you can make a case out of that!"

"I'm not the only one who noticed it!" he countered sharply.

"Oh, really? Who else, then? One of the crew?" Her eyes narrowed, and her tone became vicious. "I see. I suppose it was that woman."

"If by 'that woman' you mean Dinah Blake, yes, she mentioned something about it."

Elise was livid. "How dare she! Accusing my son—"

"She didn't accuse Andy of anything," Neil shouted, losing control. "And neither have I! She was just concerned—"

"Concerned! Ha! That's a likely story! She's obviously trying to get to you by playing up to your son!"

"Dinah's not that kind of woman!"

She threw him a scornful look. "Oh, really, Neil. You can't be that ingenuous!"

Stung by the sarcasm, he was about to make an angry reply when he realized that the conversation, as always, seemed to have degenerated into a shouting match. He hadn't come here to quarrel, he reminded himself. He'd come because he was concerned about Andy.

"Let's leave Dinah out of this," he said tightly. "You've expressed your opinion, so do you mind getting back to the problem?"

"There is no problem!" Elise cried. "How many times do I have to tell you that? Are you going to believe that... that woman instead of me?"

"I'm just trying to—"

"Because as far as I'm concerned, Miss Blake can keep her opinions to herself! She doesn't know the first thing about raising children, and she doesn't know anything about Andy. I do, and I'm telling you, I'd know if he was taking something. I'm his mother, and I'll thank her not to interfere with the way I take care of my son!"

Neil left the house in a fury. Elise had made him feel like a complete fool. He was furious with Dinah for planting those doubts in his mind and angry with himself for allowing her to do it. What had happened to his judgment lately?

He was still irate when he arrived at his apartment near the beach, and as soon as he slammed the door behind him, he headed straight to the liquor cabinet. Muttering to himself, he poured a brandy and went out onto the deck. The sound of the ocean always calmed him, but tonight the pounding surf only seemed to increase the pounding in his head. Cursing, he took a hefty swallow of the brandy, and then another, hoping it would have some effect. It had an effect, all right. The liquor settled in his stomach like an acid wash, and he cursed again as he poured the rest of it over the deck railing.

He threw himself into one of the deck chairs. This was ridiculous. There was no reason to feel as though his life had suddenly become a turmoil and he'd been thrown completely off track. Now that his doubts about Andy had been resolved, he should be relieved. He *was* relieved, about his son, anyway. But he still felt restless and dissatisfied, and he didn't know why.

"Damn it all," he muttered. He knew exactly why he felt this way. It was all Dinah's fault. She was the one who had derailed him, and it annoyed him to think that she was in better control of this...this situation than he. She'd been so cool the other night when they'd left Willowset. It was as though nothing had happened between them, and they both knew that wasn't true. But she'd been able to dismiss it with a mere shrug, so why couldn't he?

Because he wasn't cool and suave and sophisticated where Dinah was concerned. He couldn't understand why, even when he was angriest with her, he'd suddenly be overcome with the desire to kiss her. What had happened to all his self-control?

Restlessly, he went into the living room again. Chuck had given him an unedited tape of the material they'd shot so far, and for lack of anything better to do, he put it in the machine. He had agreed to produce this special, so he might as well do the preliminary editing so he could forget about it for the next two weeks. He had a full schedule until Dinah came to Los Angeles for the wrap-up, and sometime during the next two weeks, he had to get back on track.

But as he sat there and watched Dinah talking to Dr. Mason and interviewing those street kids, and buttonholing that cop, he forgot he was supposed to be editing the tape. He forgot everything but Dinah. Her camera presence was extraordinary. Without even trying, she dominated the scene, and his eyes followed every gesture she made and couldn't find fault.

Then he came to the segment they'd taped at GIT where the kids turned the tables on them and made them the subject of the interview.

"Are you married?" one of the girls had asked, and in the nonplussed silence that had followed, Chuck had turned the camera on Dinah and caught the look on her face.

Neil leaned forward, gazing intently at the screen. Dinah looked as startled at the question as he remembered he'd been. But then her expression changed, and for the merest fraction of an instant, so fleeting that he wasn't sure he had seen it at all, he saw a look of... what? Longing... wistfulness... regret? Absurdly, his pulse began to beat a little faster. Stabbing the Rewind button, he played back the tape and then froze the frame on her face.

He stared at the screen for a long time before he finally turned the machine off. Leaning back against the chair, he closed his eyes. The image of Dinah's face seemed burned into his brain: the mobile, sensual mouth that begged to be kissed, the mane of burnished hair that he loved to touch, the high cheekbones that made her face so distinctive. But the feature he saw most clearly in his mind were her eyes, those deep green eyes that she used to such advantage. He had seen them flash with anger or turn so cold they froze with a glance. But he had never seen that particular expression, for in the instant following that unexpected question, her eyes had become luminous, glowing with an emotion that stirred some deep feeling inside him. She recovered quickly, so quickly that even after staring at the tape, he wasn't sure now if he had imagined it or not.

Maybe he only wanted to believe he'd seen that softening of her expression. Maybe he had just conjured the whole thing out of some adolescent fantasy that never had a chance to begin with. Dinah had made it abundantly clear that she didn't want any involvements at this time, and he agreed wholeheartedly.

Or did he? Yes, of course he did, he thought impatiently. He'd learned the hard way that his work took precedence over his private life; he just couldn't seem to combine the two. Elise had accused him of being selfish and self-involved, and maybe he was. He'd tried hard to share his professional life with her but it hadn't worked. When he was on the trail of a new story, he forgot everything else; he became totally preoccupied...almost obsessed. What made him think it would be different with Dinah?

It wouldn't be; that was the problem. And the fact that she was in the same profession would only complicate things. He couldn't ask her to give up something he couldn't surrender himself, and he had seen how important her career was to her. She'd made that clear, too. So it wouldn't work. It couldn't.

And why was he even wondering if it could? Had he become so besotted with her that he refused to listen to his own arguments about getting involved? This ridiculous mooning around like a lovesick schoolboy had to stop. He had two weeks to conquer this puerile attraction and get himself back on track.

But as he agitatedly poured himself another brandy, he looked at the calendar on the desk and knew with a sinking feeling that two weeks wouldn't be sufficient. The way he felt now, he could take a lifetime to get over Dinah, and it wouldn't be long enough.

DINAH RETURNED to San Francisco utterly exhausted. Anger had carried her through the past two days since leaving Tahoe, but now that she was home, she felt like collapsing from the strain.

She'd still been seething the morning after that quarrel with Neil, and the thought that she had to spend two more days in his company didn't improve her temper. But they had already arranged to meet Chuck and Larry in Sacramento to interview some state officials there, and she had to go.

Andy hadn't seemed to notice the distinct coolness in the front seat as they left the resort area. Filled with enthusiasm about their skiing trip, he chatted away in back as a tight-lipped Neil drove and Dinah sat as far away from him as possible.

By the time they dropped Andy off at the airport for his flight back to Los Angeles, she was beginning to have misgivings about her suspicions. Andy had appeared so relaxed and happy during that endless drive that she wondered if she'd been mistaken about him. Cringing at the thought, she felt even worse when Andy shyly gave her a goodbye kiss on the cheek before his plane left, but after taking one look at Neil's set face, she knew an apology would be futile. His cold expression told her he was still angry, and she couldn't blame him.

The following two days had been such a strain that by the time they were over her nerves were in shreds.

She managed somehow to get through an interview with a congressman who seemed more interested in presenting his best profile to the camera than in answering questions, and another with an official who had so exasperated her with his political double-talk that she wanted to scream.

The only way she had endured it all was by reminding herself constantly what this could mean to her career, and that it was times like these that separated the professional from the amateur. With those thoughts in mind, she had dredged up enough animation to charm the governor, but that had been a hollow victory. For even as Neil stood smiling next to her at the end of the interview, the cold look never left his eyes. The tension between them had been so apparent that even the crew was affected, and they were all glad when they could wrap up and go home.

She had tried to apologize to Neil that last night; after two days of trading only the most necessary of remarks, she had decided enough was enough. They'd been invited to a cocktail party at the governor's mansion, and she'd thought that if they had to attend the function, the least they could do was be civil to each other. She should have known better. The words of apology were hardly out of her mouth before he infuriated her once more and she wished she'd never said a thing.

"Neil, there's something I want to say," she'd said, breaking the cold silence that had existed between them since they'd entered the car.

His hands had tightened on the steering wheel. "You mean without having Chuck or Larry as interpreter?" he asked sarcastically.

"Well, yes. That would help," she said, telling herself that she wasn't going to lose her temper. "This business of talking to each other only through them is childish. You're angry, and I'd like to discuss it."

"There's nothing to discuss," he said flatly.

She couldn't prevent a little sarcasm herself. "Oh, really? You might be content to work in this cold-war atmosphere, but I'm not."

"You should have thought of that before."

"Before I said those things about Andy, you mean?" She was getting angry despite her resolve, and she took a deep breath. "I only said what I did because I was concerned. Surely, you can understand that."

"I understand that you think my son is a drug addict—a druggie," he said, almost spitting the word that the kids used themselves.

"I didn't say that!"

"You certainly implied it!" he snapped.

"I most certainly did not!" she flared back. "All I did was ask if he might have taken something!" Dinah controlled herself with an effort. "I admit I might have been mistaken. If I was wrong, I apologize."

"It's a little late for that, isn't it?"

Gritting her teeth, Dinah said, "I'm sorry you feel that way."

"And I'm sorry you took it upon yourself to interfere."

"I told you—" Dinah began, and stopped, realizing the futility. He was determined to be stubborn about this, and she wasn't going to beg for his forgiveness. She had apologized; there was nothing more she could do except say coldly, "If you're going to act like this, there's no point in continuing this conversation."

"There's just one thing I'd like to say," he said tightly. They had arrived at the party by this time, and he parked the car.

Dinah refused to look at him. "Go ahead," she said stonily.

Neil stared straight ahead, too. "I'd like to think that we're professional enough to put aside our personal differences. Whether we like it or not, we still have to finish this project, so I would appreciate it if we could work out some kind of compromise."

Infuriated again at his patronizing tone, Dinah opened the car door. "How about this?" she said furiously. "You do your work and I'll do mine, and we'll leave personal opinions out of it."

And just to show him that she was just as much a professional as he, she proceeded to charm everyone at the party. She was sure that no one suspected she was fuming inside as she chatted graciously with some of the most powerful men and women in California, and when she extracted a promise from the governor himself to form a special commission on teen drug and alcohol abuse, she couldn't prevent a triumphant glance in Neil's direction.

Unfortunately he wasn't looking at her then. His dark head was lowered attentively to the silvery blonde hanging on to his arm, and when Dinah saw him laugh at something the woman said, she was furious at the swift stab of jealousy she felt. They escaped from the party an hour later and drove back to Willowset in chilly silence. Thankful that they had finished all the interviews they'd scheduled, Dinah immediately packed and left for San Francisco. She managed to say a warm goodbye to the crew, but her farewell to Neil had been cool. She knew that if she had to spend one more day in his company, she'd forget all this professional business and give him a real piece of her mind.

The chiming of the grandfather clock interrupted her gloomy thoughts, and Dinah forced herself to get off the couch. She still had to unpack and decide what she was going to wear tomorrow, but as she went into the bedroom, her steps dragged. This emotional seesaw she'd been on since meeting Neil had exhausted her, and she felt so depressed that she wanted to cry. Things were so good between them sometimes, but then he would turn inward, becoming that hard and rigid man she disliked so much and they would be at odds again.

Stop thinking about it, she told herself angrily. She'd known from the beginning that a relationship with him had no future; instead of being upset about it, she should be glad that they'd parted on such chilly terms. They still had to finish this project, and when she went to Los Angeles in two weeks, at least there wouldn't be any emotional entanglement between them to complicate things. Wasn't that what she'd said she wanted?

Sighing heavily, she threw her suitcase on the bed. But when she opened it and saw the ski jumper and parka she'd bought lying on top, an image of that first glorious run with Neil down the mountain rose in her mind, and she sank down onto the bed and buried her face in her hands.

Her life had been running so smoothly before the night of the awards dinner; she'd finally gotten herself back on an even keel. She'd defined her ambitions; she knew what her goals were. Everything had been planned and accounted for...and now she was more confused and uncertain than she'd ever been, and it was all because of Neil Kerrigan. She didn't know what she wanted anymore, and the thought that she only had two weeks to prepare herself for seeing him again depressed her even further.

Because she knew it was going to take a lot longer than two weeks to get over him. The disturbing truth was that she doubted she ever would.

CHAPTER TWELVE

DINAH WAS BESIEGED the instant she walked into the station the next morning. Naturally everyone was curious about the Willowset shoot, and in other circumstances she would have been amused at all the attention. But her sense of humor, always one of her strong points, seemed to have deserted her lately along with her good judgment, and she was annoyed instead. She didn't want to answer any questions, especially when it was obvious the big question on everyone's mind was what had happened between her and Neil.

"Damn him!" she muttered, and finally managed to escape by shutting the door of her office. Leaning against it for a moment, she told herself that she had to get a grip on herself or the next two weeks would be impossible. She couldn't avoid everyone just because she didn't want to talk about him. Gossip would run rampant then, and that would be even worse. Before any speculation began, she had to make it clear that she and Neil were colleagues, nothing more.

But not today. Every time she thought about Neil, she felt even more dismal, and she doubted she could even mention his name without bursting into tears. Hoping to distract herself with work, she glanced at the schedule her secretary had placed on her desk and groaned. The thought of plowing through a guest list composed of self-important people with little to say was so discouraging that she wanted to leave right now and never come back.

Gritting her teeth instead, she sat down and pulled one of the background folders toward her. This was her job; she was supposed to be good at it. The world didn't obligingly grind to a halt because she was depressed and out of sorts. She still had responsibilities to meet.

Unfortunately, one of them was Roger Dayton. He burst unannounced into her office before she'd read halfway through the first file, and when she saw his expression, she winced. She knew she should have gone to see him when she came in, but he would have expected a minute-by-minute accounting of the Willowset trip, and she had wanted to put the entire miserable week out of her mind.

Before he could say anything, she lied, "I was just coming to see you."

He seemed prepared at the moment to forgive her anything, smiling expansively as he lowered his bulk into the other chair. She didn't trust that smile. She knew from experience how quickly his attitude could change and she was wary.

"So," Roger said, asking the same question she'd already been asked seemingly endless times on her way in, "How'd it go?"

Steeling herself, she said, "It was fine. I haven't seen the tape yet, but I think we got some good material."

He looked relieved. "I was beginning to think you were avoiding me because there'd been some disaster."

Thinking that as far as she was personally concerned the whole trip had been a disaster, Dinah shook her head. "Of course not. We couldn't have had a better crew."

"And Mr. Kerrigan?"

"Mr. Kerrigan is just as competent as he seems. A true professional," she answered coolly.

Even Roger didn't dare challenge that tone. "Well, I'm glad the trip was a success."

Dinah couldn't help herself. "Did you think it wouldn't be?"

"No, no. Of course not," he said hastily. "I know how capable you are, Dinah."

Do you, she wondered. *Then why don't you show it by trying out some of my ideas on the show?*

She didn't say it aloud. The only reason she'd endured those two days after her quarrel with Neil was because she was determined to let the special do the talking for her. Once it aired she hoped she'd be able to deal with Roger from a new position, a position of power. Nothing spoke more loudly in this business than ratings—unless it was favors done for favors received, she amended acidly—and if the program was as good as she intended it to be, there would be a few changes made around here. Her contract had three more months to run, but this time negotiations would proceed differently, or else . . .

Or else what, she asked herself as Roger left the office. Suppose she made a stand and Roger refused to compromise? Would she go over his head and risk alienating him completely?

Roger jealously guarded his own little sphere of power; he could make life miserable for her here if he felt she'd outflanked him. Even if she did win a concession from the affiliate executives, she would have won one battle only to have lost the war. Roger would still be her immediate boss, and he was vindictive enough to make things so difficult that she'd soon wish she'd never made a stand at all.

The other alternative was to threaten to quit unless they worked something out, but was she willing to do that? One of the clauses in her contract stated that if she broke her contract and left this station for any reason, she couldn't accept a similar job within a five-hundred-mile radius for a period of five years. So if she did resign, she'd have to leave California. Did she really want to start over somewhere else?

She had some difficult decisions to make in the next few weeks, but right now she couldn't seem to think beyond getting through the next eight hours. Sighing heavily, she picked up the folder she'd begun to read before Roger burst in, then trudged down to the green room to preinterview the guest scheduled for today's show.

She still hadn't decided anything by the end of the week, and her vacillation made her impatient with herself and everyone else, especially her guests. She'd been restless and dissatisfied with the format before, but with each day that went by, it became more of an effort to hide her feelings. She'd trained herself to be tactful and diplomatic despite the way she felt, no matter how obnoxious or pedantic her guests. Yet now she felt like screaming at everyone, and it was small comfort that no one seemed aware of her inner struggle. Her audiences were unfailingly enthusiastic, the crew just as supportive, Roger just as pleased with himself. But Dinah went home every day with a fierce headache, and getting up every morning to go to the studio became an ordeal.

Wondering if she would ever be able to muster the enthusiasm she'd felt before, Dinah left the studio late Thursday night, relieved that the next day was Friday. She was exhausted and planned to sleep the entire weekend—if she could sleep at all. Despite her weariness, she hadn't been able to do much of that, either.

She was sitting at the kitchen table, picking at the dinner she'd forced herself to fix, when the phone rang. Glad of an excuse to push away a meal for which she had no appetite, she lifted the receiver, sure it was Leigh.

"Hi, doll. How're you doin'?"

"Dad!" she exclaimed in pleased surprise. "Where are you?"

"Houston. We just got back."

"From where?" Her father traveled so much that she never knew where he was or what he was doing. They'd long ago made a pact that he would call her at least every two weeks, just so she would know he was all right.

"Here and there."

Dinah smiled. "Oh, I see. Another one of those top-secret test flights, right?"

"Well, you know how it is."

"Why don't you test one of those things in the direction of San Francisco?" she asked, suddenly wanting very much to see him. For some absurd reason the sound of his voice brought tears to her eyes. Wiping them away with the back of her hand, she told herself fiercely that she wasn't going to cry.

"I might be able to get up that way in a month or so—"

"That long?" Despite her resolve, her voice quavered, and she wondered what was the matter with her. She rarely cried to her father. She'd always been proud of the fact that she could handle her problems by herself.

"Is something wrong, doll?"

Dinah closed her eyes. Her father had an uncanny ability to sense when things weren't right in her life; he often called when she least expected it just to ask if she wanted to talk. He never pressed her. He just let her know he was there if she needed him. Normally, she was grateful for his concern, but tonight she knew she couldn't talk about her problems without bursting into tears, so she swallowed and said weakly, "Why do you say that?"

"You sound a little blue."

"Oh, I'm just tired."

"That job too much for you?"

She forced a laugh. "No, of course not. In fact, things are going really well. I'm doing a special with—" to her horror, she stumbled over the name "—Neil Kerrigan."

"Well, hey! Congratulations! How'd that come about?"

Relieved that he hadn't seemed to notice her hesitation, she told him about the awards dinner, and with a great effort, even managed to make a joke about Andy getting the two of them involved. She concluded by saying, "I have to go to Los Angeles in a week to finish it, but I'll let you know when it airs."

"You be sure to do that," he said, his voice so tinged with pride that tears filled her eyes again.

"I will," she gulped, and then to her dismay, blurted, "Dad—"

"Something is wrong, isn't it?" he asked quietly when she couldn't go on. "I had a feeling there was. Do you want to talk about it?"

"I don't know," she said helplessly, and then decided to tell him the truth. "It's just that things are a little confused right now. I . . . I'm not sure I want to stay with the show."

His tone was puzzled. "I thought you liked it."

"I do . . . I mean, I did. But it just doesn't seem . . ."

"Challenging enough?" he supplied, and then chuckled fondly when he heard her sigh. "Well, you always were the first kid on the block to accept a dare. I can't imagine things have changed now. Do you have another offer, is that it?"

"No. It's just that after working with Neil on this new project, *Personalities* seems even more superficial than it did before."

"Dinah, if there's one thing you're not, it's superficial. If you don't like the way the show's going, why don't you do something about it?"

"It's not that simple, Dad."

"Well, you never liked things simple, either, did you? If there was a hard way to do something, you'd find it. It's that stubbornness of yours. . . ."

Dinah smiled. "I come by it honestly, you have to admit that."

"Your mother was the stubborn one, not me," he said with a laugh, and then sobered. "I know you'll do the right thing, doll. You always do."

"Thanks, Dad," she said softly, touched by the compliment.

But as she replaced the receiver, she wondered. What was the right thing? Her father might have confidence in her, but she seemed to have lost it herself.

Was she ready to gamble everything on one throw of the dice? There were dozens—hundreds—of other hopefuls waiting to take her place; Roger would have a replacement before the ink dried on her resignation. Was she willing to take the chance that he'd agree to anything not to lose her?

Like her father just now, Leigh had been encouraging the other night when they'd met for dinner. Dinah had to confess her doubts and unhappiness to someone, and she had always valued Leigh's advice. Her friend hadn't disappointed her. Leigh had loyally assured her that once the special was aired, it would be such a ratings success that she'd have all the leverage she needed. Dinah longed to believe that, but she knew that it would be a long time, if ever, before she had the power someone like Neil commanded.

She hadn't meant to think of Neil. She'd been trying hard all week not to think of him at all. But every time she saw a man with black hair, her heart gave a leap, and once when she thought she'd heard his voice in the corridor, she'd jumped up and was halfway to the door before she realized what she was doing. She'd wake from a restless sleep in the middle of the night realizing that she'd been dreaming about him, and when she came home after work, her eyes would immediately go to the answering machine, wondering if he had called.

It had to stop, she told herself. She couldn't go on this way or she'd drive herself crazy. Even if he did call, what did she expect him to say? What would she say herself? She only had one more week before she went to Los Angeles, and if she felt like this now, how was she going to act when she had to work with him again?

"WHERE'S YOUR SENSE OF HUMOR, Neil?" Allen Fogerty asked as the two men sat at a table at the Tavern on the Green in Central Park. "Don't you think you're taking this too seriously?"

With an effort, Neil roused himself from his contemplation of the snowfall beyond the window. Cursing inwardly, he wondered if every time he saw snow now he'd be reminded of Dinah and that ski trip to Lake Tahoe.

But then everything reminded him of Dinah lately. He'd made a fool of himself at the airport when he'd glimpsed a woman with auburn hair and had thought it was Dinah; then he'd been so unnerved by his mistake that he'd given the cabby the wrong address for the hotel. The Pentagon interview he'd mangled after coming back from Willowset still rankled, and the two days following that had been equally disastrous. He just couldn't seem to keep his mind on anything, and he'd almost missed his plane this morning because he'd completely forgotten about meeting Allen in New York to discuss the special's progress. If his secretary hadn't called to remind him, he'd probably still be wandering around his apartment in a daze.

"Neil?"

"I'm sorry, Allen. What did you say?"

Allen sighed. "Never mind. I've already said it twice, and it wasn't that important anyway. What's the matter with you? I've never seen you so preoccupied."

Neil looked down at the empty glass he held. He must have had a drink, but he couldn't remember what it was. Shaking his head slightly, he said, "I guess I've got a lot on my mind."

"I hadn't noticed," Allen said dryly. "Does it have anything to do with the special you and Dinah are working on?"

Neil glanced at him quickly. "What makes you say that?"

Allen's brows lifted at Neil's tone. "It just seemed a reasonable assumption—"

"Why?"

The brows went even higher. "Well, you have to admit, you haven't been all sweetness and light since you came back from Willowgrade."

"Willowset," Neil corrected heavily. "And who told you that?"

Allen looked amused. "Nobody had to tell me. I saw it for myself. I was at the station, remember, when you came in that first day. Looking like the wrath of God, I might add."

Neil knew it was true. He had been in a rage that morning following his ignominious return from Washington. But he wasn't about to admit that, so he said the first thing that came into his head. "I'd just had a fight with Elise."

"Oh," Allen said guilelessly. "Was it about Dinah?"

"No, it wasn't about Dinah," Neil mimicked heavily. "Why would you think that?"

Trying to cover his amusement, Allen couldn't resist a dig at his old friend. "Well, Dinah's a beautiful woman . . . or hadn't you noticed?"

"You know damned well I've noticed! So what? The world is filled with beautiful women. I had a date with one of them last night."

"Oh? Who?"

"Madelaine Chauncey."

Allen let out a low whistle. "Ah. She of the sarcastic wit and the gorgeous—"

"The same," Neil interrupted curtly, wishing he'd never mentioned it. He didn't want to discuss Madelaine's attributes, although she was a beautiful woman...in a cold sort of way, with her sharp face and even sharper tongue. She'd once amused him with her acerbic comments. Possessing the unconscious arrogance of one born to wealth and position, she said exactly what she thought and didn't care if anyone was shocked. She enjoyed shocking people, in fact; she often made a comment just to see what the reaction would be. They'd been lovers for a time, and he'd once toyed with the idea of marrying her until she'd made it clear that she wasn't interested in becoming the stepmother of a teenage boy.

"Bad for the image, darling," she drawled in that deliberately bored tone of hers. "You understand, don't you?"

He hadn't understood at all. That was the last time he'd seen her, in fact, until the other night. He hadn't heard from her in a long time, but for some reason she'd called him. He wasn't sure now why he had agreed to see her, except that he couldn't face another restless night alone in the apartment.

But he hadn't spent five minutes in her company before he wondered how he was going to get through the evening. Her sarcasm no longer amused him—it grated on his nerves. The flawless beauty he'd once admired seemed lifeless and cold. He found himself comparing her to Dinah, who could be cold and sarcastic with the best of them at times, but who had never been lifeless. Vitality radiated from Dinah; she filled a room with her presence merely by appearing at the door.

"I thought you weren't seeing Madelaine anymore," Allen commented.

With an effort, Neil thrust away images of Dinah at the governor's party. She'd been wearing a red dress that had some kind of beading over the bodice, so that when she moved, sparks of light shot away from her, glinting into his eyes. Redheads weren't supposed to wear red, he'd thought, but Dinah had, and she'd looked magnificent in it. She'd been surrounded by admiring men from the instant they walked into the party. Despising himself for the fiery jealousy he felt every time he saw her dazzling yet another male, he'd forced himself to stay as far away from her as possible. Like some demented caveman, he'd wanted to shoulder his way through the crowd and proclaim to all of them that she was his woman.

But she wasn't his woman, and that's why he'd been so surly in the car. He'd had to establish some emotional distance, or he would have found himself begging for another chance.

Abruptly he realized that Allen had made some comment again and was looking at him with that humorous expression he'd worn since they'd sat down. "What's so funny?" he growled.

"You," Allen replied, laughing. "I don't know if you realize it, but you're acting like a lovesick teenager. I can't blame you, I guess. I know what an effect she can have."

"If you're referring to Dinah, I admit she has...a certain appeal."

Allen's brows lifted again. "And that's all?"

Neil glowered. "That's all."

"I see," Allen said, laughter in his eyes. "Then unlike the rest of us, you must be immune. If she'd given me the nod, wild horses couldn't have kept me away."

Neil was silent a moment, gazing at his friend. Finally he looked away. "She didn't give me the nod, either," he said, and didn't realize how bleak his voice sounded. "She made it very clear that she didn't want to get involved."

Allen looked suddenly bleak himself. "I know. She said the same thing to me."

Avoiding each other's eyes, the two men were silent until the waiter came with the check. Beyond the frosted window, the snow continued to fall, and Neil caught a snowflake in his hand when they went outside to go their separate ways. As he watched it melt in the warmth of his palm, he didn't realize how regretful his expression was, or how sad. He caught a taxi and spent the entire flight home staring morosely out the window, trying to think of nothing at all.

That night, back in Los Angeles, he took Andy out to dinner and was pleased to see that his son was wearing the Rolex he'd given him for his birthday. That and the ski trip had been his present. Even though Elise had upstaged him with the car, he'd never believed in competing with her where gifts were concerned. He knew that Andy would appreciate his time more than any elaborate present, and it seemed that he had. Andy was still talking about Lake Tahoe as they were shown to their table at the restaurant, and Neil was only half paying attention until his son said something about Dinah. He'd been wondering how best to say what was on his mind, and the mention of her name gave him the opening he needed.

"You like Dinah, don't you?" he asked casually.

Andy rolled his eyes. "Who wouldn't?"

Who indeed, Neil agreed, and said, "Better than Madelaine?"

"Madelaine was an icicle, Dad," Andy said with the candor of the young, and shuddered. "She looked like one, too. All sharp angles and bones."

Now that he thought about it, Neil agreed with that, too. Dinah was slender, as well, but there was no comparison between the two women. Remembering the softness of Dinah's body under his hands, the warmth and silky texture of her skin, the fullness of her breasts, he felt a stirring inside him and jerked his attention back to Andy.

"Are you going out with Dinah, Dad?"

Neil saw the eager look in his son's eyes and shook his head. "Afraid not."

Andy looked disappointed. "But I thought you were friends."

Friends? He wanted them to be much more than that. "No, just colleagues," he said.

"But you'd like it to be more than that, wouldn't you, Dad?"

Startled at the wistfulness in his son's voice, Neil frowned. "It sounds like you'd like it to be," he said cautiously.

Andy sighed. "Well, you have to admit, she's pretty special. I've never met anybody like her."

Neither have I, Neil thought gloomily, and knew he never would again. "Yes, she's very good at her job," he said, trying to steer the conversation in a safer direction. "I think this special we're doing is going to have quite an impact."

"With Dinah, it will," Andy agreed fervently. "How's it coming, anyway?"

This was the opening he'd been seeking. "We finished the interviews. Now all we have to do is put it together and tape it," Neil said, and then added casually, "I think you'll find it interesting."

Andy suddenly looked guarded. "Why? It's about druggies, isn't it?"

"Yes, it is," Neil said, wincing inwardly at the term. He'd always hated it, perhaps because it was so descriptive. "It seems to be quite an epidemic."

"I guess so. I don't know. I stay away from that stuff."

Neil hesitated. Even though Elise had been so adamant, he had decided that he had to find out from Andy himself what his feelings were about drugs. "You mean you've never even tried marijuana?"

Shifting uneasily in his chair, Andy refused to meet his father's eyes. "Well, yeah. Once," he finally admitted.

Forcing himself to be calm, Neil asked, "And? What did you think?"

"I didn't like it. I don't know what the big deal is."

"So you've never tried anything else?"

"Are you kidding?" Andy said indignantly. "Coach would kill me!"

The remark seemed so genuine that Neil felt relief washing over him. "I'm glad to hear that, son," he said, and smiled.

Andy didn't smile with him; he seemed almost hurt instead. "Why the questions, Dad?" he asked in a low voice. "Did you think I used drugs? Do you really think I'm that dumb?"

"No, of course not," Neil said hastily. "But you can't blame me for being concerned, can you?"

Andy looked down at his dessert plate, absently smashing a crumb with his fork. "I guess not," he muttered. He looked up again, meeting Neil's eyes with a direct gaze. "You ought to know I'd never do something so stupid. I want you to be proud of me, Dad."

Touched by the catch he heard in Andy's voice, Neil reached out and gripped his son's arm. "I am proud of you, Andy," he said quietly. "It's just that it's hard being a father sometimes."

"It's hard being a son sometimes, too," Andy said, and looked away.

NEIL WAS THOUGHTFUL when he'd dropped Andy at home and drove back to his own apartment. After that one emotional moment, the conversation had moved on to other things—school, sports, the Lakers—and the evening had ended on a determinedly companionable note. Feeling a little guilty, Neil had debated about saying something more concerning their earlier conversation, but then he decided to leave well enough alone. He'd rather have Andy hurt that he'd asked about the drugs than think he didn't care enough to ask. But their parting was still awkward, and Neil noticed that his son avoided his eyes. Then he shrugged. He'll get over it, he assured himself, and in the meantime, he felt much better about the situation. There had been a few tense moments there when he wondered if Andy was telling the truth, but his son had never lied to him, and he wasn't going to start doubting him now. If Andy said he didn't take drugs, he believed him.

So that was one problem resolved, Neil thought as he let himself into the apartment. Now all he had to do was deal with the other one. But the problem of Dinah seemed insurmountable, and after wandering restlessly around for a while, he decided to distract himself by viewing the partially edited version of the tape from Willowset.

He'd brought both tapes, the original and the rough cut, home so he could send them to San Francisco tomorrow by courier. Even though he felt himself tensing at the thought of watching Dinah on the screen again tonight, he knew he might as well get it over with. He'd seen the tape yesterday, and it was good. Damned good, he thought, especially the interviews where Dinah had taken the initiative. She'd brought out expressions on some of those kids' faces that spoke more eloquently than words, and she'd drawn some poignant confessions from several of the teenagers they'd met on the street. Watching Dinah at work was truly moving, and Neil knew that the tape could stand as it was now. With editing it was going to be a smash.

Both tapes were on the desk, and he was about to put the cut version in the machine when he paused. Hefting it thoughtfully, he wondered if he and Dinah shouldn't view it together and then winced at the snickering ghost of a laugh that rose at the back of his mind. It wasn't an excuse to see her, he told himself angrily. It was the obvious thing to do. They could hardly edit this long distance, after all, and Dinah had just as much right as he to decide on the final cut.

The snickering laugh sounded again, but Neil determinedly ignored it. This was business, he assured himself, and decided then that he wouldn't bother with a courier. He'd take both tapes to San Francisco tomorrow himself.

Suddenly feeling as though a weight had been lifted off him, Neil returned the tape to its container. He didn't realize it, but the slow smile that had begun at the thought of seeing Dinah again had suddenly become a grin that spread from ear to ear.

CHAPTER THIRTEEN

DINAH WENT TO THE STUDIO on Friday, thankful that there was only one more day before the weekend. Her father's call the previous night had buoyed her spirits somewhat, and she felt she could face the day without falling apart completely. Then she met the guest scheduled for that day's taping, and her mood plummeted again. Marvin Beeson was an overweight, officious osteopath who claimed that the current national fitness craze was dangerous to everyone's health, and by the time Dinah excused herself from the preinterview in the green room, she was gritting her teeth. Returning to her office, she sat down and put her head in her hands.

Where did Roger find these people? She'd thought at first that Beeson had to be joking with his sedentary theory, but when she realized he was serious, she knew she was in trouble. The guests so far this week had been uphill work, but this osteopath was the last straw. She'd barely been able to remain in the green room five minutes with him; how in the world was she going to endure an entire show?

There was a quick rap on her office door. "Five minutes, Miss Blake."

Dinah slumped in the chair. Was five minutes long enough to write a letter of resignation? Since Roger was so fond of digging up these individuals, maybe he'd like to go on the air with them, too. It would serve him right, she thought, and went out to meet her own fate.

The show was as bad as she thought it would be—worse. Marvin Beeson waxed eloquent on the dangers of exercise, citing as the basis for his theory everything from heart attacks while running to sprained ankles while climbing stairs. When Dinah tried to point out that most physicians advocated exercise in some form or another, Beeson dismissed the statement with a wave of a meaty hand.

"Why do you think the medical profession tries to interest people in exercise, Miss Blake?" he asked.

Morbidly fascinated by this time, Dinah said, "I presumed it was because of the increased health benefits to their patients. Obviously you have a different explanation."

"Indeed, I do," Beeson said in all seriousness. "There are benefits, all right, but not to the patients. Who do you think sets all these broken bones or tends to the sprains and splints? It's the physicians, Miss Blake, that's who—"

Dinah saw where this was going and interrupted hastily. "Oh, I hardly think—"

Beeson overrode her. He had his forum now and was running with it. "The same doctors who tell their patients to go out and break and strain everything in the first place. If you ask me—"

Dinah cut in sharply. She could imagine the switchboard starting to flood with calls from irate practitioners, and she said, "I would love to give you the chance to expound on your theory, Dr. Beeson, but unfortunately—"

To her dismay, he overrode her again. "You mark my words, Miss Blake. It's all a plot by the medical profession to..."

Dinah rarely had occasion to use the signal she'd established with the director when she needed instant response. She used it now, gratified to see camera two swing at once into a tight shot of her face. Such was her control that no one in the audience knew how much she longed to turn to this pompous man beside her and blast him with a few well-chosen words. With her instinctive sense of timing, she filled the remaining two minutes of the show by giving a brief history of osteopathy, compelling Beeson to silence by her glowing account of the service osteopaths had done for mankind. Relief on his face, the floor director finally signaled her and she went smoothly into the wrap-up, graciously acknowledging Beeson as her guest without giving him a chance to say another word.

The girl who had taken her place as guest-relations director took one look at Dinah's expression as the houselights came up, then bore Beeson away. Dinah didn't care where the obnoxious man went, just as long as he was out of her sight. Not trusting herself to say anything to anyone, she headed straight to Roger's office.

She didn't bother to knock; she was too angry. Flinging the door open, she said, "If you *ever* do that to me again, I'll—"

It was then that she realized Roger wasn't alone. Neil sat in the chair at one side of Roger's desk. When Dinah saw him, she stopped in her tracks.

"What are you doing here?" she blurted.

He came smoothly to his feet. "Watching the show."

Her eyes flew to the monitor on the desk. Naturally it was tuned to the studio; if Roger didn't oversee the show from the control booth, he watched it here. Mortified at the thought that Neil had witnessed that debacle, she said stiffly, "If you don't mind, I'd like to talk to Roger alone."

Neil inclined his head. "Not at all," he replied gravely, but with a twinkle in his eye. "I can see that you have, er, something to discuss. I'll be glad to wait in the hall."

"Oh, please don't let me detain you," Dinah said acidly. "I'm sure you must have other appointments."

"Well, actually, I did," Neil said with that maddening calm. "But I've taken care of those already, and since I brought the Willowset tapes with me, I thought we might make arrangements to go over them. If you have time, that is."

Nearly exploding with rage and embarrassment and a variety of other emotions she didn't care to identify, Dinah said between her teeth, "I thought you were going to send the tapes by courier."

He shrugged. "I had to come to San Francisco for business anyway. It was just as easy to bring them myself. It seemed like a good idea to edit together."

Dinah didn't want to edit the special with him. She didn't want to spend any time with him at all beyond that which was absolutely necessary to finish this misbegotten project. Torn between wanting to see how the interviews they'd done appeared on tape, and her desire to give Roger a piece of her mind, professional curiosity finally won out. The damage today was already done; she could deal with Roger later, when she was in better control. The special was more important right now. The way things had gone this week, it might be the only thing that would salvage her career.

"All right," she said curtly. "We might as well do it now then."

Neil seemed unperturbed at her tone, and for some reason that irritated Dinah even more. She was seething as they walked down the hall toward the editing room, but even through her irritation, she was keenly aware of Neil sauntering along beside her, and she was careful to stay as far away from him as possible. She was infuriated that he had witnessed the fiasco with Marvin Beeson. That particular show seemed to prove exactly how shallow and superficial her series could be, and the contrast between *Personalities* and the work they'd done in Willowset had never been more glaring.

The fact that Neil hadn't commented on the disaster made it even worse. She knew what he had to be thinking, and as they entered the editing room and she introduced Richard, the editor, and asked if they could use his equipment for a while, she vowed that no matter how tempted she might be, she would not ask Neil's opinion. The last thing she needed right now was to see that superior, smug expression on his face— or to hear a lecture about talk shows.

"Sure, Miss Blake," Richard said at once, obviously awed at the presence of Neil Kerrigan. "I'm finished for the day, so you can have the place to yourselves. Unless you want me to stay, that is."

Of course, she wanted him to stay. The thought of being alone with Neil so dismayed her that she knew she'd never be able to maintain her equilibrium without the distraction of a third party. Then Neil said calmly, "Thanks, but I've spent some time in editing. I think we can manage. We're just going to rough it out, anyway."

"Sure thing, Mr. Kerrigan," Richard said respectfully, and before Dinah could object, he grabbed his coat and was gone.

Dinah waited until the door closed behind him before she dared a look at Neil. "So you're an editor, too."

Raising an eyebrow at the edge in her voice, he answered mildly, "It doesn't hurt to be familiar with as many aspects of the job as possible, does it?"

"No, it doesn't," she said frigidly, and held out her hand for one of the tapes.

As she expertly threaded the end of the tape into the machine, she was aware of Neil's surprise and couldn't prevent a smug smile. He wasn't the only one who had familiarized himself with the different facets of the job, she thought in satisfaction, and when the tape was ready to run, she glanced at him again and gestured toward the chair beside her. "I've spent some time in here myself," she said curtly. "Shall we begin?"

A few minutes later, Dinah nearly forgot he was there. She'd begun with the unedited version, and as it unfolded before her, she became completely absorbed. She'd always had an eye for editing. One of her college professors had been so impressed with her ability he'd tried to encourage her to make a career of it. She'd spent many hours in here with Richard, and it hadn't taken him long to realize how adept she was. He'd often joked that she didn't need him at all. That wasn't true, of course. As much as she enjoyed the editing process, she didn't have time to do it on a regular basis. But it was nice to know she could handle the job if necessary, and so every once in a while she joined Richard here, just to keep her hand in. Now she was glad she had.

The tape ended finally, but instead of asking for the edited version, Dinah went through the original again. She'd made some mental notes on the first viewing, and she wanted to confirm her own ideas before she went on. As the tape rolled again, her excitement grew. She'd deliberately dampened her enthusiasm the first time, forcing herself to watch with a clinical eye, but now that she had a clear picture of how she would edit the material, she couldn't prevent a smile of pure delight. It was going to be good, she thought. She knew it; she could feel it. As far as she was concerned, it was the best work she'd ever done, and when the tape ended the second time, she almost felt like shouting with joy.

Then she remembered that Neil was sitting beside her, and so she turned coolly to him. Surprised to find that he was staring at her intently, she drew back a little and said, "Is something wrong?"

He looked amused again. "I was just wondering why I bothered to come."

Her flush deepened. "I'm sorry. I was just so absorbed...."

"So I see. Do you always apply such intense concentration to your work?"

"If it's important, yes. And this is important." Suddenly she couldn't hide her enthusiasm any longer. She was so pleased with what she had seen that if she didn't share it, she'd explode. "I think we've got it, Neil," she said excitedly. "When this material is edited, it's going to be really good."

"It's good now."

Carried away by her excitement, she blurted, "Do you think so. Honestly? It's not just me?"

"It's not just you," he said. "I thought the same thing when I first saw it."

Their eyes met, and in their shared glance, Dinah saw something that shifted her excitement to another plane. Suddenly they were more than colleagues discussing their work. They were a man and a woman who had shared an experience that had changed them in some profound way. Disturbed by the rush of emotion she felt, Dinah looked away. But she could feel his eyes on her, and the silence that fell between them was electric.

"I'd . . . I'd like to see the edited version now," she made herself say. She didn't want to look at him again. She was afraid that something in her eyes, or her face, or the sudden trembling of her mouth, would betray her.

Neil seemed somewhat shaken himself. His hand was unsteady as he handed the tape to her, and she was careful not to touch him as she accepted it. It took all her control to thread the machine this time; she willed her hands not to shake and betray her even further. Cursing the effect he had on her, she was about to start the machine when there was a knock on the door and one of the assistants poked her head in.

"I'm going now, Miss Blake," the girl said, trying not to look admiringly at Neil. "Is there anything I can do before I leave?"

"No, I don't think—" Dinah began, and then happened to glance at the clock. Startled to discover that it was already after seven, she looked uncertainly at Neil. "Maybe we should send out for something to eat," she suggested. "It looks like we're going to be here for a while, unless you want to finish this at another time."

He shrugged. "I've got the time if you do."

They ordered sandwiches and coffee, and by the time the food arrived, they were both intent on the second tape. The interruption had enabled Dinah to compose herself again, and if she concentrated fiercely on the viewer, she could almost pretend that this was a normal situation and that there was nothing out of the ordinary in spending an evening in the editing room with a man who set her pulse racing every time she permitted herself to look at him.

After a while, though, she again became absorbed in what they were doing. It was thrilling to discover that they both had the same approach to editing their show. She admired Neil's suggestions, and he seemed just as pleased with her ideas, and she was elated to find that if she focused only on the tape, she could almost forget how many other things they disagreed on.

Finally, after they'd gone through the material for the third time, Neil sat back and stretched. "I don't know about you, but if I look at this anymore, I'll start to see double."

Now that they had paused for a few minutes, Dinah was surprised to realize that it was nearly midnight. Sometime during the past few hours, the sounds of activity in the station had faded, and she knew that everyone had gone home for the night. Except for the security guard, they were alone. Trying not to feel uneasy at the thought, she took a sip of the cold coffee by her hand and grimaced before putting the cup down again. Sitting back herself, she massaged her temples.

"I know what you mean," she said, forcing a small laugh. "Maybe we should quit for the night."

"How about a nightcap?"

She dropped her hands. "Oh, I—"

"We still have to discuss the narrative," he said persuasively.

She couldn't look at him. Now that she wasn't distracted by the tape, she was too aware of his presence again, of the fact that they were alone. Turning away, she began to fiddle with the equipment to give herself something to do.

"We can't decide on that until we have the final cut," she said, trying desperately to concentrate on anything but the realization that he was sitting right beside her, and that if she wanted to, she could reach out and touch him. She didn't want to touch him; she knew what would happen if she did.

She stood instead. "It's been a long week," she said evasively, still avoiding his eyes. "I really don't think I could concentrate on the commentary right now. I'll make some notes this weekend and send them to you."

He stood with her. "Perhaps you're right," he agreed. "It is late."

Relieved that he hadn't pressed his invitation, she asked impulsively as they left the studio, "Are you flying back to Los Angeles tonight?"

"No, I think I'll just grab a hotel room and go back tomorrow."

They were outside by this time, and as they walked to their cars through the deserted parking lot, Dinah felt even more awkward. It seemed churlish not to have a nightcap with him after they'd spent all evening together, but the thought of going to a bar at this late hour was unappealing. Wondering if she should invite him to her house instead, she was standing there indecisively when he said, "Well, good night, then."

"Good night," she said uncertainly. Then to her horror she heard herself add, "Would you like that nightcap after all? We could go to my house if you want."

He looked surprised. "I thought you were too tired."

"I was...I am..." Wishing she'd never said anything, she knew it was too late to backtrack now, so she floundered on. "Tiburon is only about fifteen minutes away, and I...I could show you the notes I've got so far on the narrative."

Mercifully he didn't remind her that she'd promised to send those notes to him next week or that she'd said she was too tired to concentrate on the narrative now. His smile wasn't even mocking when he said, "Fine. I'll follow you in my car, then."

What could she say after that? Climbing into her car, she watched as Neil went to his, admiring despite herself that easy, effortless stride, the lift of his head. Imagining the hard, lean body under his suit, she bit her lip. What was she doing? It had been an act of pure folly to invite him to her house!

One drink, she told herself as she drove out of the parking lot, Neil following behind. One drink and then he'd leave. She didn't owe him anything, and she absolutely was not going to put herself into a position where she'd do something rash. She'd managed by some miracle to keep her distance tonight, and when they finally arrived at the house, she vowed it would stay that way.

Leading the way into the living room, Dinah went immediately to the liquor cabinet against the far wall. "What would you like?"

"Brandy is fine."

Dinah rarely drank anything stronger than wine, but tonight she poured two snifters, hoping the brandy would give her courage. Turning with one in each hand, she was surprised to see that Neil hadn't moved since coming in. He was standing in the middle of the room gazing around with interest, and Dinah involuntarily looked around, too, trying to see the familiar objects through someone else's eyes.

Like the rest of the house, she had decorated the living room herself, and she'd been pleased with the effect. Knowing it was completely impractical, she hadn't been able to resist the white wall-to-wall carpet because it set everything else off so perfectly. The room was a mixture of styles and periods, from the delicate Queen Anne desk on one wall, to the contemporary salmon-colored modular sofa with its throw pillows in aqua and deep persimmon on the other. Blown-glass lamps on the hand-rubbed oak end tables gave the room a soft glow, and hidden spots in the ceiling highlighted the woven wall hangings and the few paintings she'd chosen with such care. Neil walked over to one tapestry, a four-by-five-foot abstract over the sofa that incorporated the colors in the room, and murmured, "This is beautiful."

"Thank you," Dinah said. "I did that during one of my weaving phases."

"You did this?"

Smiling at his astonishment, she gave him one of the brandies. "I did all the wall hangings."

He glanced admiringly at the tapestry again. "A woman of many surprises," he said. "What other hidden talents do you possess?"

Seating herself gracefully on the couch, Dinah answered, "I wouldn't say it was a talent, exactly. It's more a form of therapy. Setting up a floor loom is a tedious process, but the actual weaving seems to help me work out...problems." She hesitated, taking a sip of brandy before she gestured at the wall hanging. "I did that when I was going through my divorce."

He sat on the couch with her, a careful few feet away. "Did it help?"

"Yes," she said, wondering why she was telling him this. "It gave me something to concentrate on besides myself."

He smiled briefly. "I could have used something like that. My solution was to work twenty-four hours a day."

"I did that, too," she admitted. "The house seemed so empty after Ted left that I didn't want to come home. If I hadn't had the show—" She stopped abruptly. She didn't want to talk about her work at the station, not after the fiasco today. "Anyway," she went on hastily, "I got through it somehow. Now it all seems like a bad dream." She shuddered. "One I never want to go through again."

His look was both curious and intent, a disturbing combination. "You don't intend to get married again?"

Just for an instant, Dinah thought she sensed something deeper behind that seemingly idle question. Then she scoffed at the notion. He was simply making conversation, she told herself firmly, and shrugged, as though amused at the idea. "I might consider it if the right man came along," she said lightly. "But I doubt that will happen. Didn't someone once say that lightning doesn't strike twice?"

"I think that depends on where you're standing," he said with a smile. "If it's in the middle of a field during an electric storm, maybe it could happen."

Now she was sure there was something behind that penetrating blue glance, and she looked away confusedly. She had the sudden thought that she had found herself in the middle of that field, and that he had been that lightning bolt out of the blue, and the image was so disturbing that she took a quick swallow of brandy. Then, to her dismay, she heard herself say, "What about you? Or are you married to your career now?"

His smile this time was bitter. "Elise says I've always been married to my profession."

She couldn't seem to stop herself. "Is it true?"

He hesitated, swirling the amber liquid in the snifter. "My work has always been important to me. Maybe too much so."

"I know what you mean," Dinah said impulsively. "I was shocked when Ted filed for divorce. Until then, I'd thought that we could work it out somehow." Now her voice was the one tinged with bitterness. "We could have, I guess, if I'd agreed to give up my job."

"Was that what he wanted?"

"I'm not sure what he wanted," Dinah said. "He was proud of my success. It was just that he couldn't handle it."

Neil nodded briefly. "Couldn't handle being known as 'the husband of,' you mean. In a way, I can sympathize."

She looked at him sharply. "Why?"

"Even for the most liberated male, that's a tough thing to accept."

"I don't know why it should be," she said in annoyance. "I was expected to support him in his career. Why couldn't he support me in mine?"

He shrugged. "I don't know. I had the same problem with Elise, remember?"

They were silent after that, until finally Neil placed his empty snifter on the coffee table. "It's late. I'd better be going."

She didn't argue. Something about the conversation had disturbed her, but she wasn't sure what it was yet. She couldn't think with him so near. She could already feel herself weakening, wanting to make up some excuse to ask him to stay just a little longer. Before she could say anything, she led the way to the front door and then was completely taken aback when he said quietly, "You're not going to forgive me, are you?"

She made herself look up at him. "I don't know what you mean...."

"I'm talking about the things I said at Lake Tahoe—about you interfering." He hesitated. "I'm sorry, Dinah. I shouldn't have said those things. I know you were just concerned about Andy, so will you accept my apology?"

She didn't know what to say. She wanted to look away and found she couldn't. "Yes," she said faintly. "I accept it."

"Do you?"

She didn't want to discuss this anymore. She could feel herself being drawn inexorably to him, and she didn't want that. It had been so hard to get herself back on an even keel after that skiing trip that she just couldn't put herself through it again. Opening the door, she grasped the edge of it tightly to prevent herself from reaching for him.

"I understand," she made herself say. Her mouth was suddenly so dry she could hardly speak, and her pulse was hammering in her ears.

"I wish I did," Neil said hoarsely, and took an involuntary step toward her.

"What...what do you mean?" she stammered. She looked into his eyes again and knew instantly that she shouldn't have. There was no mistaking the desire she saw there, and her thudding heart skipped a beat.

"I mean that I don't understand what's happening to me," he said raggedly. "Ever since my divorce, I've been able to walk away from any woman I chose. I didn't want to get involved, and I didn't. But then I met you, and suddenly I can't walk away. You're in my thoughts, my dreams. You've become a part of me that I can't deny. I didn't want it to happen, but it did, it has, and now..."

Unable to finish, he reached for her, and there was something so poignant in the gesture that Dinah felt herself responding instantly to it. His arms trembled as she stepped into them, and she closed her eyes briefly when he buried his face in her hair.

"Just tonight," he whispered, his voice shaking with the force of his desire. "Just tonight, that's all I ask...."

The sensation of being in his arms again was so exquisite that Dinah began to tremble violently herself. Somehow, she lifted her head. "And tomorrow, Neil?" she whispered. "What about tomorrow?"

His arms tightened around her. "We'll work it out," he said huskily. "Whatever it is, we'll work it out."

She wanted to say something more, but the contact of his body against hers was like a flame to a candle. The spark he'd ignited became a conflagration the instant his mouth claimed hers, and she could no more have fought it than she could have doused a raging forest fire with a teacup. Uttering a helpless sound, she clung to him as he reached back and shut the door.

CHAPTER FOURTEEN

DINAH WOKE EARLY the next morning, remnants of the dream she'd been having still clinging mistily to the edges of her mind. Now that she was awake, the fragments drifted away and she felt cheated. She'd been dreaming about Neil and she wanted to remember every detail.

Then she turned over and realized it hadn't been a dream at all. Neil was sleeping beside her, his face buried in the pillow, and as she gazed at him, her expression became tender. His jet-black hair was tousled endearingly, and when she reached out to touch it, he shifted position and opened his eyes.

"Good morning," he murmured, and smiled.

"Did I wake you?"

"No, but you should have," he said, and slid an arm under her to pull her closer to him. "Do you know you're just as beautiful in the morning as you are the rest of the day?"

"Even without lipstick?" she teased.

"You don't need lipstick," he replied, kissing her lightly. "Or anything else, for that matter. You're lovely the way you are."

"My, how gallant—and so early in the morning."

"I get better as the day goes on," he murmured, stroking her back.

Remembering the intensity of their lovemaking the night before, Dinah wondered how he could improve. She was still awed by what had happened, and the gentle touch of his hand on her back now conjured up memories of the heights those hands had taken her to last night. When they had both finally collapsed of exhaustion, she'd known that there would never be another man who could begin to compare with Neil.

Without warning, she suddenly wanted him again, and when she looked into his eyes and saw that he was gazing hungrily at her, too, she smiled. "Wasn't there something about a plane you had to catch?"

"There are always planes," he said huskily, and rolled over, taking her with him.

Last night they had both been overwhelmed by the power of their desire. Passion had swept them almost into a frenzy, and after fighting it for so long, their hunger could no longer be denied. But this morning they were able to prolong the anticipation, building their excitement by exploring each other, delighting in the sensations they aroused.

Neil threw back the covers to gaze at her, his eyes traveling slowly over her body, his fingers lightly grazing her slender thighs and the curve of her hip.

"You are beautiful," he whispered, tracing her shoulder and the line of her throat. Murmuring endearments, he pressed his lips against the fullness of her breast, causing her to utter a soft sound and twine her fingers in his hair. When his tongue began to circle her nipple, she shuddered with the aching awareness he aroused and tried to lift his mouth to hers. He shook his head and moved lower, tracing with his tongue the line of her torso, down to her stomach, pushing her legs apart with one hand, and slowly, agonizingly, moving still lower.

He put his mouth to the soft, sensitive flesh of her inner thighs, and then, rolling her over, against the backs of her knees, then upward again to the small of her back. He followed the line of her spine with his tongue until she moaned again and twisted around to touch him, too.

Now it was her mouth, her tongue, her hands, exploring him, and he was the one to shudder under her caresses. Marveling at the width of his shoulders and the breadth of his chest, she placed her hands on his arms, enjoying the feel of the hard biceps, before she abruptly straddled him and looked down into his flushed face.

This time, it was he who reached for her, and she who shook her head. Placing her hands on those powerful shoulders, she slowly bent down and teased one nipple with her tongue, and then the other, before she moved lower, to the hard, contracted muscles of his belly. Lightly stroking his thighs, she brought one hand up to encircle him, caressing him slowly at first, and then more rhythmically, until his breathing became ragged and he groaned and reached for her again.

Anticipation had become torture, and when he rolled over on top of her, she clung to him. He looked down at her, his eyes black with passion, and she could no longer prolong the moment. When she guided him inside her, the sensation was so blissful that she uttered a choked sound. His mouth crushed hers, his tongue probing deep inside, and they were swept away. Her hips rose to meet his, and with every thrust of his body and every answering lift of hers, she could feel that heat spreading inside her. Her entire body throbbed with sensation, and she strained to draw him even deeper within her, so that he filled her being. She wanted to engulf him and to be surrounded by him and to immerse herself in him. She wanted to revel in his desire because it was she who had driven him to it, and he who had aroused such passion in her. She had never felt such blind desire for any man, and the hot touch of his frenzied hands, his tongue twining with hers, added to the agonizingly sweet intensity of the moment.

Gasping as the first shuddering wave of climax claimed her, she called out his name and arched against him, wanting him to come with her. It was her last coherent thought before she was carried away, tossed like a leaf in a storm. Sensations pounded her, and she surrendered to the indescribable pleasure bursting inside her. His hoarse cries were matched by her own, and in that moment, they were truly one.

At last, their ragged breathing quieted, they lay with arms and legs still twined together, and Dinah raised her head. Smiling tenderly when she saw him lying there with one arm flung across his face, she traced the line of his jaw with a fingertip. When he raised his arm slightly and peered at her, she murmured, "If you get better as the day goes on, I'm not sure I'll be able to endure it...."

Dropping his arm over his eyes again, he muttered, "That might have been an empty boast. What did you do to me?"

Laughing throatily, she reached up and kissed his cheek. "I think it was a draw, don't you? How about some breakfast?"

He groaned. "I'm not sure I can get out of bed."

"I thought you had a plane to catch," she teased.

His lips quirked. "Don't start that again. That's what got me into trouble in the first place."

She laughed again and threw back the covers. "I'm going to take a shower, and then we'll have something to eat. Do you think you'll be recovered by then?"

"I don't know," he said, watching her as she shrugged into a short silk robe. "Maybe you'll have to bring me breakfast in bed."

"Fat chance!" she said, and threw one of the pillows at him before she ran into the bathroom.

When she emerged ten minutes later, flushed and rosy from the shower, with tendrils of hair escaping from the hasty knot she'd tied atop her head, the bed was empty and the tantalizing smell of sizzling bacon was drifting up the stairs. Shaking her head wonderingly, she went down to the kitchen and paused on the threshold, smiling at the sight of him by the stove, a fork in one hand and a towel draped casually around his trim waist.

"I see I can add cooking to your list of accomplishments," she said, accepting a cup of coffee from him. "I had no idea you were so versatile."

"I'm afraid my culinary efforts only extend to bacon and eggs," he cautioned as she seated herself on one of the bar stools in front of the kitchen counter. "Anything fancier than that, and we'll have to send out."

"I don't know," she persisted, gazing at him over the rim of the cup and enjoying the nonsense. "You make a mean cup of coffee."

Grinning, he put a full plate in front of her. "I thought I might need it after what you did to me this morning."

She looked at him innocently. "It's too bad that we won't have time for a repeat performance."

Pausing in the act of loading his own plate, he turned to look at her. "Oh?"

Reveling in the disappointment in his voice, she took another sip of coffee. "Well, you did say that you had to fly back to Los Angeles this morning," she said demurely.

"Did I?" he said in mock consternation. "You must have misunderstood."

"Then you don't have to go back right away?" she said mischievously. "You have time to do all the tourist things, like Union Street and Jackson Square and Chinatown? I'll be your guide, and we can spend the whole day just walking around, seeing the sights."

Setting his plate down, he came around the counter. Grasping her shoulders, he lifted her to her feet, and his eyes glowed as he gazed down at her. "The only sight I want to see is you," he said huskily.

Suddenly breathless, she looked up into those compelling eyes of his, and her voice shook slightly when she said, "But don't you want to see—"

She never finished the sentence. His lips stopped her mock protest, and she learned to her delight that he wasn't as exhausted as he'd claimed. She also discovered that her impractical white carpet hadn't been so impractical after all. It wasn't as soft as the king-size bed upstairs, but after a while, she didn't notice the difference at all.

Their lovemaking was just as passionate as it had been before, but there was something so different about making love in the middle of the living-room floor that they were more playful with it, and this time when the climax came, they both laughed exultantly as they collapsed in each other's arms. Dinah couldn't remember ever being so happy, and as she snuggled against him, she never wanted this day to end. Whatever problems they had could be dealt with later. Right now, she intended to enjoy herself, and to surrender to the bliss of being with him and in his arms. He seemed to feel the same way. As he held her close, he sighed in pure pleasure.

In the end, they did go out, Dinah dressed in jeans, an oversize rust-colored jacket, huge sunglasses and an even bigger hat; Neil clad in the change of clothing he'd brought in an overnight bag—jeans faded to a silvery-gray, battered running shoes and an Irish sweater that made him look like one of the fishermen who inhabited the wharf. His sunglasses weren't quite so huge, but every time Dinah looked at the improbable baseball cap he'd added to his disguise, she burst into laughter.

They walked through Fisherman's Wharf like genuine tourists, and quite a few people stared at them as they passed. But it was obvious from the doubtful looks they received that their disguises were successful, and Dinah thought it delicious fun. Neil enjoyed himself, too; it wasn't often that he could go out in public without being recognized. Dinah was amused to think how surprised these people would be if they knew that the man standing at one end of the crowded market eating crab out of a paper boat was the hardnosed journalist, Neil Kerrigan. She could hardly believe it herself. She had never seen him so relaxed and at ease, not even at Lake Tahoe. He was quick to smile, and every time he casually put his arm around her waist as they walked along, she felt a new thrill.

Resolutely, she put aside all her questions and doubts. It was inevitable that this fairy-tale day would come to an end and certain realities be faced, but she wanted to pretend for a short time at least that there were no problems at all between them. Neil had said that somehow they'd work things out, and last night she'd been so hungry for him that she'd been willing to believe anything. But she knew from bitter experience that problems didn't just go away; they had to be dealt with.

But not today, she thought, melting in the warmth of his smile. And maybe not even tonight. Dinah knew that the longer she delayed the realities, the more difficult it would be to face them, but she didn't care. She'd held herself on such a tight rein for so long, corraling her emotions and denying her feelings, that it was a relief to let go for once. Her work and her career had been the sum total of her existence ever since her divorce, but now she saw how empty that life was, how sterile. She felt alive again today, and the feeling was too euphoric to spoil.

So they went to Chinatown and Union Square and Telegraph Hill, with its narrow alleys and small frame houses, and by the time Neil pointed the car toward Tiburon and home again, they were both pleasantly tired and bathed in the warm glow that an unexpected, frivolous day off can bring. Dinah realized with a start that she hadn't thought about the studio for hours, and the ghastly week she'd endured almost seemed like a bad dream.

And then reality raised its ugly head, and she knew the fantasy had come to an end.

"I talked to Andy," Neil said as they sat on the couch before the fire in the living room.

Dinah had made espresso, and at his comment she set the tiny cup aside. The thick dark liquid seemed suddenly bitter. Neil's arm was around her shoulders, and she felt herself tense.

"Oh?" she said, trying to speak casually. "About what?"

"About drugs and drinking. I thought I should hear what he had to say on the subject."

She didn't want to pursue this conversation. Remembering only too well what had happened the last time they had discussed Andy, she wanted to avoid the subject altogether. But she made herself ask, "What did he say?"

"He admitted he'd tried marijuana—but only once."

Dinah looked up at him. "How did you feel about that?"

He smiled sheepishly. "Well, I was ready to lay into him right there, but then he said he hadn't liked it, thank God. I don't know what I would have done if he'd tried to defend it."

Dinah was silent, thinking of some of the kids they'd interviewed. Several had agreed to talk to her only on the condition that they wouldn't appear on TV, and after what they told her, she knew why. They had been devastatingly honest, and she had been horrified.

"Oh, yeah, I can come home totally stoned out of my mind," one girl of about fourteen had said. She'd been dressed in designer clothes, with guileless blue eyes and a face that belonged on the cover of a magazine. "In fact, I do it sometimes just to see if my parents will notice. They never have."

"I haven't been to school all semester," a boy of sixteen, Andy's age, had bragged. When Dinah had asked how he explained his report card to his parents, he'd looked at her disdainfully. "It's easy to change *F*s into *B*s. My old lady thinks I'm a genius because I'm keeping my grades up."

Another girl had laughed slyly. "My mom thinks that smell in my room is incense. Can you believe that?"

And on it went. Dinah had been shaken by the scorn and contempt those teenagers had felt for their parents who didn't know, or refused to believe, how deeply involved their children were in the drug scene, and it distressed her to think that Andy might be part of that. Even though she still had doubts, she tried to take comfort in the fact that Neil had talked to his son about it and was apparently satisfied with the answers he'd received.

"Well, I'm glad you discussed it with him," she said lamely.

"He's never lied to me, Dinah. I believe him when he says he wouldn't touch the stuff."

"Then so do I," she replied, and tried to. But she couldn't rid herself of the image of Andy that night at dinner. She hadn't imagined that feverish look in his eyes, and she could still remember the agitated tapping of that spoon.

"Well, I'm glad that's settled," Neil said with satisfaction.

Is it, Dinah wondered, and avoided his eyes.

"It *is* settled, isn't it?" he asked when she was silent.

"Yes, of course," she said with a quick smile, and hastily changed the subject. "I was just thinking that we haven't discussed the narrative for the program yet.''

He groaned. "Do we have to talk about that now?"

She laughed, relieved to have diverted him success-fully from the subject of Andy. "Would you rather just wing it on Friday?" she teased.

Sighing, he shook his head. Reaching forward, he retrieved his cup from the coffee table. "All right. But I already know what approach I'm going to take."

"What?"

"I'm going to lay it right on the line. As far as I'm concerned, a lot of this abuse is the fault of the par-ents.''

She was startled. "You're going to say that?"

"Indeed, I am," he replied, suddenly grim. "If parents wouldn't let their kids run around like little hellions, they wouldn't get into trouble."

"But most of those teenagers we interviewed came from good homes, with caring parents—"

"How caring can parents be to allow that type of behavior?"

Dinah could feel herself getting frustrated. This was the Neil she liked the least, the inflexible, narrow-minded man who refused to consider any view that collided with his. Dismayed that the conversation had taken such a turn, she began, "I'm sure that they're just as concerned as you would be—"

"If they were concerned, they'd do something about it," he said uncompromisingly. "I did."

Dinah swallowed a reply to that, wondering if other parents had confronted their children just as Neil had, and had been just as satisfied at the answers because they couldn't face the truth.

Neil smiled suddenly and put his arm around her again. "Let's not argue," he said persuasively. "Haven't we got better things to do?"

She wanted to give in to him, to let it go, to pretend that this conversation had never taken place. Their rocky relationship seemed to have smoothed out today, and she didn't want to stir things up again. She could feel the warmth of his body against her side as he held her close, and the pressure of his arm told her that all she had to do was turn her head and their lips would meet.

But if she did that, they would never resolve their differences. She'd be lost in the taste and touch and sensation of him and forget everything else, as she had last night. But they couldn't avoid discussing any issue that might lead to an argument. If their relationship could be destroyed by that, it was no relationship at all.

"I don't want to argue, Neil," she said. "But we do have some things to talk about."

"What things?" he murmured, his lips against her hair.

Closing her eyes against the sensations he was evoking even with that simple gesture, Dinah pulled away. Turning to face him, she curled her legs under her, hoping it would be an effective barrier.

Taking a deep breath, she plunged in. "You've told me what approach you intend to take with this program, but you haven't heard mine."

He shrugged. "It's obvious that you sympathize with these kids, Dinah. I'm sure you'll say something about how tragic the situation is—"

"It *is* tragic!"

"Sure it is. But the problem isn't going to be solved unless we present the facts. You've seen the statistics..."

Annoyed by his attitude, she spoke more sharply than she intended. "I know how statistics can be twisted. I've seen it done too many times."

"Then it's our job to make sure that doesn't happen, isn't it?"

She tried again. "But this special isn't only about facts, Neil. I thought we agreed on that in the beginning."

"You agreed on it. I said I had to report it as I saw it."

"All right, then, so will I. As I told you before, Neil, I don't believe that the situation is as simple as you make it out to be. It's not that black and white."

"It is to me."

Her frustration growing, Dinah tried to remain calm. "I still think your attitude is too harsh."

"Why? Because I believe in facing issues squarely and dealing with them? That's why I talked to Andy, why I asked him straight out if he was involved with drugs."

"And you were satisfied with his answer."

"I told you I was."

She took a deep breath. "What if he wasn't telling you the truth?"

The first hint of coldness entered his eyes. "I told you, Andy doesn't lie to me."

She couldn't stop herself. "I talked to other parents who said the same thing. And their kids weren't telling the truth at all."

The blue glance had turned frosty. "Are you saying that's the case with Andy?"

Despite herself, her voice took on a pleading note. "Of course not. I was just using that as an example, trying to show you that sometimes facts have to be tempered with—"

"I don't understand you," he interrupted. "When are you going to realize that you can't allow sentimentality to interfere with your job?"

She was stung into a sharp reply. "And when are you going to realize that there's more to life than cold facts?"

He was annoyed at that. "Facts are what I deal with every day," he said. "And if you don't mind my saying so, you'd be better off if you dealt with them, too."

"What does that mean?"

"Take your show, for instance," he said, ignoring the sudden edge in her voice. "The other day is a perfect example. That guest, Beeman, or Bateman—"

"Beeson," she said through her teeth. "His name was Marvin Beeson."

He waved a dismissive hand. "Whatever. The point is, you let him get away with murder. He spent the whole time promoting the most outrageous, ridiculous theory I've ever heard, and you didn't call him on it. Why, Dinah? Were you afraid of hurting his feelings?"

"Of course not!"

"Oh, I see," he said. "Then you didn't want to embarrass him in front of your audience."

"No, I didn't," she snapped. "But that's beside the point."

"It's exactly the point," he said calmly. "If you had made him defend his theory instead of just allowing him to promote it, you would have been doing your viewers a service. You would have been doing him a service, by forcing him to reevaluate his opinions. I know you're capable of it, Dinah. I saw you do it in Willowset with that police officer. Why don't you do the same thing on your show?''

"It's not that simple—"

"Why not? Don't tell me you're happy doing that kind of thing, because I won't believe you. You're too intelligent, too perceptive—"

"Well, thank you for that much at least," she said scathingly. "I was beginning to think I had no good qualities at all."

"That's not what I meant, and you know it."

"I don't know what you mean, Neil. I don't know why we're having this discussion at all!"

"Don't you? I'm trying to help—"

"By criticizing everything I say?"

"By showing you that you have the capability to do more."

He was right and she knew it. He hadn't said anything she hadn't thought herself a hundred times or more, just this week. She'd agonized over it and shed tears over it and been frustrated to the point of quitting over it, and Neil's comments touched a raw nerve.

An image of Marvin Beeson's fatuous, vacuous face rose in her mind, and it seemed to Dinah in that moment that he represented everything that was wrong with her show. She'd wanted to destroy the pompous man's satisfied, superior expression with one word. But she hadn't been able to do that. Roger Dayton had effectively tied her hands by refusing to allow her more latitude, and her frustration finally erupted.

"Don't you think I know what I'm capable of?" she said again, bitterly. "If I could change the format of the show, I would!"

"Then why haven't you?"

She'd gone too far; she might as well tell him everything. "Because I don't have the power you do, that's why."

"Then go somewhere else."

She looked at him as though he were out of his mind. "Go somewhere else," she repeated incredulously. "You make it sound so easy!"

"That's what I'd do."

"But you don't have to!" she cried. "That's the whole point! You can do whatever you want to with your show, and no one says a thing!"

He didn't deny it. "It wasn't always that way, Dinah. I had to fight for it. You can, too."

She lifted her head against the sudden sting of tears in her eyes. She would not cry, she told herself. "Yes, but it was a little easier for you, wasn't it, Neil? After all, you're a man."

"That's beneath you, Dinah, an excuse other women might use, but not you. You deserve better than what you're doing with *Personalities* and we both know it. And if you can't change it, do something about it.

"What?" she said acidly. "Quit? Admit defeat, and start all over somewhere else? I don't imagine even you would do that!"

"If I wasn't getting the recognition I deserved, I would." He reached suddenly for her hand. "I know a lot of people in this business, Dinah. I can help...."

It was so tempting to let her fingers lie in his, to accept his comfort and support. She wanted to fling herself into his arms and weep with frustration, allow him to wipe her tears away and tell her that everything would be all right. But then her pride came to her rescue, and she reminded herself how high a price she'd paid for her career. She'd sacrificed her marriage for it, and she couldn't negate that sacrifice now by clinging to Neil. She might want to right now, but she knew that she'd hate herself for it later, so she took her hand away.

"I don't need your help," she muttered. "No one helped me get where I am now, Neil, and even though that might not be much to you, it is to me."

His eyes darkened. "I didn't say that, and you know it. Why are you being so stubborn about this? Haven't you heard anything I've said?"

"Oh, I think you've made yourself very clear."

"Obviously, it didn't do any good."

"Why? Because I don't agree with you? I have a right to my opinion, Neil."

"I never said you didn't."

Suddenly Dinah just wanted him to leave. She hadn't meant to say all the things she had earlier, and she was mortified and angry with herself. Her thoughts were whirling in so many directions that she didn't know what she thought anymore. She needed time to think, to sort things out. And this time, she wouldn't allow herself to be so overwhelmed by her feelings for him that she ignored their fundamental differences that had made her so unhappy before.

"I think you'd better go," she said.

He hesitated, obviously wanting to say something more and then deciding against it as he stood. "I'm sorry, Dinah."

She wouldn't look at him. "Let's just drop it, shall we?"

He gazed down at her a moment longer, then said quietly, "I'll see you in Los Angeles next week, then."

"I'll be there," she muttered, feeling like a fool. She knew she had overreacted, but it was too late now. If he didn't leave soon, she would burst into tears and that would be the final blow to her pride.

But after he had gone, she sat bleakly on the couch, staring vacantly into the dying fire. It was all her fault, she thought. She'd been a fool to think that they could work this out. The only thing they had proved tonight was that they would never agree on anything. He'd accused *her* of being stubborn, but he was the most inflexible man she'd ever met, and she doubted that he would ever change. Sobbing, Dinah knew that the fantasy had suddenly come to an end.

NEIL WAS STILL ANGRY with himself when he arrived at the airport and boarded his flight. Feeling like a fool as he strapped himself in, he knew he never should have offered to help Dinah. Now that he thought about it, he realized how condescending he'd sounded, how patronizing. No wonder she'd reacted the way she had; if he'd been in her position, he would have been furious.

Damn it to hell, he cursed silently. He should have known better; next time he would.

If there was a next time, he thought morosely, and absently accepted a drink he didn't want from a flight attendant without even noticing her admiring smile.

CHAPTER FIFTEEN

"IF YOU ASK ME," Leigh said the night before Dinah was due to leave for Los Angeles, "you're going about this all wrong."

Dinah turned from her self-inspection in the three-way mirror. It was after-hours at Leightique, and she had come in to choose what she was going to wear for the final taping of the special. She'd already tried on six different outfits, but nothing pleased her, including the pink-and-white polka-dot dress she currently had on.

"If I wear this, I'll look like a clown," she said crossly.

Leigh looked exasperatedly at her. "If there's one thing you never look like, Dinah, it's a clown. Aren't you going to answer me?"

Grabbing the next dress Leigh held out, Dinah headed toward the fitting room again. "No," she said, and jerked the curtain shut.

Leigh wasn't intimidated by the gesture. She immediately jerked the curtain aside again and stood in the doorway, arms akimbo. "Do you know what I think?"

Dinah sighed. Glancing at her reflection as she buttoned the new dress, a periwinkle silk with gold trim, she thought this one might do. "No," but I'm sure you're going to tell me."

Ignoring the sarcasm, Leigh stepped forward, automatically adjusting the shoulders on Dinah's dress. "I think you're in love with him and just don't want to admit it."

Dinah tightened the belt another notch. "That's ridiculous," she said, looking over her shoulder for a back view. "What shoes should I wear with this?"

Leigh handed her a pair of heels that matched the gold piping on the dress. "Try these. And what's ridiculous about it? The fact that you're in love with him, or the fact that you don't want to admit it?"

Slipping the heels on, Dinah gazed critically at the effect. Yes, this was the one—finally. "Both," she said and began to unbutton the dress again. "If I was in love with him, why would I be afraid to admit it?"

"Don't take that off yet. We still have to find some accessories. And you wouldn't admit it because of what happened with Ted."

Dinah looked at her disdainfully before she brushed by and went out to the jewelry case by one wall. "Neil is definitely not Ted," she said, and pointed to a pair of earrings the same shade as the dress. "What about those?"

Leigh crossed her arms. "Those will be fine. And now that you're dressed, will you stop a minute and talk to me?"

Sighing again, Dinah leaned against the jewelry counter. "There's nothing to talk about. I told you about the argument we had."

"From the sound of it, it seems that you were the one doing the arguing. He was only trying to help."

"That's not the way I saw it," Dinah said sullenly.

"Of course not," Leigh said, sounding exasperated again. "If you weren't so busy trying to deny your attraction to him, you would have—"

"I haven't denied that I'm attracted to him," Dinah interrupted.

Leigh rolled her eyes. "Oh, yes. I believe you said the man had a certain…fascination. But isn't it more than that? Come on, Dinah. We've been friends for too long. I know you, and you're in love with Neil. Why can't you admit it? What are you afraid of?"

Dinah looked down at the earrings in her hands, rolling them over and over between her fingers. "I am afraid," she said slowly. "I don't want the same thing to happen with Neil that happened between me and Ted."

"But you've admitted they're two entirely different men."

"Yes, and the problems are different, too. But they're problems, all the same."

"What problems?"

Dinah sighed again. She wondered how she could explain her feelings to Leigh when she wasn't sure she could explain them to herself. She'd thought a great deal about that conversation she and Neil had had the other night, and the more she thought about it, the more their differences seemed insurmountable. He was so inflexible on the issues that were important to her. She couldn't help but wonder if in the future their opposing viewpoints would become even more incompatible, until they had nothing in common at all.

Then, too, there was the issue of her career. Neil had expressed sympathy for Ted not being able to handle her success, and she wondered if he would resent her competing in the same profession. If they became even more deeply involved, would he one day expect her to sacrifice her ambitions for his larger, more important ones? Ted had, and at the time he'd demanded that of her, his career was nowhere near the height of success that Neil enjoyed. Oh, it was all so complicated, so seemingly hopeless.

"Have you tried to talk to Neil about some of these things?" Leigh asked quietly, after Dinah had tried haltingly to explain. "Because if you haven't, I think you should. Maybe you'll be surprised at the answers."

"And maybe I won't want to hear them at all," Dinah said depressingly.

"Well, isn't it better to know?"

As Dinah drove home, she realized Leigh was right. She couldn't go on this way, and at least if she confronted Neil, she'd know where she stood. She hadn't spoken to him since that night, and she dreaded the inevitable awkwardness of their first meeting tomorrow. They had agreed to hammer out the final draft of the script at the station before the taping on Friday, and she'd spent hours forcing herself to concentrate on writing her part. Leigh had read a copy of what she had written and had been deeply moved, but Dinah doubted that Neil would feel the same way.

No doubt he'd accuse her of being sweet and sentimental, she thought in sudden irritation and decided right then that if he demanded an entire rewrite, he'd have a fight on his hands. She wasn't going to defer to him, not on this. She knew her approach was right for her, and she wouldn't change it just because he was too pigheaded and narrow-minded to see things any other way!

THE NEXT MORNING, in Los Angeles, Neil was waiting for her when she arrived at the station. Before she could say anything, he took her arm and practically dragged her into his office. As she turned indignantly to him, he closed the door and said, "Dinah, we have to talk."

She was instantly wary. "Why? Has something gone wrong? Aren't we taping tomorrow?"

He looked exasperated. "It has nothing to do with the show. Well, in a way it does, but it's not that."

He stopped abruptly and ran a hand through his hair. It was a gesture she had rarely seen him use, and she asked, more sharply than she intended, "What is it, then?"

"It's you and me . . . us!"

She was so surprised that she just stared at him. Sinking back against the edge of the desk for support, she thought confusedly that this wasn't the scenario she had imagined at all. She'd geared herself up for a fight with him, and this had caught her completely off guard.

"What about . . . us?" she asked cautiously, and then understood. *He's decided against doing the special after all,* she thought. *He's going to tell me that they've postponed it indefinitely and that I shouldn't have come.* Her eyes blazing with sudden anger, she pushed herself away from the desk again. "If you're trying to get out of doing this program at this late date—"

Startled by her challenge into a quick response of his own, he interrupted, "I told you, this has nothing to do with the damned show!"

She stared at him defiantly. "What then?"

"It's . . . it's . . . Oh, hell!" he said, and took a step toward her.

She wasn't prepared for the look on his face, and she tried to back away. But the desk pressed into her, and when he put his hands on her shoulders, she nearly cried out.

"What are you doing?"

"I wish to hell I knew," he said. "I've just spent the most miserable week of my life, and I don't know why. If we don't get this straightened out between us soon, I think I'll go out of my mind!"

Dinah felt mesmerized, hardly able to breathe. The pressure of his hands on her shoulders increased, but she hardly felt it. She couldn't believe this was happening; she didn't know what to say.

"Well, say something!" he demanded, when she continued to stare dazedly up at him.

She shook her head slightly, trying to free herself of the spell she seemed to be under. "I don't know what to say," she said faintly.

"Do you want me to apologize again, is that it?" he demanded. "Because if it is, I will. I'm sorry, Dinah. It seems like every time I turn around I'm apologizing to you for something or other, but if that's what it takes . . ."

She couldn't help it. A smile tugged at the corners of her mouth as he spoke, and he looked so anxious and aggrieved and angry all at the same time that she wanted to laugh. Instead, she shook her head again and started to say, "You don't have to apologize, Neil. I—"

He released her so abruptly that she nearly staggered back. Grasping the edge of the desk for balance, she looked at him in dismay as he said, "I'd like to know what you find so damned amusing!"

She was appalled. "I wasn't laughing at you, Neil!"

"Forget it!" he snapped. "I'd thought we could talk this out like two reasonable human beings, but I should have known better!"

To her horror, she saw him reaching for the door. Without thinking, she flung herself toward him and grasped his arm. "Wait!"

He jerked his arm away. "Why, so you can laugh at me again?"

"I told you, I wasn't laughing," she said desperately. "It was just that you looked so...so... I've never seen you look like that before, and I—"

"I've never felt this way before," he growled. "Half the time I don't even know what I'm feeling. Damn it, Dinah, I..."

He turned to her then, and the look on his face was her downfall. Without even being aware of what she was doing, she stumbled into his willing arms. The tightness of his embrace was the sweetest sensation she'd ever felt, the more poignant because she'd thought never to experience it again. Clinging to him, she looked up into his eyes and started to say, "Oh, Neil..."

She never finished the sentence. His mouth came down hard on hers, and there was such a sense of urgency in the pressure of his lips that she responded in kind. All the longing she'd felt for him burst inside her, and she wound her arms around his neck, pressing her body tightly against his. His hard thighs were against hers, his chest crushed her breasts, and yet it was more than a kiss of passion and desire. It was a meeting of two hearts that had been fighting too long against love. As her lips parted under his, Dinah knew that she had lost the battle and didn't care.

Dazed when they finally broke away, Neil shook his head as if to clear it. Still holding her tightly, it was a moment before he could speak. "Do you think we can talk now?" he asked raggedly.

Too breathless to answer, Dinah looked up into his handsome face and nodded.

BUT THEY DIDN'T HAVE TIME to talk until that evening, and in a way, Dinah was glad. She'd been so swept away by her feelings that she needed time to regain her perspective, and the two production meetings that had been scheduled for them gave her the opportunity. She viewed the final cut of the tape with Chuck and Larry and then met with the writers who would polish the script. The necessity of attending to these details gave her breathing space, time to get her thoughts in order again.

Because as much as she would have liked it to, one kiss couldn't banish the problems that still had to be resolved. But whenever she felt Neil's eyes on her that day or heard the warmth in his voice or saw his quick smile, she became determined that they would work things out somehow. They had to, she thought; she couldn't go on this way. They seemed to have come to a crossroads, and she knew that if they didn't discuss their differences now, they never would.

But she was apprehensive when they were finally able to leave the station at the end of that long day. As the Ferrari roared along the coast highway toward his home where Neil had promised to cook dinner for her, Dinah tried to tell herself there was no reason to be nervous. Neil himself had said that they had to talk, so he clearly realized there were certain difficulties to be faced. He wouldn't have said that if he hadn't intended to try to come to some compromise. It was a beginning, she thought; it would be up to them both to make it something more.

Neil's apartment was a surprise. Dinah had expected a typical bachelor's pad with leather furniture and dark colors, but when she walked in, she exclaimed with pleasure at the rusts and golds and greens of the decor and at the abstract paintings on the off-white walls. Track lighting illuminated the living room in a warm glow, and she laughed when she realized one wall was entirely covered by stereo and television and recording equipment. It looked like a jet's cockpit, and she couldn't resist teasing him about it.

"Do you need a license for all that?"

He looked at her loftily. "I'll have you know that's the latest in high tech."

"It looks like it. Does it work?"

Indignantly, he reached out and fiddled with a few dials. The room filled with glorious sound, and Neil grinned at her expression. "Steaks all right for dinner?"

She smiled back. "Can I help?"

"You can do the salad."

They seemed to have an unspoken agreement to wait until after dinner for any serious discussion, and

Dinah was glad of that, too. As they worked side by side in the kitchen, she couldn't help thinking how wonderful it would be if it could always be this way. Then she pulled herself up short. They had a long way to go before they reached that stage, she reminded herself, if they ever reached it at all.

They ate in the dining room, and Dinah was touched when Neil set the table with linen and silver and candlesticks. Their conversation ranged over a number of subjects, each of them avoiding the one most important until the candles had burned halfway down and Neil brought in coffee.

"I was impressed with the narrative you wrote for the show," he said casually, after pouring them both a cup.

Dinah knew the comment was anything but casual, and she tensed. This was the opening she'd been waiting for, and he'd deliberately given it to her. She had no choice but to take it. She knew if she delayed discussing their relationship any longer, she wouldn't want to discuss it at all. He looked so handsome in the candlelight that every time she glanced at him, her throat ached with longing.

"I wasn't sure you'd like it," she said carefully.

His eyes met hers. "Why?" he asked.

"Well, the last time we talked about it, we didn't . . . agree."

He was silent for a few seconds, studying her face. Finally he said, "The last time we talked about it, I wasn't thinking straight." He leaned forward suddenly, as though to convince her of the truth of what he was about to say. "I know you think my views are harsh, Dinah, and maybe they are. But I don't think I ask any more of anyone than I do of myself.''

"But not everyone is as strong as you are, Neil," she pointed out. "Your standards are so high—"

"I don't expect everyone to meet my standards," he protested.

"Yes, you do," she said, smiling faintly to take the sting from her words. "You have such a clear idea of what's right and wrong that you have no patience with what the rest of us call human weakness."

He sat back. "I can't deny that. I've always thought that the most insidious phrase in the English language is 'I'm doing my best.' It just seems to be an excuse not to do better."

She smiled again at that. "You see what I mean? That's where we're so different. I can always see all the shades of gray between your black and white."

He leaned forward again, this time covering her hand with his. "But that doesn't mean we can't compromise," he said softly.

Her heart leaped despite herself. Those were the words she had longed to hear, but she had to know if he really meant it. "I didn't think that word was in your vocabulary," she said quietly.

"It is now," he answered, his fingers tightening over hers. "Dinah, I don't want to lose you. I know we view things differently, but is that really important?''

"Yes," she said steadily. "It is."

"But why?"

She forced herself to meet his eyes. "Think back to the argument we had the other night, Neil. You were upset with me because you told me what your solution was and I didn't agree."

"I told you I wasn't thinking straight that night. I know I went about it the wrong way, Dinah, but I did want to help. You're too good to waste your talents on a show like *Personalities*. I just wanted you to realize that."

"Don't you think I do? I've wanted to change the format for a long time, Neil, but—" She shook her head slightly. "Let's not talk about the show right now, all right? Another problem is that I'm just not sure I want a long-distance relationship—stolen weekends here and there when you're not off on assignment somewhere, hurried phone calls now and then. It just won't work."

He looked uncomfortable. "We could make it work. You could come to Los Angeles. The network will give you something here."

She felt the first stab of irritation at that and tried to suppress it. She had promised herself she'd be calm about this. "Why? Because you ask them to?"

He heard the edge in her voice and tried to recover. "No, because you're good at what you do, Dinah. You said yourself you weren't happy with your show."

"I'm not, but my career is just as important to me as yours is to you, Neil. How would you feel if I asked you to come to San Francisco?"

He looked startled at that. Obviously, the idea had never occurred to him. "But my show originates in Los Angeles."

"And mine is based in San Francisco," she said evenly. "Is your work more important than mine?"

"I didn't say that," he protested, but she saw by his expression that it was, and she began to get angry despite her resolve.

Neil tried again. "I know how important your work is to you, Dinah. I accept that. It's just that you should be doing something more with your talents than interviewing people like Marvin Beeson."

"I intend to," she said. "But I can't do a hard-news show like yours."

"I'm not asking you to."

"Aren't you? Have you changed your opinion about talk shows?"

He looked uncomfortable again. "No," he admitted. "But after the work you did in Willowset, I'd hoped you would have changed yours."

"But I haven't, Neil, and that's just the point. I want to have guests on my show like Dr. Mason and Mark Delaney of Get In Touch—people who have made a difference. Not generals and senators and governors like you interview, but men and women who work quietly behind the scenes accomplishing things that improve the quality of life." This time it was she who leaned forward to emphasize her point. "Human interest, Neil. That's what I want to explore on my program. Because there's more to life than digging up cold facts."

He was silent at that, obviously wanting to say something and debating about whether to say it. "Oh, Dinah." He sighed, and she knew by the tone of his voice that she hadn't gotten through to him after all.

Before he could say anything more, the ringing of the phone interrupted them. As Neil muttered something and got up to answer it, she slumped in her chair. She hadn't realized how tense she'd been until they were interrupted, but now she felt exhausted. Trying not to feel hopeless, as well, she took a sip of coffee, and wondered what more there was to say.

NEIL WAS IRATE when he went to answer the phone. The interruption had come at an awkward time and he would have let the damned thing ring if he hadn't been about to say something stupid. But he didn't want a repetition of last weekend when he'd made a fool of himself. He had to think about what Dinah had said and gather his own thoughts. *Human interest!* he thought, and barked a hello into the receiver.

"Neil, something terrible has happened," Elise cried hysterically as soon as she heard his voice. "I just don't know what to do! You have to come over here right away!"

"What is it? Is it Andy?"

"Of course it's Andy! Why else would I call you? Oh, Neil, I'm so frightened! I didn't even recognize him. He was like a stranger!"

"Calm down," he ordered curtly, aware of Dinah turning to look at him before he jerked his attention back to the phone. "Is Andy hurt?"

"Yes...no...I don't know!" Elise gabbled. "Oh, Neil, I found all sorts of pills in his room, hidden in a drawer. I wasn't looking for anything, I was just putting some of his clothes away, and I...and I found them. Dozens of them! I don't even know what they are!"

Neil tried to remain calm. "It must be a mistake."

"That's what I thought!" she cried. "But when I asked him, he...he... Oh, Neil. It was awful. He flew into a rage and told me it was none of my business!"

"Where is he?" Neil demanded. "Put him on the phone right now!"

"I can't!" Elise wailed. "He took my car. I couldn't stop him!"

Forcing himself not to panic, Neil took a deep breath. "Think carefully, Elise. Was he on something?"

"He must have been. He wasn't himself, Neil. You know Andy would never do anything like that. What are we going to do?"

Neil didn't hesitate. "I'm calling the police," he said grimly.

"The police! Oh, Neil, you can't!"

"What the hell else can I do? We don't have any idea where he is, and if he's..." He couldn't say it again. The thought that his son was involved with drugs enraged and horrified him at the same time, and his voice was harsh when he amended, "He's obviously in no condition to drive. He's a menace to himself and everyone else."

"But, Neil!" Elise wailed.

"How could you have let this happen?" he shouted suddenly. "Goddamn it, Elise—"

"How could *I* have let it happen?" she screeched. "He's your son, too! Maybe if you had paid a little more attention to him, instead of running around with that...that *woman*, none of this would have happened!"

Elise's shrill accusation reminded him that Dinah was still there, and he flicked a glance in her direction. She could hardly have missed the gist of the conversation the way he'd been shouting, and the thought that she'd witnessed this enraged him all over again.

With a fierce effort, he controlled his impulse to smash the phone through the wall.

"We'll talk about this later," he grated to Elise. "Right now the important thing is finding Andy."

Her voice was a quaver. "Are you still going to call the police?"

"Yes," he said tautly. "And I hope to hell they find him. As far as I'm concerned, they can lock him in a cell and throw away the key."

"Oh, Neil! You don't mean that!"

His jaw was clenched so tightly that it hurt. "Oh, yes, I do!"

Crashing the phone down on another wailing protest, Neil closed his eyes. This wasn't happening, he thought. It had to be some ghastly mistake.

But he knew it was no mistake. Elise had found the pills, and there was only one reason for Andy to have them. So he'd lied the other night. He'd sat right across the table and lied when Neil had asked him about drugs. Staring blindly down at the phone, his fingers clenched around it until the knuckles were white.

"Neil," Dinah said quietly from somewhere behind him. "Is there anything I can do?"

He couldn't seem to make himself turn and face her just yet, so he kept his back to her and muttered, "No. There's nothing you can do."

"I'd like to help."

He whirled around then, his expression so filled with rage and pain that Dinah paled. "I said there's nothing you can do! There's nothing anyone can do! He took Elise's car!"

"We could go looking for him."

His eyes blazed. "And just where do you suggest? In case you haven't noticed, Los Angeles is a big place. For all we know, he might have splattered himself all over a freeway by now!"

She flinched at that. "Neil, I know you're upset—"

"Upset! *Upset?* My wife calls to tell me she found dozens of pills in my son's room, and you think I'm upset?"

"Neil, please," she said desperately. "You have to calm down."

"Calm down?" he shouted. "Andy's driving around somewhere stoned out of his mind on something, and you want me to be calm?"

She tried to take his arm. "Come and sit down."

He jerked his arm away so savagely that she nearly fell. "I don't want to sit down! I just want my son found!"

"We'll find him, Neil," she said urgently. "We will. You have to believe that."

"I don't know what to believe anymore," he said, and was appalled when his voice broke. Trying to control himself, he went to the liquor cabinet and poured himself a straight Scotch. The alcohol burned going down, but it didn't make him feel better, and in a sudden violent movement that was so foreign to him even he was shocked, he took the glass and threw it as hard as he could against the wall.

It shattered into a million pieces, and as he looked at it in horror, a new voice said, "Good shot, Dad. Want to try it again?"

Dinah and Neil both whirled around. They'd been so intent that they hadn't heard the door open. When

Dinah saw Andy on the threshold, that feverish look in his eyes and a sneer on his face, she blanched. It was even worse than she had thought. She couldn't imagine how Andy had even gotten here in this condition, and when he staggered into the room to face his father, she wrenched her eyes away to look at Neil.

He seemed carved of stone.

CHAPTER SIXTEEN

IF DINAH lived to be a hundred, she knew she'd never forget the look on Neil's face as Andy swaggered into the living room. His anger was all the more frightening because it was so controlled, and even though she'd been shocked when he'd thrown that glass across the room, she would almost have preferred another violent outburst to the deadly silence that fell.

Not knowing what else to do, she placed a hand on Neil's arm. It felt like granite, and that frightened her even more. He hadn't moved or spoken since Andy had come into the room, and in an effort to defuse some of the tension, she said desperately, "Neil, please. I'm sure there's an explanation...."

Neil's eyes never left his son. The words ground out of him one by one, forced between lips that barely moved. "There...is...no...explanation."

Andy laughed suddenly, a high, shrill sound that was chilling. "That's right, Dad. There never is an explanation, is there? No excuse is ever good enough for you. Well, you want to know something? I don't have an excuse. I don't have any explanations! So what do you think of that?"

The challenge rang out in the room. Dinah hadn't believed it possible, but Neil became even more rigid.

"What have you taken?" he demanded harshly. "What are you on?"

"I haven't the faintest idea," Andy sneered. "I just took a handful, and that was it." He laughed again, teetering back and forth, trying to focus. "Don't you know that's the only way to fly?"

Dinah had promised herself she wouldn't interfere, but she couldn't just stand there and do nothing. Alarmed by the pallor of Andy's face and by the glittering look in his unfocused eyes, she tightened her grip on Neil's arm. "Maybe we should take him to the hospital."

Neil shook her off. "We'll deal with this right here," he grated, and turned to his son. "You dare to stand there and tell me you took a handful of pills and don't even know what they are? I can't believe you would be so stupid! Where did you get them?"

Andy's lip curled. He seemed to have trouble standing; he braced himself against the side of the couch. "You really think I'm going to tell you that?"

"Before this evening is over, you will," Neil grated. "In addition to everything else, you've broken the law."

"Which law is that?" Andy asked derisively. "Neil Kerrigan's law? The one that says, 'no son of mine is going to step out of line'?"

Neil looked nearly apoplectic at that. "What's the matter with you?" he shouted suddenly, losing control. "Don't you realize what a terrible chance you're taking with your health? If you don't care about yourself, at least think of your mother. She's almost out of her mind with worry!"

Just for an instant, Andy looked young and vulnerable. The corners of his mouth trembled and he seemed about to cry. Then that frightening stranger's mask slipped down over his face again and his expression became contemptuous.

"But you're not worried, are you, Dad? You're so furious I'll bet you even called the police!"

"I was going to," Neil said inexorably. "I wasn't going to allow you to drive around in this condition. You're obviously not yourself."

Andy laughed again. "Is that what you're really worried about? Isn't it more how the headlines would read if I cracked up? Imagine, the son of the great crusader busted for drugs! What would happen to your saintly image then?"

Neil was so furious he took a step toward him, his hands clenched. Dinah had listened in appalled silence, telling herself after that one outburst that she couldn't intervene, but she was so afraid of what he might do that she put her hand on his arm again. "Neil, please! This isn't doing any good. Can't you see he needs help?"

He shook her off as though she were a fly. "He needs help, all right," he snapped. "Maybe a few months at a work farm will rearrange his priorities."

She looked at him in horror. "You don't mean that!"

His expression was so fierce that she shrank back. "Don't I?" he shouted. "Well, maybe you'd rather deal with this on one of your programs, then! Is this what you meant by human interest stories? Take a good look, Dinah, and tell me I should feel sorry for him! Go ahead, tell me that he deserves any sympathy at all!"

She was appalled. "How can you be so unfeeling?"

"I'll tell you how," Andy said fiercely. "Because the only thing he cares about is performance, and I haven't performed very well tonight."

His blue eyes, so like his father's, shifted to Neil, and his bitterness was like a physical blow. "In fact, I haven't performed very well my entire life, have I, Dad? Nothing has ever been good enough for you, has it? I not only had to make the honor society, I had to be captain of the team. Straight *A*s and a thirty-point game average, that was all you cared about, wasn't it?" With each word, his voice had risen until he was nearly screaming. "Well, you want to know something? I haven't been to school in weeks, and coach kicked me off the team. What do you have to say about that?"

Neil was stunned. "What do you mean you haven't been to school in weeks? Someone would have called. They would have let your mother know!"

"Oh yeah? You think they care about that? All I had to do was forge your name on a pass!"

"You did *what*!"

Andy looked insufferably pleased with himself, enraging his father even further. "The name Kerrigan is magic, Dad," he said derisively. "I just had to say that you wanted me to go on assignment with you somewhere, and they couldn't let me go fast enough. Because isn't that always where you are—on assignment?"

"How dare you forge my name on anything!" Neil roared. "Where were you all that time? What were you doing?"

"What's it to you?"

Neil's face was crimson. "You'll find out, young man! You tell me this instant!"

"And if I don't?"

Neil took a step toward him. "This is your future you're fooling around with, and I'm not going to let you waste it!"

"You don't have any choice!"

"You bet I do!"

Dinah wanted to put her hands over her ears and run from the room, away from the ugly words they were hurling at each other, away from the hurtful things Neil had said to her. But she seemed caught between these two powerful opposing forces: Andy, so belligerent and hostile; Neil, so furious he wasn't listening to anything his son was trying to say. She had to do something; she couldn't let this confrontation escalate further.

Stepping between them, she cried, "Stop it! Stop it! Screaming at each other isn't going to solve anything. Can't you just talk—"

Andy flung up his head. "Talk!" he spat. "He never listens to anything I say. He's so sure he's right and the rest of the world is wrong that I could talk until I'm blue in the face and it wouldn't make any difference!"

She turned frantically to him. "But have you ever tried, Andy? Have you ever told your father what you really feel? I'm sure he would listen—"

Neil interrupted then, his voice so harsh she hardly recognized it. "I've listened to enough tonight to last me a lifetime. It's beyond me that a son of mine could behave so irresponsibly, and I'm not going to tolerate it. Do you hear me, Andrew? I'm not going to tolerate it!"

Dinah looked at Neil in dismay, unable to believe he could be so unforgiving. Hadn't he heard anything his son had said? The pain and anguish in Andy's voice, the terror of not being able to live up to his father's expectations, had been so clear to her....

"Neil," she said helplessly. "Can't you—"

He looked at her, his eyes blazing. "Is this enough human interest, Dinah?" he shouted. "Would you like to call Chuck and Larry and do another interview right here? Think what it would mean to your precious career if you were the first to get the scoop about the Kerrigan family! You might even get an Emmy for it, because God knows, it would be the talk show of the year!"

Dinah was so shocked she was speechless. The absolute contempt with which he had flung those last words at her was like a knife through her heart. She couldn't believe that even in his own rage and pain he could deliberately hurl such hurtful accusations at her, as though her career was uppermost in her mind right now. The thought so appalled her that she stumbled back from him.

"Way to go, Dad," Andy sneered. "Just because you're mad at me—"

"Stay out of this!" Neil snapped, and took a step toward Dinah. "I didn't mean—"

Dinah didn't trust herself to speak. Whirling around, she grabbed her coat and purse, and then her suitcase, which mercifully, Neil had left by a chair. Her only thought was escape, and before either Andy or Neil could move again, she had jerked open the door.

"Dinah!" Neil shouted.

But she was gone, running away from the terrible scene she had witnessed, fleeing from the pain threatening to overwhelm her. Choking with sobs, she ran down the stairs and out into the night.

He didn't mean it, she tried to tell herself as she found a phone booth and called a taxi. He was just upset, so distraught over Andy that he didn't know what he was saying.

But as the cabby took her to a motel near the station, she could still hear Neil's harsh words, still see his face, cold and set. It was all she could do not to burst into tears as she registered with a shaking hand. By the time the bellboy left her alone in the room, she was trembling from head to foot.

How could this have happened, she wondered, sinking down onto the edge of the bed. Why had it happened? An image of Andy's face rose in her mind, and she bowed her head. She'd suspected this all along, but she hadn't wanted to believe it, not even when she'd seen the evidence of it with her own eyes. It seemed so unlikely that Andy could be involved with drugs: she knew what a good student he was, how fine an athlete...

Just like Dean Mathews, she thought suddenly, remembering the boy in the clinic. Shuddering, she closed her eyes. Why do they do it, she wondered agonizedly. Can't they talk to someone—anyone—before it's too late, like it is for Dean?

She knew Neil was a good father; she had seen for herself how deeply he loved his son. He had told her how much he regretted not having more time to spend with Andy, and she knew that the time he did spend with him was the best he could give.

But it hadn't been enough. Somewhere along the line, Andy had begun to believe that his father didn't love him, that unless he lived up to Neil's expectations, he wasn't worthy of that love.

And what about her, she wondered, and then despised herself for being so selfish at a time like this. How could she think of her relationship with Neil when Andy was in such despair?

But as concerned as she was about Andy, she was deeply hurt, too. Neil had taken everything she had said and had used it against her, and the knowledge that he could do that was so devastating that she began to sob again.

Had she really been so foolish to think she could change him? After what had taken place tonight, she saw only too clearly how little influence she had on him. She'd fought so hard against admitting that their relationship had no future, but it seemed that she must accept it now. If the incident with Andy hadn't changed Neil's inflexible attitude, there was no hope that anything else would. Surely, not she.

Drawing in a shuddering breath, Dinah closed her eyes against the pain of loss that swept over her. Life goes on, she told herself, and at least she had found out now, before it was too late.

Too late, she thought, and wanted to laugh bitterly. It had been too late the instant she had met him. She'd felt that attraction even then, and as much as she'd tried to battle it, she had lost. The lightning bolt had struck.

How can I love a man like that, she wondered, and knew that even after what had happened tonight, she still did. Somehow, she'd have to deal with that, and she had to do it by morning; rehearsal and final taping for the special was scheduled for tomorrow.

Forcing herself, she got off the bed and into a hot bath, hoping it would make her feel better or at least give her time to gather her thoughts. But the only thoughts she had were of Neil and Andy, and by the time she dragged herself out of the bath, she felt so discouraged and depressed that she ordered a glass of wine from room service. After it arrived, she sat by the window in the darkness, staring vacantly out at the lighted pool, wishing futilely that she could just fall asleep, wake up in the morning and discover that this had all been a bad dream.

It had been a bad dream, a nightmare, but it was real, and she knew that this desolate feeling wouldn't be gone when she awakened. Neil was a harsh man, an unforgiving man—of himself, perhaps even more than others—and behind the anger he'd displayed was an even deeper humiliation. In his eyes he had failed with his own son, and he would never forgive himself for that. He wouldn't forgive her, either, for witnessing his humiliation. He was too proud. He would remember the things she had said about other parents not realizing their children were involved with drugs; he would remember his own unyielding response. He'd been so sure of himself, so arrogant when he'd flatly stated there was no excuse, and finding himself in the same position for which he'd condemned others was intolerable to a man of his pride.

But understanding why he'd behaved as he had didn't make it any easier to bear. He'd been deliberately cruel to her, and she wondered how she was going to face him tomorrow. They still had the show to do together—or at least, they were supposed to do it. If she doubted she could get through the taping, how must Neil feel? Could he actually get up on that set and say the things he'd planned, knowing his son was one of the statistics?

Recalling the script he had written, which the show's writers were polishing now, Dinah shook her head in despair. In true Kerrigan style, it was a brilliant blending of facts and statistics that stated his position on the issue without personal comment. It was Neil at his best, a stunning example of investigative reporting.

But as she had tried so many times to convince him, the solution to teenage drug abuse wasn't only a matter of dealing with facts. Real people were involved—the teenagers and their families—and as they had discovered so tragically tonight, the reasons for abuse were complex. Andy wasn't a statistic, he was Neil's son, an unhappy, driven boy so afraid he couldn't live up to his father's standards that he sought relief from the pressures in a handful of pills. How many more young boys and girls felt like that?

"There is no explanation," Neil had said. But there was, and if he couldn't see that, not only was there no

hope for Andy, but their own relationship was doomed, as well.

Because it was inevitable that one day she would disappoint him, too. She couldn't live up to Neil's standards while trying to fulfill her own. Either she would collapse under the strain, as Andy had, or she would become so resentful of Neil's demands that their relationship would become a battleground. Just as it had with Ted.

Her glass of wine was empty. It was two in the morning, and she knew she should get some rest. Rehearsal was scheduled for ten o'clock with the final taping after that, and even though she doubted that they'd tape tomorrow after what had happened tonight, she had to make an appearance. She was a professional, she thought with a bitter twist of her lips, and no matter how desolate and defeated she felt inside, the show must go on.

But as she continued to sit there, too weary and too heartsick even to move, she wondered bleakly if it would.

AFTER CALLING ELISE to tell her that Andy was with him, Neil drove most of the way back to the house in taut silence with a sullen Andy sitting as far away from him on the front seat as possible. For the first few miles his anger was still so great that he didn't dare look at his son. But then, when he covertly glanced over and saw that Andy had put his head back and that his eyes were closed, concern began to thread its way through his rage and he wondered if Dinah had been right. Andy didn't look well at all. Maybe he should take the boy to the hospital.

"I'm taking you to see a doctor," he said abruptly. "God knows what you've done to yourself by taking all those different drugs tonight."

"I only took a few uppers," Andy muttered.

Neil looked at him sharply. "You said you took a handful of pills and didn't know what they were."

"I only said that to bug you."

Neil suddenly slammed his fist against the steering wheel. "I just don't understand," he said hoarsely. "Your mother and I have tried to give you everything! How could you do this? Don't you realize what you're doing to yourself? How could you jeopardize your health, your whole future?"

Andy turned sullenly to look out the window. "If you don't understand, I can't tell you."

Neil looked across at him again, torn between frustration and failure and a dozen other conflicting emotions. The pain that he felt won out over the rest, and he said, almost pleadingly, "Talk to me, Andy. Tell me why."

Andy refused to look at him. "I can't talk to you," he muttered. "You only want me to say things you want to hear."

Is that true, Neil wondered abruptly. *Is that really what he thinks of me?* "I've always been willing to listen to you...."

Andy did turn his head then, his eyes fierce and bleak at the same time. "Have you, Dad? When? Between assignments? Between catching a plane for somewhere else? You've always been more interested in talking to senators or generals than you have me. As long as I was doing what I was supposed to, you thought everything was fine!"

Stunned by the attack, Neil didn't know for a moment what to say. "But everything was fine," he said bewilderedly.

"Oh, sure. But only as long as I kept my grades up and participated in every sport in school!"

Wondering if he knew his son at all, Neil said, "But you've always been a good student, and you enjoy sports."

"That's because I thought if I was good enough at everything, you'd come home again!"

The agonized words reverberated throughout the car. They had left the freeway by this time and were almost at the house. Neil immediately pulled over and stopped, but before he could turn to Andy and say anything, his son had jerked open the door and started to run.

Neil didn't hesitate. Flinging himself after him, he caught up half a block later. "Andy!"

Andy pulled his arm away from his father's restraining hand. They were passing under a streetlight just then, and when Neil saw the shine of tears on his son's face, he was appalled.

"I'm ... sorry ..." he said, not knowing what else to say. "I didn't know you felt like that. Andy, listen to me—"

Hunching his shoulders, Andy kept walking. "Forget it," he muttered. "I don't want to talk about it. It was a stupid thing to say."

This time when Neil reached out, his grip was so firm that Andy couldn't break away. "I don't think it was stupid," he said quietly. "And I want to talk about it. I think it's about time we did, don't you?"

Andy rubbed a forearm across his face, scrubbing away his tears. Wisely, Neil didn't offer him his handkerchief. Instead he put his arm around his son's shoulders and said softly, "Let's walk."

And so they walked for blocks, eventually finding a small park where they sat on one of the benches. Neil was silent as he allowed Andy to pour out the bitterness and resentment he had kept so well hidden since the divorce, but as he listened to his son, he began to feel more and more sick at heart. He had tried to explain to Andy his reasons for leaving Elise, but what twelve-year-old boy could really understand the failure of a marriage when the participants couldn't understand it themselves?

"I thought it was my fault," Andy said agonizedly at one point. "I thought that I'd disappointed you so much you didn't want to live with us anymore."

Neil closed his eyes against a spasm of pain. "You've never disappointed me, Andy. I've always been proud of you...so proud that you were my son."

"Then why didn't you want me to live with you?" Andy cried.

"I did," Neil said, and knew he could never tell his son about the bitter custody battle he and Elise had waged. "But your mother and I felt that with my being gone so much, it would be better for you to live with her."

"But I wouldn't have minded staying alone! At least we would have been together when you came home!"

"You were so young, Andy. I had to think what was best for you. But I...I did want you with me. I would have given anything if it could have been that way."

Andy's voice was bitter again. "But you had your work."

"Yes, I had my work," Neil agreed. "And sometimes I think your mother was right when she said my work took precedence over everything else."

"Even us? Even Mom and me?"

Neil closed his eyes again, thrust suddenly back into the jungles of Vietnam, where the noise from the guns almost, but not quite drowned out the screams from wounded and dying men. With an effort, he thrust the horrible images away. He knew now that it was time he tried to explain to his son the reasons he'd become so involved in his work; time to come to grips with it himself. Andy was so like his brother, he thought. Andy's uncle had been so kind and generous; he'd felt things so deeply.

Just as he had once himself, Neil thought, before he had learned to shut off his feelings because he couldn't bear the pain. He didn't know if he could bear it now, but he had to try. He wasn't going to lose his son as he had his brother.

"You never knew your uncle, Andy," he said after a moment, when he could speak again. His throat was tight with emotion; it was difficult to force the words out. "I named you after him, not only because he was my brother, but because he was one of the finest men I've ever known."

Aware that Andy had straightened and was looking at him intently, Neil went on, his voice taut with remembered pain. "When he...when he died in Vietnam, I was so consumed with rage and pain and guilt that I wanted revenge on everyone. I decided then that I'd use all my skills as a reporter and journalist to force politicians to be responsible for their decisions, to defend those decisions to me and to the people they were charged to guide and protect. It . . . it became an obsession with me, that work, and I expected my family to understand. But I was wrong, Andy. It was my obsession—not yours, not your mother's.''

And not Dinah's, he thought suddenly, and felt a pang. Forcing himself to continue, he said huskily, ''I'm not offering that as an excuse, Andy, but that's what happened. And I . . . I'm sorry.''

Andy was silent for a long moment, staring down at his long legs, which were thrust straight out in front of him. Finally, in a voice so low Neil had to strain to hear it, he said, ''You never told me that before, Dad. Why now?''

Neil was silent for a few minutes, too. ''Because I want you to understand,'' he said slowly. ''It wasn't right, and I know that now. But I want you to understand. I always felt so guilty, as though it should have been me.''

''But it wasn't your fault that Uncle Andy died.''

Neil shook his head. ''No. But I was the one who wanted to go, Andy didn't. The only thing he ever wanted to do was stay home and run the farm.'' Despite himself, his voice turned bitter. ''I was the one who couldn't wait to get away, and yet it was Andy who was drafted . . . Andy who died in a war he never wanted to fight.''

Andy sighed. Looking off into the distance, he said, almost more to himself than to his father, ''It's funny, isn't it? Here you've been trying to deal with Uncle Andy's death by wrapping yourself up in your work, and I've been trying to deal with my problems by getting involved with drugs.''

Startled at this mature observation, Neil said carefully, "I don't think either of us has found the solution, do you?''

Andy sighed again, his expression so despairing that Neil wanted to take him in his arms and cradle his head against his chest. He forced himself to remain still as Andy said, "I don't know why I did it in the first place...take drugs, I mean. I thought it would help, but it didn't, and the more I took, the lousier I felt. And now—''

He stopped abruptly, biting his lip as tears filled his eyes.

"And now?'' Neil asked gently.

The tears spilled over. "And now I don't know whether I can stop,'' Andy said, his voice breaking. He turned to his father, his eyes agonized. "Oh, Dad,'' he sobbed. "I don't know what to do!''

"I do,'' Neil said quietly, and as if Andy were a small child again, he unhesitatingly gathered his son into his arms and held him tightly. And for the first time in years, his own cheeks were wet with tears.

CHAPTER SEVENTEEN

DINAH ARRIVED AT THE STATION the next morning sick at heart, ill at ease, and not sure what she would find when she got there. It was even worse than she had anticipated, for she learned that Neil had come in some time before and had gone straight to his office without speaking to anyone. He'd been locked in there since, and his expression had been so grim that his secretary hadn't dared interrupt him even to bring in coffee. The tension in the studio was almost palpable, and everyone she met seemed on tenterhooks except for Allen Fogerty, who had flown in from New York to watch the taping. He seemed blithely unaffected when he found Dinah in Makeup going over her script.

"Ah, looking radiant as always!" he exclaimed, kissing her cheek.

Dinah looked at her reflection in the mirror, wondering if she was the only one who could see the circles under her eyes and the waxen cast to her skin. Feeling as though she had aged twenty years overnight, she thanked Allen for the compliment, and then, before she could prevent herself, asked, "Have you seen Neil yet?"

"No," he said cheerily, dropping into the empty chair beside her. "I just got here. Why?"

Dinah didn't want to say anything in front of the young woman who was doing the set makeup she'd always detested. She knew how easily gossip spread in television stations, and because it was obvious to everyone that there was some kind of problem, she knew, too, how avid they all were to find out what it was. Aware that the woman was listening intently despite her seeming preoccupation with applying blusher, Dinah made herself shrug. "I just wondered."

"We saw a duplicate of the tape yesterday," Allen said, and Dinah knew the casual "we" meant that Daniel Rawlings had seen it, too. She tensed. "You two sure put together some great material from those Willowset interviews. The feeling in New York is that this is going to be some program."

Dinah closed her eyes briefly. If they completed it, that was, she thought, and made herself smile. "That's nice to hear."

"Nice?" Allen lifted an eyebrow. "That's certainly less than enthusiastic." He looked at her closely for the first time. "Is anything wrong?"

Averting her eyes, Dinah pretended to study her appearance in the mirror. "No, of course not," she said, fluffing her hair with one hand. "Why do you say that?"

Allen jerked his head at the cosmetician, indicating that he wanted to be alone with Dinah. Sighing, the young woman put down her brushes and reluctantly left the room.

As soon as the door closed behind her, Allen said, "All right. What is it?"

"It's nothing, Allen," Dinah evaded. She remembered the script in her lap and gestured faintly at it. "Just preshow jitters, I guess."

"Come on. We know each other better than that."

Dinah started to bite her lip, remembered that she'd have to have her lipstick redone if she did, and muttered, "Honestly, I'm just a little nervous. I'll be glad when this whole thing is over and I can go back to San Francisco."

He looked at her in consternation. "I thought you were looking forward to doing this."

"I was.... I—I am. But Neil isn't the easiest person in the world to work with, you know, and it's been...a strain."

"Ah."

She looked at him sharply. "What does that mean?"

He seemed amused. "Nothing. It was just a comment."

"I'm not sure I like the tone of that comment," she said with a frown.

His smile faded, and he suddenly looked concerned again. "Have you and Neil had a fight?"

She couldn't help it; a bitter laugh escaped her. "You might say that. But it's not going to affect my performance, if that's what you're worried about."

"I wasn't thinking of that at all," he said, sounding hurt. "I know what a professional you are. I was just thinking of you."

"I'm sorry," she said, suddenly feeling close to tears. "I told you I was nervous."

He leaned forward suddenly, placing a hand on hers, forcing her to look at him. "The problem with Neil isn't professional, is it?" he asked quietly.

She couldn't meet his glance. "I really don't want to talk about it, Allen."

"It's almost comical, you know," he said with a fond smile. "Seeing the two of you together, I mean. You're both trying so hard to deny the fact that you're in love that you can't see what's right under your own nose."

"You're imagining things," she muttered.

"I see," he said. "Then if you're not in love, there's no reason for him to be locked in his office, refusing to speak to anyone, and there's no reason for you to be sitting in here looking like you want to cry." He tapped the binder she was suddenly clutching so tightly. "You should be on top of the world right now, you know. You've got some great material, and the script is fantastic. Even Mr. Rawlings is so sure the show is going to be a success that he—"

He stopped so abruptly that Dinah's curiosity was aroused despite her misery. "He what?"

But Allen had said enough. He stood, gripping her shoulders as he smiled down at her. "You have your secrets—I have mine," he said. "Break a leg on this show, Dinah. You won't be sorry."

He was out the door before she could ask him what he meant, and she was about to get up and go after him when one of the production assistants stuck his head in the door and said, "Five minutes, Miss Blake."

Dinah sank back into the chair again, suddenly paralyzed with fear. She couldn't go out onto that set.

What would she say to Neil? How would she act? She couldn't pretend that nothing had happened, and now it was too late to go to his office and ask if they could talk. She'd wanted to when she'd first come in, but she had delayed, hoping he would come to her. It was obvious that he wasn't going to now, and somehow she had to go out there and—

Stop it, she told herself frantically. *Just stop it!* Panicking wasn't going to solve anything. An entire crew was on the set waiting for her and Neil to act like the professionals they were supposed to be. She had to do her job, no matter what she felt like inside.

Raising her eyes to the mirror, she tried to summon a smile, but her reflection stared bleakly back at her, and as she forced herself out of the chair, she couldn't look that way again. What, she wondered, would she do when she entered the studio and Neil wasn't there?

Neil wasn't there. The silence on the set was deafening as Dinah took her place; the tension so thick it could almost have been cut with a knife. Dinah was so taut herself that she nearly shrieked when someone approached her from behind to fit her with a microphone, and she knew her voice was shaking badly when she spoke into it for a sound check. She'd placed the script in front of her, and as she looked down at it, she realized frantically that she couldn't remember a word she'd written. Resisting the impulse to rifle through the pages, she clasped her hands tightly and waited. Her eyes, like everyone else's, went to the big clock on the wall, and as the second hand ticked inexorably toward ten o'clock, she held her breath.

Neil appeared one minute before ten. Grabbing a microphone, he pinned it on his suit lapel himself and took his place beside her. The set had been designed so that it appeared as though they were both seated behind a huge desk, and behind them the station's logo blazed in the network's rainbow colors. The floor director, looking vastly relieved and about to have a heart attack at the same time, cleared his throat, and the sound was like the crack of a rifle. Glancing around, he was about to raise his arm as a signal for them to begin, when Neil spoke.

"This will be a take. We don't need a rehearsal."

Dinah looked at him in dismay. She didn't dare argue with him; she couldn't. The thought that they were doing this cold made her feel so panicked again that she wondered if she'd even be able to speak at all.

Then Neil looked at her, and something in his eyes made her go very still. "I've got my reasons," he said. "Will you follow me?"

Suddenly, without even knowing how, she understood. Hardly able to breathe, she slowly inclined her head. Had she misinterpreted that expression in his eyes? Was she seeing something that wasn't there because she wanted so desperately to believe it was? Summoning every ounce of poise, she turned to face the camera as he began.

"Good evening, ladies and gentlemen," Neil said in that rich voice that had enthralled so many millions. "This is Neil Kerrigan, together with my cohost, Dinah Blake. Tonight, we're going to bring you a very special program about teenage drug and alcohol abuse."

And then, as the crew began to look confused, and upstairs in the control booth, Allen Fogerty and the director glanced at each other in puzzlement, Neil departed from the prepared script. It had been decided that he would give the introduction, citing the facts and figures they had uncovered—reporting, as he did so well, the hard, unvarnished realities of such abuse. Dinah had been scheduled then to take over with the second part of the story—the effects of this abuse on teenagers and their families—and both narratives would form the backdrop for the interviews they had taped. They would each summarize at the end, and that would be it.

But Neil set aside the script now, and as he leaned forward to gaze directly into the camera, only Dinah guessed what he was about to say. Her expression was composed, but her heart was beginning to pound. Would he say it? Could he? She knew how hard it would be for him, how fierce a battle would have been fought between last night and this morning, and if he had succeeded, how hard won had been the victory? Tears in her eyes, she listened as Neil's voice, so quiet and intense, filled the room as he finally spoke from his heart.

"I'd like to dedicate this program to two very special people," he began. "One, who recently demonstrated to me more clearly than facts and statistics ever could, the dangers and despairs of addiction. And the other—" he turned to look at Dinah then, the expression in his eyes more eloquent and heartfelt than the words he spoke "—and the other who taught me that while facts are never wrong, people can be."

Dinah was so choked with emotion when he turned to face the camera again that she wondered if she'd be able to speak. But then, in a solemn voice that vibrated with emotion, Neil said, "Ladies and gentlemen, my cohost, Dinah Blake."

She didn't have to glance at the pages on her lap or at the teleprompter in front of the camera. Neil had asked if she could follow him, and she knew without question that she could. She began to recite the facts and figures he had been scheduled to relate, her clear tones running counterpoint to Neil's recital of the heart-wrenching effects of drug abuse on children and their families.

As they went on, a team who understood each other so clearly and effortlessly that they didn't need a script at all, the atmosphere became even more charged. The expressions of the crew, the faces of Allen and the director, became awed as they listened to the brilliant and unforgettable display of talent and ability from two professionals who had suddenly become much more than that. The set fairly vibrated with the power of their personalities, and no one could say which one of them dominated the other. Their strengths were separate and equal, and by the time Neil said a solemn good-night, the set was so quiet that the ticking of the clock could be heard.

Into that awed silence the director said in a hushed voice, "That's a wrap...."

Dinah couldn't look at Neil; she was too overcome with emotion. She lowered her head to take off the microphone, but her hands were trembling so badly she couldn't undo the clip. Suddenly Neil's strong fingers covered her own, and as he unhooked the microphone, she slowly raised her eyes to his.

"Can we talk?" Neil asked wryly, and forgot that his own mike was still on.

"Boy, you sure can!" someone yelled exuberantly.

Then, as they both looked up, startled, someone started to clap. Another joined him, and soon the entire set reverberated with whistles and cheers and the roar of a thunderous ovation. Every member of the crew was on their feet applauding them, offering the only tribute they could to two people who had given them something beyond compare.

Dinah looked at Neil, and when he met her eyes, their shared glance seemed to go on forever. They were surrounded by a cheering crew, but it seemed to Dinah that she and Neil were on an island alone. She saw herself reflected in the brilliance of his eyes, and she knew that her own eyes were brilliant, too. Neil took her hand, and as they both stood to acknowledge the rousing ovation, it was a moment Dinah knew she would never forget.

It was more than an hour before they were able to talk. Trays of food had magically appeared at the conclusion of the taping, and a long trestle table was set up to accommodate the brunch buffet Allen had ordered to celebrate. Dinah was still too excited to eat, but the earlier tension seemed to have made everyone else ravenous, and as she was surrounded by well-wishers holding loaded plates and toasting her with champagne punch, she was separated from Neil.

She saw him in an intent conversation with Allen some time later, but they were on the far side of the room, and the press of people who had come down from their offices to join the party was too great for her to make her way over to him. As she watched him, his dark head lowered attentively to whatever Allen was saying, she felt a strong wave of love for him.

When he happened to glance up just then and meet her eyes, his smile made her heart turn over. Then the station manager came up to her and she was just turning politely to him when she saw Neil nod, shake Allen's hand and start toward the door.

He couldn't be leaving, she thought in dismay, and was about to go after him when she stopped herself. The experience they'd shared just now had been an emotional high, but it had also been an exhausting assault. She couldn't blame him for wanting to escape the crowd; as much as she appreciated the tribute, she longed to have a few moments alone herself. She still felt breathless, as though she had climbed a high mountain and was resting on a shallow ledge before making the final ascent.

The past twenty-four hours had been even more draining for Neil, and she knew how wrenching this past hour, especially, had been for him. The fact that none but she knew why he had changed the script hadn't made it any easier for him. In a way it had made it even more difficult. She had been there last night; she knew.

She could only imagine the soul-searching Neil must have done, the pain he must have felt at having to come to grips with a problem he had managed, even during all those interviews, to keep at arm's length. If thoughts of Andy had never been far from her mind during the miserable night she had spent, how much more deeply had Neil felt the strain?

Suddenly wanting very much to be alone herself, Dinah was just excusing herself from the happy clutches of the station manager when Allen came up.

His eyes sparkling, he murmured, "Boy, when you break a leg, you really do, don't you?"

She shook her head. "It's Neil who deserves the credit."

"Is that so?" he asked, looking smug. "Well, I thought you did a creditable job yourself." He paused and then added deliberately, "So does the head of programming, in case you're interested."

She was startled. "Mr. Rawlings?"

Allen nodded. "The same. He's on the phone right now, in fact. He wants to talk to you."

"But how—"

He looked smug again. "There are ways. Come on, do you want to talk to him or not? I think you'll be interested in what he has to say."

She tried to pump him as they found a phone away from the noise of the party, but Allen just smiled as he handed her the receiver. Her heart thumping, she held it to her ear and willed her voice not to shake when she said, "Mr. Rawlings? This is Dinah Blake."

"Well, congratulations, Dinah," the rich, mellow voice said. "Allen tells me you and Neil did quite a job."

Dinah glanced up, but Allen gave her a brief wave and a smile before he closed the door behind him. "Thank you, Mr. Rawlings."

"Call me Dan," the man who was rumored to detest nicknames said. "I think we know each other well enough by now, don't you?" He chuckled. "Or we will, if you accept the job I'm about to offer."

"Job?" Dinah repeated faintly. She couldn't believe this was happening.

"How would you like to live in New York?"

"New York?" she squeaked, and made a fierce effort to compose herself. She sounded like a parrot, she thought frantically. The man would think she was a fool.

Rawlings seemed not to notice her confusion. "We have a time slot opening here," he said smoothly, "and I've been thinking for quite a while about adding an informational news program to the schedule." He coughed delicately. "The competition seems to have done quite well with theirs, you know."

Dinah knew. But she also thought privately that in the past few years that popular program had splintered into too many components, so that the issues covered weren't examined as closely as they had once been. Before she could think what response to make, Rawlings went on, uncannily echoing her own thoughts.

"What I had in mind was something like you and Neil have done with this special—one issue a segment, examined in depth. Not unlike Neil's *Kerrigan Report*, but with a broader scope."

Dinah tried in vain to suppress her rising excitement. Her voice trembled slightly when she said, "I think that's a wonderful concept, Mr. Rawlings."

"Dan," he corrected her gently. "And I thought you would, since the idea seemed to have originated with you."

"With me?" she exclaimed, startled. How in the world had Daniel Rawlings found out that she longed to implement this on her own show?

His voice was dry. "Of course, I only made that my concept after Neil told me about the conversation he had with you. Rank has its privileges, you know."

She didn't care who took credit for it; she was too stunned at what he had said. "You talked to Neil about this?"

"Well, I suppose it would be more accurate to say that he talked to me," Rawlings admitted wryly. "I called him after I'd had a chance to see the tape this week, and he mentioned it. We, er, discussed the possibility then of teaming the two of you on a show like this."

"The two of us!"

"Well, yes, of course," Rawlings said, as though the thought should come as no surprise.

"But Neil has his own show!"

"And so do you," Rawlings said smoothly. "Are you ready for a change?"

"Well, yes, but—"

"Then perhaps Neil is, too."

She couldn't believe this. Neil giving up *The Kerrigan Report*? It was inconceivable.

"Mr. Rawlings...Dan...I don't know what to say."

"Say yes," he said calmly. "I know your contract has several more months to run, but that will give us time to work up the concept and for you to start looking for a place in New York." He chuckled again. "Of course, the network will be happy to help you with that, and naturally, the increase in salary will be, er, substantial enough for you to find something quite suitable."

"I'm sure it will," Dinah said faintly, and was too stunned to ask anything more. In a daze, she said goodbye and hung up the phone.

"Did you accept?"

Dinah had been so intent on the conversation that she hadn't realized anyone had entered the room. Whirling around, she saw Neil lounging against the doorjamb, a broad grin on his face.

"You knew about this all the time!" she accused.

He shut the door behind him. "Just for the past few days. Dan didn't want me to say anything until it was official."

"I'm not sure it's official now."

Neil's grin faded. "What do you mean?"

"I don't like being manipulated," she said resentfully. "I feel like this decision was already made for me."

He began to look bewildered. "But it's what you said you wanted."

Dinah didn't know what she wanted. In fact, she couldn't imagine why she was acting like this. After what Rawlings had offered her, she knew she should be jumping with joy. It was the chance of a lifetime, a career opportunity she'd be crazy to turn down.

But she was being assaulted with too many decisions at once, pulled in too many directions at the same time. And uppermost in her mind right now was the thought that Neil had outmaneuvered her. Did he still think that only he had the right to make decisions? Didn't he think her capable of making any herself?

Ignoring the fleeting thought that she couldn't seem to make any decisions at all right now, she glared at him. "Why did you talk to Daniel Rawlings without telling me?"

"It didn't start out that way," he protested. "He called me about the tape, and...and during the course of the conversation—"

"You just happened to mention how nice it would be if he asked me to do another show!" she said bitterly. "I told you that in confidence, Neil. I didn't expect you to go running to the head of programming and beg him to give me a chance!"

"That's not what happened, Dinah. It was his idea, not mine!"

"Only after you talked to him about it!"

Looking bewildered again, Neil ran an agitated hand through his hair. "Why are we arguing about this? I thought you'd be pleased."

"I am pleased!" she shouted. "It's just that I...that I don't understand this relationship at all! You do something like this for me on the one hand and then on the other, you...you..." Frustration and anger and despair were threatening to overwhelm her, and she had to make a fierce effort to go on.

"I can't live on gestures, Neil," she said wrenchingly. "I need more than that."

He reached her in one stride and grasped her shoulders, forcing her to look up at him. "I thought that the show today proved what I'm willing to do for you, Dinah," he said fiercely. "Do you think that was easy for me?"

Tears filled her eyes. "No, I know how hard it was."

"I did it for Andy, Dinah, but I also did it for you. I thought that if anything could show you both that I've changed, that I'm trying to change, that would. You've made me see so many things differently, things I never wanted to see before. You made me—"

He stopped abruptly, lifting his head against the glitter of tears in his eyes. Controlling himself with an effort, he finally went on. "Last night I told Andy why my work has obsessed me all these years, and why I viewed things as I have. I want to tell you..."

And so he told her about his brother, about the rage and the overwhelming sense of loss he had felt when his brother died and why it had led to his becoming the person he had been. He made no excuses; he didn't try to rationalize. He told the story so simply and poignantly that Dinah was deeply touched. He'd opened his heart to her today on the show, but this painful recounting of his past moved her even more profoundly, because at last he was sharing that private part of him that he had kept hidden all these years.

"But you never told me," she whispered, when he concluded. "I would have understood."

He smiled wryly. "I never told anyone, not until I told Andy last night."

She was stricken at that. How could she have forgotten about Andy? "How is he?" she asked urgently. "Oh, Neil, I've been so worried about him!"

"He's going to be fine," Neil answered, and then smiled again, this time a little ruefully. "We're both going up to Willowset tomorrow."

"Willowset?"

Neil's eyes began to twinkle. "Your friend Mark Delaney agreed to admit him to Get In Touch."

Dinah was so thrilled she could hardly contain herself. Her own eyes sparkling, she said, "I thought you didn't believe in that program."

"I didn't believe in a lot of things until last night," Neil said somberly. "Least of all that today I'd give up *The Kerrigan Report*."

"You what? Oh, Neil, you can't give up a show like that!"

He smiled. "I already have," he said so easily that she knew it no longer mattered to him. "Now all we have to do is decide what you're going to do about *Personalities*."

"We?"

"A mere figure of speech," he corrected hastily. "You have just as much right to decide about your career as I do mine."

She looked at him closely. "Do you mean that?"

"Of course I mean it," he said indignantly. "Don't you think I've learned anything these past weeks? And if you don't want to take the show in New York, I'll understand." Pausing, he added sadly, "I'm not sure Andy will, though. After he graduates from Mark's program, he's going to move to New York with me for a while, and I know he was looking forward to seeing more of you."

"That's blackmail," Dinah said warningly. "You know how fond I am of Andy!"

Neil smiled. "He's fond of you, too. And wasn't he the one who first suggested we'd make a good team?"

Dinah pretended to consider that. "Well, we managed fairly well today," she said, outwardly calm while within her pulse was beginning to race. "But what about the future? We might be too competitive...."

His hands moved from her shoulders to her waist, and she could feel herself yielding to him, wanting to move closer so that they touched. "There's no competition between equals,'' Neil said quietly. "And that's what we'll be, Dinah. We always have been. I just had to beat down my pride long enough to admit it. I . . .'' He had to pause to clear his throat. "I love you, Dinah,'' he went on intensely, those incredibly blue eyes of his holding hers. "I want to marry you. I know you said you didn't want to get involved, and if you say no to that, too, I'll understand. I won't like it—'' his expression became suddenly bleak "—but I'll understand. I'll try, anyway.'' He smiled, forcing himself to add. "I'll do my best . . .''

Before Dinah could say anything, before she could even begin to speak over the lump in her throat, the office door opened and Allen walked in. A slow flush spread over his fair skin when he saw Neil standing with his arms around Dinah, and when he looked at her, his expression was regretful. "I see the best man won.''

Dinah laughed as she stepped even closer into Neil. She'd made her decision long ago, a decision that had nothing to do with careers or ambitions but had only to do with a choice of the heart. Neil had shown his willingness to compromise today, and even though she knew there would be storms ahead, she was convinced now that they could weather them.

Because at last, Neil had glimpsed those shades of gray, the fine lines that made life a compromise and a relationship a thing of joy, and her eyes shone as she glanced up at him. "Not the best man, Allen,'' she said wickedly. "But a different one.''

Allen cleared his throat. "Uh . . . I came to tell you that they're going to run a tape of the show in a few minutes," he said, backing away. "But I can see that you're...uh..."

Dinah smiled as the door closed behind him and the noise of the celebration still going on in the studio faded. "Don't you think we should join the others?" she whispered. "After all, the party is for—"

She never finished the sentence. Neil lowered his dark head, and the instant his lips claimed hers, she forgot everything but the blissful sensation of being kissed by him, loved by him.

"Who needs a party," he murmured, his mouth moving on hers, "when we can celebrate on our own? I love you, Dinah. I'm only sorry it's taken me so long to admit it."

Dinah pulled away from him for just an instant to search his face. "Are you sure?" she whispered.

"I've never been more sure of anything in my life," he answered simply, and his expression was such that she knew she'd never doubt it again.

"Neither have I," she said, and drew his head down to hers once more. She returned his kiss with all the power of her passionate nature, and as Neil lifted her effortlessly in his arms to hold her even more tightly to him, she smiled in delight.

Who ever said that lightning doesn't strike twice?

Harlequin Superromance

COMING NEXT MONTH

What readers say about SUPERROMANCE

"Bravo! Your SUPERROMANCE [is]...super!"
R.V.,* Montgomery, Illinois

"I am impatiently awaiting the next SUPERROMANCE."
J.D., Sandusky, Ohio

"Delightful!...great."
C.B., Fort Wayne, Indiana

"Terrific love stories. Just keep them coming!"
M.G., Toronto, Ontario

*Names available on request.

Take 4 best-selling love stories FREE
Plus get a FREE surprise gift!

Harlequin Intrigue

WHAT READERS SAY ABOUT HARLEQUIN INTRIGUE . . .

Fantastic! I am looking forward to reading other Intrigue books.

*P.W.O., Anderson, SC

This is the first Harlequin Intrigue I have read . . . I'm hooked.

*C.M., Toledo, OH

I really like the suspense . . . the twists and turns of the plot.

*L.E.L., Minneapolis, MN

I'm really enjoying your Harlequin Intrigue line . . . mystery and suspense mixed with a good love story.

*B.M., Denton, TX

*Names available on request.

WORLDWIDE LIBRARY IS YOUR TICKET TO ROMANCE, ADVENTURE AND EXCITEMENT

Experience it all in these big, bold Bestsellers— Yours exclusively from WORLDWIDE LIBRARY WHILE QUANTITIES LAST

To receive these Bestsellers, complete the order form, detach an send together with your check or money order (include 75¢ postag and handling), payable to WORLDWIDE LIBRARY, to:

In the U.S.
WORLDWIDE LIBRARY
901 Fuhrman Blvd.
Buffalo, N.Y.
14269

In Canada
WORLDWIDE LIBRARY
P.O. Box 2800, 5170 Yonge Street
Postal Station A, Willowdale, Ontari
M2N 6J3

Quant.	Title	Price
_____	WILD CONCERTO, Anne Mather	$2.95
_____	A VIOLATION, Charlotte Lamb	$3.50
_____	SECRETS, Sheila Holland	$3.50
_____	SWEET MEMORIES, LaVyrle Spencer	$3.50
_____	FLORA, Anne Weale	$3.50
_____	SUMMER'S AWAKENING, Anne Weale	$3.50
_____	FINGER PRINTS, Barbara Delinsky	$3.50
_____	DREAMWEAVER, Felicia Gallant/Rebecca Flanders	$3.50
_____	EYE OF THE STORM, Maura Seger	$3.50
_____	HIDDEN IN THE FLAME, Anne Mather	$3.50
_____	ECHO OF THUNDER, Maura Seger	$3.95
_____	DREAM OF DARKNESS, Jocelyn Haley	$3.95

	YOUR ORDER TOTAL	$_____
	New York residents add appropriate sales tax	$_____
	Postage and Handling	$___ .75
	I enclose	$_____

NAME _____

ADDRESS _____ APT.# _____

CITY _____

STATE/PROV. _____ ZIP/POSTAL CODE _____

WW-1-3